THE JUDGE'S DAUGHTER

RAINE STOCKTON DOG MYSTERY #15

By Donna Ball

www.donnaball.net

Published by Blue Merle Publishing

Drawer H
Mountain City, Georgia 30562
www.bluemerlepublishers.com

Cover art by www.bigstock.com

A Note to Readers

The events of this book take place in the year between the end of *Murder Creek* (Raine Stockton Dog Mystery #14,) and the end of *Unfixable* (Blood River Mystery #1), but before the holiday anthology *Deck the Halls*. Many of the events referred to in this book occurred in *High in Trial* (Raine Stockton Dog Mystery #7). While it's not necessary to have read any of those mysteries before this one, they would undoubtably enhance your enjoyment of *The Judge's Daughter.*

DONNA BALL

PART ONE

DONNA BALL

CHAPTER ONE

They took my earrings, my watch, my phone, my purse. They took my engagement ring. They took my photograph and my fingerprints. Then they took me to my cell.

The Hanover County Detention Facility had been recently upgraded and it wasn't that bad, as jail cells go. Certainly, I'd stayed in worse shelters along the Appalachian Trail. At least this place looked clean—kind of—and didn't smell too bad. There was a cot bolted to the wall and a metal toilet and sink. There was even a small television high on the wall and a laminated sign instructing you to call the guard station to turn it on. Next to the sign was a much-worn red intercom button that connected you to the guard station. The deputy who had escorted me here, a pleasant young woman whose name tag read "Ledbetter," had explained all this to me, along with something about mealtimes and when I would be allowed to shower and exercise. There was a small square window in the middle of the metal door, and when she closed it, I was alone in a concrete walled room that wasn't much bigger than one of my dog kennels.

Up until then, I hadn't really been scared. Now I was.

I sat on the edge of the cot with my hands twisted tightly between my knees to keep them from shaking, and I waited. I didn't call the guard station. I didn't ask for the television. And I tried, as best as I could, not to think. I just waited.

After what might have been hours but probably wasn't, a sharp buzz made me bolt to my feet. A voice from the intercom said, "Stockton, your lawyer is here."

"O-okay," I stammered, but I had barely finished speaking before the lock clicked open and Deputy Ledbetter stood there again, ready to escort me to the conference room.

She tried to make conversation and I tried to respond, but I didn't have much to say to her and my answers were mostly monosyllabic. There was a time when I knew everyone in the Hanover County Sheriff's Office, but not anymore. And, really, what could I possibly have said to her that she would want to hear? Or, for that matter, what could she say to me?

Except one thing.

"Well, look at that," she declared in an amused tone as she opened the conference room door. "Looks like you have a special visitor."

At the sound of her voice my beautiful golden retriever spun around and raced toward me, his toenails scrabbling on the linoleum floor, his leash trailing behind him. I dropped to my knees and opened my arms and he flung himself into them. "Cisco!" I whispered, burying my face in his sweet-smelling fur. "Oh, Cisco!"

I hugged him and hugged him, and he wriggled his delight, warm, excited breath panting onto my face, drying tears I didn't even realize I had cried. I wrapped my hand around his leash and stood up. The deputy smiled at my lawyer. "I'll be right outside, Miss Brightwell." She closed the door.

Sonny, who was really more of my friend than my lawyer, had pulled her wheelchair up to the table and was watching us with a beneficent expression. She had a degenerative joint disease that was remitting and relapsing, and she'd admitted to me that, while her mobility devices could be a necessity on bad days, she wasn't above using them to garner sympathy from people she wanted to underestimate her. I suspected today might be one of the latter cases.

I said a little breathlessly, "How did you get him in here?" I bent to drop a kiss atop Cisco's head and to hug him one more time before sitting down. "And thank you! Thank you so much!"

She waved a hand, smiling. "Please. He's a therapy dog, isn't he? And, as you've told me a dozen times, the average person doesn't know the difference between a therapy dog and a service dog. I didn't think any of these jokers would try to stop a lawyer in a wheelchair from bringing her assistance dog into the building, and I was right. It was Miles's idea," she added. "They wouldn't let him in to see you, so he sent the next best thing."

Another quick hot flash of tears, which I blinked back determinedly. Cisco put his paws on my knees, and I dropped my face to his neck once again, hugging him, inhaling the warm, reassuring fragrance of him. "Or maybe *the* best thing," I said, and even managed a thin smile as I straightened up again. "Tell him thank you."

"It's the least I could do," she replied. She took a legal pad and a pen from the soft leather satchel she wore on a cross strap over her torso and placed them both on the table. "Now, Raine, you know I'm not a criminal lawyer, so there's not a lot I can do for you tonight. I'm just here to make sure you're okay and to get the process started, but by agreeing to meet with me, you've assigned me to your legal team. I assume that's okay."

She glanced at me, and I nodded numbly. I don't think I'd ever been in the kind of trouble that Sonny couldn't handle before, nor had I ever imagined the time I would need a legal team. Legal teams were what criminals had, if they could afford them. I wasn't a criminal.

"Miles has one of the best defense attorneys in the country coming up from Atlanta in the morning, and he'll assemble your team and decide on our strategy. I'll bring him up to speed as soon as we finish our conversation, so he'll be ready for your bond hearing in the morning."

"Wait." I stared at her. "In the morning? But—aren't you here to get me out? What do you mean, morning?"

She looked at me patiently. "Raine, you know the judge has to set bond. As soon as he does, and it's paid, you'll be released under the terms the court sets until your court date."

I stared at her. "But—I didn't do anything!" I protested stupidly. How many times had she, as a lawyer, heard that? How many times had I heard it, sitting in my father's courtroom? *I'm innocent!* they'd cry as they were being cuffed and dragged off to jail.

But I really was.

She went on calmly, "Generally in a case like this I'd expect bond to be set at $20,000 to $50,000, but it could be as high as $250,000. Not that it matters," she assured me quickly, "Miles is prepared to pay it immediately and you'll be home by lunch. The only problem could be that new prosecutor wanting to make a name for himself, trying to argue you're a flight risk…"

"Me?" I blinked, feeling overwhelmed. "I've lived here all my life. I own a business. Where would I go?"

"You're engaged to a man with access to a private jet," she answered simply. "Anywhere you want."

I wound my fingers into Cisco's silky fur, trying to ground myself. "This is crazy," I managed in a moment. "This can't be happening."

"Raine," Sonny replied solemnly, "the charge is murder. And I assure you, it is happening. Now." She picked up her pen and turned over a page on the legal pad. "Why don't you tell me what happened? Start at the beginning."

A long time ago a bad man by the name of Reese Pickens had said to me, *Someday your uncle is not going to be sheriff anymore, you won't be married to a deputy anymore, and nobody will care that your daddy was a judge. Let's see how smart you are then.*

I had poked my nose into a lot of places it didn't belong since then and had had more than a few brushes with the law. Jolene had threatened to arrest me more than once and had actually even taken me into custody one time—for a traffic violation, which was quickly dismissed. I had always thought of things like that as part of the job, part of being who I am. I had never considered the fact that I had gotten away with so much *because* of who I am, who I knew. And the truth is, a lot of those times I had been wrong.

This time I was right. This time I was innocent. And this time, that long ago prediction had come true. Nobody cared.

My fingers tightened in Cisco's fur. He looked up at me with an expression very much like alarm.

"Raine," prompted Sonny gently.

I cleared my throat. I tried to think.

"I guess," I said eventually, "it all started back in January. When Jolene told me about the process server."

CHAPTER TWO

It hadn't been a great couple of weeks for me. My internet server and my business phone had gone down, dumping all of my e-mails and voice messages, as well most of my contacts, into the great cloud void. This is no fun for anybody, but for a small business owner like me it can be disastrous. Fortunately, I'm engaged to a man who may not be a tech wizard himself but who employs dozens of them. Eventually my contacts were restored, but the e-mails were gone forever. In the midst of all this my general manager, Corny, had slipped on the ice and broken his wrist. He's the kind of person who wouldn't let a little thing like that slow him down, and I'm the kind of person who will work twice as hard just to make sure he doesn't overdo it. The final blow came when I started working on my taxes, as I routinely do every January. The good news was that I made more money last year than I'd expected. The bad news was that I owed more taxes than I was prepared to pay.

It was definitely time for an evening out.

There aren't that many places to dine out in the rural mountain community of Hanover County, North Carolina, so the chances are that wherever you go, you're going to see somebody you know. It wasn't that I was particularly surprised to see Jolene Smith walk into the Pizza Palace that evening just as Miles, Melanie and I were settling into our booth, but I was very surprised to see who she was with.

Melanie, my eleven-year-old stepdaughter-to-be, was trying to wheedle her father out of some cash for arcade games as he helped her out of her puffer coat and hung it on the peg beside our booth. "What happened to your own money?" he asked her.

Aside from a hefty allowance, Melanie picked up extra cash by working for me a couple of hours a week at Dog Daze, my boarding kennel and training facility on the outskirts of town. Not that she needed it, of course, since her dad was richer than God, but it was important to Miles for his daughter to learn to make her own way in the world, and that was a sentiment with which I wholeheartedly agreed.

"I'm saving it to buy a VR headset," she said. "Glasses, earphones, microphone, IOS compatible."

I lifted an eyebrow but said nothing. When I was a kid, the most I could hope to afford on my allowance was a new basket for my bike. Pink, with multicolored handlebar streamers. I saved for it all summer.

Miles took my coat and hung it beside Melanie's, then shrugged out of his own jacket. "Well, I'm saving my money to buy a boat," he replied, "so I'm afraid I can't help you out."

"Daaad," she started to whine, then her curiosity was piqued. "What kind of boat?"

"Yeah," I agreed, because that was the first I was hearing of it. "What kind of boat?"

Miles grinned at us both and was about to reply when a gust of cool air from the front of the building signaled a new arrival and he glanced toward the door. "Isn't that Deputy Smith?"

It's always a little strange to see a law enforcement officer out of uniform, but Jolene Smith would have turned heads however she was dressed. She was a tall, striking African American woman with one of those figures that was made for the form-fitting jeans and V-necked sweater she wore beneath her leather jacket. Tonight, she accessorized with a gorgeous pair of stack-heeled boots that practically made me salivate with envy. In full makeup and gold hoop earrings that almost touched her collarbone, she was, in a word, beautiful. Her mother and her little boy came in behind her as I turned in my seat to follow Miles's gaze, but that was not what made me stop and look twice. Buck Lawson, my ex-husband, came in with them, holding the little boy's hand.

Buck bent to unzip the child's coat and didn't notice us at first. It was Friday night, and the Pizza Palace was near capacity. Conversation buzzed, silverware clinked, bells dinged from the arcade games in the adjacent room. Garth Brooks was on the speakers, people laughed, a baby squealed. The air was thick with the mouth-watering aromas of olive oil and garlic, and that moment, as I twisted in my seat just in time to meet Jolene's eyes, was like a snapshot. I would remember it.

Jolene touched Buck's arm and said something to him. He glanced over at our table and acknowledged us with a smile. I thought he'd come over, but just then the hostess appeared, menus in hand, to take them to their table. Jolene said something else, and he nodded. He gestured the little boy and his grandmother to precede him, and they followed the hostess toward a table in the back. Jolene did not accompany them but started across the room. Maybe she was going to the ladies' room. But I didn't think so.

I ducked back around quickly, feeling a little foolish for doing so, but my attempt to avoid her was futile. Miles, who had barely taken his seat, stood up again, and I could tell by the direction of his gaze that she was coming this way. "Great," I muttered under my breath. A perfectly nice evening ruined.

Miles said, "Deputy Smith. Good to see you."

She replied, "Mr. Young."

I pasted on a smile and looked up at her. "Hi, Jolene."

She nodded at me. "Stockton."

Jolene Smith was an interesting woman. Aside from being the only Black person *or* female person in the sheriff's office, which was a challenge in itself, she had done two tours of duty in Afghanistan and had worked for Homeland Security before settling in our little town in the middle of the Smoky Mountains. She had been here little over a year before being promoted to chief deputy, which meant she now outranked all those good old boys who had been on the force a lot longer than she had and who probably resented the hell out of her for it. Until recently, she had also been one half of our only K-9 team. Since my dog, Cisco, and I are the only wilderness-certified search and rescue team in the county, she and I had occasion to work together now and then, and you'd think that would give us something in common. I had tried to be her friend, I truly had. But the fact of the matter was Jolene Smith was not a very likable person. And she had made no secret of the fact that, for some unknown reason, she did not like me.

So why couldn't she just let us have our dinner in peace?

She said to me, "Have you got a minute?"

I tried not to let my surprise show. "Sure, I guess."

She glanced at Miles, indicating this was to be a private conversation, and he took the hint. "Come on, hotshot," he said to Melanie, sliding out of the booth. "I'll go halvsies with you on some game tokens."

"Dad," she replied with one of her signature eye-rolls, "nobody says 'halvsies' anymore."

"I just did," he pointed out, and they moved off toward the arcade room, bickering good-naturedly.

Jolene took the seat across from me that Miles had just vacated, perching on the edge, clearly not intending to stay long. When she didn't speak immediately, I felt compelled to fill the void.

"I was sorry to hear about Nike," I said.

Nike was Jolene's Malinois, a highly trained munitions-sniffing dog who had been funded—along with her handler, Jolene—through Homeland Security. When her contract was up and Jolene accepted a permanent job with the Hanover County Sheriff's Office, Nike had been reclaimed by the government that had spent tens of thousands of dollars on her training.

Jolene frowned impatiently. "She didn't die, Stockton. She was reassigned."

So much for trying to be nice. The waitress stopped by then, pad and pencil in hand, and I was happy to ignore Jolene while I ordered three Cokes, a large pepperoni pizza and a salad bowl for the table. The restaurant was busy, and I was hungry. Maybe Jolene would take the hint and get to the point.

She waited until the waitress had hurried off to say, briskly, "I need to tell you something. The sheriff has a policy about employees disclosing personal relationships within the office. Since you were bound to hear about it anyway, I wanted it to come from me first, woman to woman." Before I could even begin to wonder what this had to do with me, she said, "Buck and I are dating."

I stared at her, completely without words as she lifted one shoulder in a gesture of irritation and added, "Dating is such a stupid word. Makes us sound like a couple of teenagers. But we're together. We have been for a while. We're not trying to keep it secret but..." She nodded her head toward the table in the back, where Buck had gone with her family. "I guess you noticed that."

It started to come together in my head. Buck Lawson, chief investigator with the Hanover County Sheriff's Office, had been critically wounded back in May, and every time I went to the hospital to visit him, Jolene had been there. But then, so was most of the department. Law enforcement was like that; there was no question about them circling the wagons when one of their own was down. But even later, after he was recuperating at home and pretty much everyone in town was on rotation to bring him meals or make sure his laundry was done and his house cleaned and his garden watered, she would often be leaving just as I was arriving or arriving just as I was leaving. I figured it was a work thing, since Jolene was chief deputy and Buck was chief investigator and the sheriff had promised to keep Buck in the loop while he was out of work. Not that I was at his place that much, but he *was* my neighbor, and we *had* known each other since we were kids and been married to each other for just about a third of our lives and…

"Buck wanted to talk to you himself," she said, regarding me calmly, "but I know we have a history and I thought I owed you this much."

History, I thought. That was one word for it.

"It's a small town," she added. "I didn't want there to be any hard feelings."

I knew I should say something. She was trying very hard to be civilized. Maybe I should thank her for the effort. Maybe I should warn her about what she was getting into. But something told me Jolene Smith knew exactly what she was signing up for with Buck, and, oddly enough, she might be the only woman in the world who could handle it. That was reassuring, in a way.

So, what I said was, "Is this why you never liked me? Because you had a crush on Buck and you thought I was, I don't know, competition?"

She gave a small, surprised laugh and a shake of her head. "Stockton, you're just like one of those golden retrievers that are always jumping up on people and getting muddy pawprints all over a person's clean suit. They mean well, but they're a pain in the ass. The way we got along never had anything to do with Buck. You're just a little annoying, that's all."

I started to object indignantly that my dogs never jumped up on people but thought better of it. She had met Cisco, after all. I said, scowling, "You're no Miss Congeniality, you know."

She seemed amused by that. "Never tried to be." She placed her hands on the table, palms down, in preparation for rising. "Well," she said, "I guess I'll see you around."

I muttered, "I'll try not to be too annoying."

She stood to leave, then seemed to remember something. "Say, did that guy ever find you?"

I looked up at her, wishing she'd just go. "What guy?"

"Some man stopped by the office as I was leaving, asking for directions to your place. Looked like a lawyer, or maybe a process server."

Terrific, I thought. Could this evening get any better?

It wasn't that unusual for me to be summoned to a court appearance, but it was never any fun. Usually, the summons had something to do with my search and rescue work, but only last month I had been called to give testimony regarding a vicious dog, who, as it happened, had once been one of my students. I really, really hoped this wasn't something like that.

She shrugged. "On the other hand, he had a dog crate in the back of his car, and he did ask for your business, not your personal address. Too bad they're the same thing. Maybe he just wanted somebody to take care of his dog. Annabelle gave him directions but told him you were closed until morning."

"So that's what the sheriff's office does now?" I returned, disgruntled. "They give out information on private citizens to strangers?"

She replied easily, "Always happy to direct lost tourists to local businesses. Just part of the service. Enjoy your meal, Stockton."

I suspected Miles of waiting for her to leave, because he came back alone and slid into his seat almost as soon as she vacated it.

"Buck is dating Jolene," I said without waiting for him to ask.

He lifted an eyebrow appreciatively as he watched her cross the room, long legs, high-heeled boots, swinging hips and all. "And this surprises you because?"

I kicked him under the table, and he looked back at me with laughing eyes. But he was right. Jolene was gorgeous, and she had to be the only pretty woman in town Buck *hadn't* dated. I guess the only thing that surprised me was that it had taken this long for them to get together. And that it had taken me this long to notice.

"It was nice of her to tell you in person," Miles added.

"Classy."

The waitress returned with our drinks and a basket of breadsticks. "I guess." I took a breadstick and added uncomfortably, "When Buck married Wyn, I found out by practically walking in on their wedding reception. Everybody knew but me. It was humiliating. Jolene was there, and I guess even she felt sorry for me. So, yeah, maybe she remembered that and tried to do the decent thing for once."

Miles is far too confident to be jealous of Buck, and he always goes out of his way to be civil to him. He has understood from the beginning that Buck would always be a part of my life, just like Aunt Mart and Uncle Ro were. There are things he doesn't like about my ex—mostly the same things I don't like about him— and I know he gets impatient with him. But Miles makes it easy to talk about Buck without feeling I have to watch what I say, and I appreciate that.

I mulled the whole thing over for a moment, and added thoughtfully, "You know something funny? I have a feeling Buck just might have met his match. I mean, they're complete opposites, and I don't just mean the race thing. She's a Yankee, he's a southern boy. She's a soldier, he's a charmer. She's a rottweiler, he's a cocker spaniel."

Miles smothered a chuckle. "Buck Lawson is no cocker spaniel."

I considered that. "All right, a Labrador retriever, then. Friendly, easygoing, but always ready to get the job done. The point is, they couldn't be more different, but sometimes people like that are made for each other."

He smiled at me across the table and caught my finger with his, the one that wore his engagement ring. It was a marquis cut solitaire surrounded by chocolate diamonds that made me feel like a princess whenever I looked at it. "Sometimes they are," he agreed.

I smiled back at him, but the smile faded as I crunched down on my breadstick. "Jolene said I was like a golden retriever with muddy paws."

He kissed my fingers lightly. "I've never known your paws to be muddy, sugar," he said and sat back. "So, what kind of dog am I?"

"Border collie," I replied immediately. "Quick, smart, energetic, and you only bite when you have to."

Melanie, having spent all her tokens, arrived in time to hear the question and demanded, "What about me?"

"You're a poodle," I told her. "Intelligent, agile, versatile..."

"And high maintenance," her father put in. He stood to let her into the booth beside him.

Melanie replied archly, "Also the smartest dog in the world."

"Next to the border collie," I corrected.

Melanie helped herself to a breadstick. "Did you order extra pepperoni?"

"I did." I took another bite of my breadstick and added to Miles, "Jolene also said a process server was looking for me. She was good enough to give him my address."

"What a sweetheart." He took a breadstick from the basket. "What did you do now, if you don't mind me asking?"

I shrugged elaborately. "But your lawyer is standing by, right?"

"Always on speed dial for you, darlin'," he returned.

A short time later, that wouldn't seem so funny, but right then we just grinned and toasted each other with breadsticks and forgot about the whole thing as soon as Melanie began to regale us with stories of her day at school. It turned out to be a nice evening, after all, and when we got back to Miles's house not one but two gorgeous retrievers galloped to greet us: Melanie's dog, Pepper, and my guy, Cisco. One of them, temporarily forgetting his manners, almost jumped up on me in his excitement, but quickly remembered himself and sat for a treat.

Furthermore, his paws were *not* muddy.

CHAPTER THREE

J anuary is the slow season in the mountains, particularly if you're in the dog training and boarding business. Classes were suspended until spring, and the kennel was closed for cleaning and maintenance for the entire month. Miles kept insisting this would be a perfect time to take a vacation to some place with beaches and palm trees, but when you're rich, that's how you think. When you're not, you actually do spend the time cleaning and maintaining your place of business.

Well, that, and teaching your dog to read.

Aside from being trained in search and rescue, my golden retriever, Cisco, is a certified therapy dog. He's also registered with the R.E.A.D. program, which helps children improve their literacy and communication skills by having them read aloud to therapy dogs. Personally, I'm not wild about kids—Melanie is the only one I've ever really liked—but Cisco is great with them. He and I go into schools and libraries where children who were once reluctant readers can't wait to choose a book to read to Cisco. Sometimes Cisco helps them along by turning a page with his paw or "whispering" a word in my ear when a young reader finds it too difficult to pronounce. But this new skill, assuming I could teach it to him, would definitely be the crowning jewel of his repertoire.

It all started, as so many things do, when Melanie saw a video on the internet. According to it, you start by holding up a piece of paper with a simple command written on it, like "down" or "sit." You repeat the command out loud and reward the dog when he performs. Then you gradually fade the verbal command until the dog performs the behavior simply by seeing the paper with the word written on it. According to the trainer who was demonstrating the technique, dogs could eventually be taught to identify and differentiate between the shapes of letters that form words and make the association between those words and objects or behaviors, which is more or less what people do when they read. It's pretty exciting stuff.

Now, I'll be honest. My two Aussies, Mischief and Magic, have more visual acuity than Cisco does, just because they're herding dogs. And because translating signals and symbols into action is pretty much a basic job requirement for a herding dog, they would probably both be naturals at the reading game. But my particular two Aussies, as smart as they are, have the attention spans of a couple of gnats when it comes to anything that isn't immediately self-gratifying for them. They are agility champions, because running and jumping, for them, is its own reward. But reading to children... not so much.

Cisco, on the other hand, could be led around the world and back with a treat in front of his nose. He has his share of impulse control and attention span issues, but almost all of them can be overcome with the aforementioned treat. And with his flowing golden coat, happy grin and big, sparkling dark eyes, he's a guaranteed heart-melter even if he'd never learned a single trick, which is one of the things that makes him such an outstanding therapy dog.

Fortunately, he excels at tricks, and the reading game, to him, was just another fun way to earn a treat. He had already mastered "down" and "sit" without the verbal cue, but those words are fairly easy because they look entirely different when written down. Today I wanted to teach him another short word, "paw," and once he had learned to offer his paw when I held up the paper with the three letters written on it, I could teach him to tell the difference between "paw" and the other three-letter word he knew, "sit." From there his potential for recognizing new words, or even combinations of words, was unlimited. I could hardly wait to begin.

We were all set up in my freshly painted training room and had just finished a rousing game of chase-the-ball to get Cisco revved up for even more fun to come when Corny poked his head inside the open door. "Excuse me, Miss Stockton? I hate to interrupt, but there's someone here to see you."

I had put Corny in charge of inventory, which I thought would keep him too busy to attack the kennels with a bottle of disinfectant and a toothbrush, as he was anxious to do, or worse yet, to sweep the snow off the walkway. I have no doubt he could have done either job better with one hand than I could have with two, but I already felt bad enough that he had gotten hurt while working for me. Since I couldn't force him to take the rest of the month off, assigning him to the front office was the next best thing.

I said, surprised, "With a dog? Did you tell him we're closed?"

Cisco, sensing a chance to show off, grabbed his ball, raced around the room with it, and skidded to a stop in front of Corny. He dropped his ball on the floor and looked up at Corny expectantly. Corny, who always had his priorities right, addressed Cisco before he answered my question. "Now then, young sir," he told my golden sternly, "I thought we were in school."

Corny was what some people might call an "odd duck"— but never within my hearing, unless they wanted to be on the receiving end of a few sharp words about their own pedigree in return. With his fuzzy orange hair, oversized glasses and penchant for dressing in primary colors, Corny was definitely the center of attention in any room he entered. He was also one of the most efficient, energetic young men I'd ever met, and the way he had with dogs was nothing less than magical. Since he had moved into my back room and taken over the grooming and kennel management duties, my business had improved forty percent, and I actually had free time for the first time in years.

I held out my hand. "Cisco, here."

Cisco picked up the ball and brought it to me with considerably less enthusiasm than he had shown Corny. He cheered up when I tossed him a treat, though, even though it meant the ball went back onto the toy shelf.

"He said it was a personal matter," Corny told me. Today he wore black and white striped pants with a bright yellow shirt and red suspenders. His broken wrist was encased in a matching yellow cast cover printed with pawprints, and he wore his signature red baseball hat that was covered with pins depicting various breeds of dogs. Cisco appeared to be fascinated by all the colors and watched Corny fixedly.

"He has a dog with him," Corny went on, his brows knitting in mild bafflement, "but I'm not quite sure what kind. Or if it *is* a dog, to be honest."

Corny was something of a purebred snob. I was too, but he had better credentials than I did. His grandfather had been one of the all-time great AKC handlers and best-of-show judges, and if Corny didn't recognize the breed on sight, it very likely didn't exist. I was intrigued.

"I thought he might be an associate of Mr. Young's," Corny added helpfully. "He looks very... businesslike."

That was when I remembered what Jolene had said about the process server, and my lips took a downward turn. "Right," I muttered. But what a jerk to use a dog to get close enough to me to serve a summons.

I tossed Cisco a stuffed toy from the basket on the shelf and left him to entertain himself while I followed Corny back to the office. The man who waited there wore a knee-length all-weather coat and oxblood loafers that were already stained with melted snow from the short walk to the door. He held a briefcase in one hand and a leash in the other. At the end of that leash was a shaggy, medium-sized, golden-haired dog with floppy ears and a tail that waved gaily over its back. It strained at the leash and snuffled happily at the floor, tongue lolling. I shared a puzzled glance with Corny. I couldn't determine what breeds had gone into its making, either. Its coat was curly in places and wavy in others, and far too long to be a standard anything. It had the muzzle of a Labrador and the ears of a spaniel. Its paws were as big as a Newfoundland's, but its legs long and gangly. Part bear, part jack rabbit?

I knelt down to greet the dog and it tried to bound over to me, quickly hitting the end of its leash. His nails scrabbled on the floor as he tried to get to me.

"Sorry about that," the man said. He jerked on the leash. "Rags, stop it!"

I moved closer and offered a treat from my pocket, which the dog quickly gobbled up, panting eagerly and straining at the leash for more. I stood up, intrigued enough by the dog to forget I was supposed to be annoyed with the man who had almost certainly come here to ruin my day. He surprised me by shifting his briefcase to the hand with the leash, almost losing control of his dog in the process, and offering not a court document, but a handshake. "Miss Stockton?" he said. "Raine Stockton?"

I shook his hand warily. "That's right."

"My name is Leon Whitmire. I'm an attorney from St. Petersburg, and also Maude Braselton's nephew."

I stared at him, my confused thoughts scrambling to rearrange themselves. Maude Braselton was my oldest friend. She'd been my father's court clerk for as long as I could remember, a fixture at every holiday table, a mother to me after my own mother died. She was also a brilliant trainer and breeder of golden retrievers and had introduced me to the world of dogs at a young age. She had given me my first golden retriever, the ancestress to Cisco. She had been my partner in Dog Daze from the beginning; in fact, the kennel and training business had been her idea.

Then I had discovered her betrayal, and I couldn't forgive her. I said things I couldn't take back and dissolved our partnership in Dog Daze. She moved to Florida, and even though, after a long time and a lot of help from my friends, I was able to make peace with what had happened and even talk to her now and then, things were never the same between us. The last I heard she was living with her brother in Tampa and breeding goldendoodles, of all things.

My eyes snapped to the shaggy creature who was bouncing and lunging at the end of the leash. Could it be a goldendoodle? Could *that* be one of Maude's dogs?

Impossible, I thought. Maude was one of the most fastidious breeders in the dog world. Nothing in her breeding program—even a breeding program built around designer dogs—could produce such as mishmash of colors and textures. It was cute, but it was no purebred.

Corny, sensing that the lawyer was struggling to maintain his composure as well as his grip on the leash, stepped forward. "Would you like me to take him?" he offered. "I'd be happy to take him out to the play yard while you talk with Miss Stockton."

The other man's shoulders practically sagged with relief, but he looked dubious as he looked at Corny's casted arm. "Are you sure? He's, um, a bit of a handful."

Corny extended his hand for the leash with a confident smile, and the other man couldn't turn over the leash fast enough. "Thank you," he said. "He's just a puppy, and I'm afraid I don't know much about dogs."

Corny took the leash and got the puppy's attention with a single lift of his index finger. The dog eagerly bounded up to him and slid clumsily into a sit, panting happily. Corny rewarded him with a treat, and the next thing we knew the dog was trotting contentedly beside Corny, eyes fixed on him worshipfully, as the two of them left the room. Like I said, magical.

I turned back to my visitor, now thoroughly confused. "We're closed for the winter," I said, "but if you're interested in private lessons..."

As soon as I spoke, I felt foolish. Surely the man didn't

drive all the way from St. Pete just to have me train his dog. And even as I thought that he shook his head. "Miss Stockton, I'm so sorry. I left several voice messages on your business number, tried to reach you by e-mail and direct message on Facebook... I didn't have a personal phone number for you, or a way to text you, and I finally decided that since I had to drive to Virginia this week anyway, it would be easier to simply stop by in person."

I blinked, not following at all. So, he *had* come all this way to ask me to train his dog? Why?

I said, "I'm afraid I didn't get any of your messages. We had a little tech glitch and I lost just about everything that came through in the past ten days. So." I glanced toward the door through which Corny had exited with the dog. "Is that one of Maude's dogs? Why would you bring it here when Maude is a much better trainer than I am?"

His expression was solemn. "Miss Stockton," he said, "I'm so sorry to tell you this, but Aunt Maude passed away Thursday a week ago." He shook his head sadly. "I tried to reach you. Again, I'm sorry."

I stared at him for a very long time—long enough to almost, but not quite, convince myself I hadn't heard him correctly. Maude was in her late sixties, younger than my father had been when he died. Younger than Miles's mother was now. She was fit, active, and, when last I had seen her, in perfect health. How could she be dead?

Finally, I managed a soft, "Oh." I went behind the counter to my desk and sat down hard. I said again, "Oh."

He followed me behind the counter and stood there uncertainly, his hands wrapped around the handle of his briefcase, while I struggled to find my way back from the shock. Finally, I took a deep breath, blinked my eyes into focus, and managed, "How, ummm..." I cleared my throat. "How did she die?"

"Ovarian cancer," he replied. "She was diagnosed about a month ago and it was quite advanced. She went downhill very quickly."

I nodded slowly, still trying to find a way not to believe what I was hearing.

He said, "As you might know, my father—Aunt Maude's brother—passed away last year and she had no other relatives except me. She asked me to draw up her will and execute her estate. That's why I'm here, Miss Stockton."

I took a moment to process the words, then gestured him to the yellow plastic chair where clients sometimes sat to fill out paperwork on their dogs. "Please," I said, "sit down. And you can call me Raine. I should offer you coffee." I looked around distractedly, as though a coffeepot might magically appear. If Corny had been here, it would have, but the actual coffeepot was back in the kitchen, two rooms away.

He sat down and assured me, "No, thank you, I'm fine." He opened his briefcase on his lap and began to shuffle through papers. "This shouldn't take long. Again, I apologize for just showing up like this. My daughter just spent a semester abroad, and she's flying into Dulles from Germany tomorrow. I was planning to spend a week with her before attending a conference in Washington. I'm hoping to get to Richmond before it gets too late tonight. Ah, here we are." He drew out a folder.

"What about her dogs?" I interrupted, because that was really all I could think about just then. "Her golden retrievers, River and Rune, and wasn't she breeding goldendoodles?"

He nodded. "As it happens, the dog I have with me— she called him Rags for pretty obvious reasons—was from her last litter. Her puppies are usually spoken for well in advance, but this one, apparently, wasn't up to standard. I was hoping to find someone to take him before I left, but no such luck, and I hated to turn him over to a shelter. I do remember the two golden retrievers you're referring to, but they were quite old, you know, and I believe they passed. She had three male goldens and several female poodles, all of which lived with foster families when they weren't actively being bred. When

Aunt Maude became ill, she arranged for those families to formally adopt the dogs."

I nodded. That policy, sometimes known as a "guardian" or "family care" program, was becoming more and more popular among breeders. The breeder, while retaining full ownership of the dogs in her program, placed them as puppies with qualified families to be raised as pets. The breeder paid for all the dog's needs except food, and the dog stayed with its foster family for all but a few weeks of the year. After a specified number of years—usually three to four—the dog was taken out of the breeding program and formally adopted by the foster family. It was a great deal for the family, who got an expensive purebred dog with virtually no expenditure on their part. Great deal for the dog, who got to spend his life as a cherished member of a family rather than as one of a multitude of kennel dogs. And a great deal for the breeder, who did not have the hassle or the expense of running a kennel.

I swallowed, but my voice was still a little hoarse as I said, "She should have told me. I would have come if I'd known."

He nodded sympathetically. "Aunt Maude was..." He searched for the word. "Stalwart. And private. She wanted to handle things her own way."

I fixated on the dog, probably because it kept me from fixating on why he was really here. "So, you're going to keep the dog? Rags?"

He gave a small, soft laugh and shook his head. "Good heavens, no. I live in a tenth-floor condo downtown. I wouldn't know what to do with a dog. I was hoping one of my daughter's friends might be able to find a home for him. At any rate, she said she'd try."

I managed, "That was nice of you. To drive all this way with him, I mean."

He smiled sympathetically. "Miss Stockton—Raine," he corrected. "I'm not sure if you're aware that Aunt Maude held on to the property she owned here. A three-bedroom house, five acres, a small barn located on Deer Run Trail. I believe it was rented until recently."

I said uncertainly, "Yes. I might have heard something about that."

"She left the property in its entirety to you." He handed me a heavy, blue, legal-sized folder with the name of his law firm embossed in gold on the outside. "This is a copy of her will, the deed to the property and the transfer of ownership documents." He leaned forward to open the folder for me. "I'll need you to sign all three copies of this set of documents where indicated and return two to me. The taxes for this year will be paid out of Aunt Maude's estate. Apparently, there is some back rent owed—the last tenant skipped out—but it was such a small amount we've written it off. There's a letter you'll need to sign to that affect, forfeiting claim to monies owed."

His voice droned on, his hand turned pages, and I just stared. Finally, I said, "She left me her house?"

"Yes, that's right. I believe Aunt Maude intended to write you a letter explaining everything, but I didn't find anything in her belongings. Obviously, I'll forward it to you should I come across anything." He glanced around. "Do you suppose we could ask that young man who was here before to come in and witness your signature? Then we can finalize all this, and I can get out of your way."

Corny returned with the scruffy-looking goldendoodle, assuming our visitor was ready to go. His expression was stricken when I explained to him what had happened.

"Oh, Miss Stockton," he exclaimed softly. "I am so sorry!"

Corny had never met Maude, but he knew about her. It was basically her job that he had taken over when he came here, and he knew she had once been my partner in Dog Daze as well as an old family friend. He also knew, because his immersion in the world of dogs was as intense as mine, that she had been quite prominent on the dog show circuit in her time. I'd always thought the two of them would like each other if they ever met. But now they never would.

I signed the papers in something of a daze, and Corny put

his signature next to mine. Rags snuffled Corny's pockets for treats, searched the floor for crumbs, and put his big, shaggy paws on my desk—a move that Corny quickly corrected with a stern look. The dog, while lacking Cisco's obvious good looks and charm, reminded me a lot of Cisco at that age. Or maybe I was just projecting. He was one of Maude's dogs. So was Cisco.

Leon Whitmire packed up his briefcase, stood and offered his hand again. "It's been a pleasure meeting you, Miss Stockton. Raine. I'm sorry it had to be under these circumstances. If you have any questions, you have my card."

I nodded, still feeling dazed. "Thank you," I managed, "for coming all this way."

His smile grew a little wry as he turned to take the bouncing puppy's leash from Corny. "I don't suppose you know anyone who wants a goldendoodle, do you?"

I said impulsively, "I do." I stepped from behind the desk and added, "I mean, we do. That's what we do, what Maude and I used to do, and I still do. Breed rescue. And if you're just going to turn him over to rescue when you get to Washington anyway..."

"Seriously?" The surprise in his expression was all but lost in the overwhelming relief that flooded his face. "If you could save me driving the rest of the way with a puppy in the car, I can't tell you how grateful I'd be. I have his food and bedding," he added quickly, as though afraid I'd change my mind. "Vet records, too. I'll go get them."

When the supplies were delivered, the surrender papers signed, and Rags the goldendoodle was settled in his crate beside my desk, wagging his shaggy tail and watching the proceedings with interest, the lawyer was clearly eager to be on his way. "Again," he said sincerely, "thank you." He nodded to me, and then to Corny. "Good to meet you both."

I wished him a pleasant trip, and when he was gone, I turned to look at the eager young pup in the crate. I looked at him for a long time. "Well," I said at last.

Corny agreed, "Well." He looked at a loss for further words

for a moment, and then he brightened. "It looks like you have a new dog."

I managed a weak smile. "Yes," I said. "So it does."

CHAPTER FOUR

Buck Lawson turned up the collar of his fleece-lined denim jacket and slammed the door of his cruiser. He waited a moment for the throbbing ache in his bad leg to subside, refusing to bend and rub out the stiffness. His boots crunched on the frozen, snow-spattered ground as he made his way carefully past the fire engines, the other police cars, an ambulance, the coroner's van. Red and blue lights strobed across the dull winter day. Radios crackled. A rural postal delivery vehicle was parked at the edge of the dirt road in front of the house, its yellow dome light still turning. Buck shoved his hands into his pockets and suppressed a shiver when the cold wind hit him. He wished he'd worn gloves.

The house sat at the end of a mostly deserted road called Quail Pass. The only neighbors were a tire shop and wrecker service a mile away, an abandoned lumber yard, and a couple of mobile homes with leaky roofs and rusty window frames. None were within shouting distance. This was not exactly one of Hanover County's premier neighborhoods.

Buck made his way up the drive to the house, past an old washing machine, a pile of trash lumber that might once have been a shed, and a rusted-out Chevy on blocks. The coroner was waiting for him on the porch of the unpainted house, shoulders hunched against the cold, blowing on his cupped hands to keep them warm. Since all the doors and windows of the house were open for ventilation, it probably wasn't any warmer inside.

"How's it going, Sam?" Buck greeted him. "Bitter day, huh?"

"At least we're not standing on the side of the road waiting for the guys to pull bodies out of some wreck," the other man replied glumly. "I hate those calls."

"Yeah, me too." Buck nodded toward the house. "What've we got?"

"Carbon monoxide," replied Sam without hesitation. "Lord knows I've seen enough of that over the years. One victim, male, fifty-six years old. That propane heater has got to be as old as he is. Looks like he fell asleep on the couch last night watching TV and never woke up. The postman found him a few hours ago." He glanced toward the yard, where a deputy was interviewing a shaken-looking Carter Frank, the rural carrier for this part of the county. "I figure he's been dead less than twenty-four hours."

"Okay, Sam, thanks." Buck moved toward the door. "Let me make sure the boys have got all the pictures they need, and you can take charge of the remains."

"Thanks, Buck." He blew again on his hands and shivered. "Anything you can do to speed things along will be greatly appreciated."

Buck started to go inside and then, with an apologetic glance at Sam, stepped off the low porch and crossed the yard to the mail carrier who had discovered the body. "Sorry to keep you from your route, Carter," he said, "but, believe or not, we can get you on your way a lot faster if you'll just tell me one more time what you've been telling the deputies since they got here."

Carter Frank was a slim man with a balding head and a prominent Adam's apple. The Adam's apple bobbed noticeably now as he swallowed. "Hell of a thing, Buck," he said. "Hell of a thing."

The deputy who had been interviewing Carter finished jotting down the last of his notes and asked Buck, "You need me to stand by, Major?"

Buck said, "Get a couple of the boys and start canvassing the neighbors. The houses are pretty far apart, but somebody might've seen something that can give us a better idea of the time of death."

"Yes, sir."

He turned back to the postman. "About what time did you get here?"

"One fifteen," Carter replied. "I know because I only had a few more stops and was thinking I might be able to sign out before the diner stopped serving lunch at 2:00. He had a package that was too big for the mailbox, so I went to leave it on the stoop there. That's when I saw him, plain as day, through the window there..." He gestured to the grimy window beside the front door, its bottom pane now raised to let cold wind blow through. "I could tell something wasn't right, just by the way he looked, the way he was lying, you know?"

Buck gave an encouraging nod. "The house was shut up when you got here?"

"Yes, sir, it was. I started knocking and calling out, but he didn't move. I even tried the front door, but it was locked. I must've knocked for a good five minutes. That's when I figured I better call 911. I mean, you remember a few years back when I found old Miz Kellogg face down in her garden. It was just heat stroke, but they said she might've died if I hadn't come along when I did. I was afraid of something like that, so I called."

"You did the right thing, Carter." Buck glanced around the yard. "Did you see anybody coming or going when you got here? Any vehicles that aren't usually here when you make your rounds?"

"No, sir, nothing like that. Just that old pickup truck of his, and it's almost always here. Now, yesterday," he added helpfully, "seems like he might've had company when I came by. Some kind of dark-colored SUV in the yard, but of course it was too cold for anybody to be outside, and I wasn't really looking. Nothing but junk mail yesterday."

"What time was that?"

"About the same time; 1:00 or so. But like I say, I wasn't really paying attention."

Buck said, "Okay, Carter, thanks. You can go on, now. If you think of anything else, give me a call."

"Hell of a thing," Carter repeated and shook his head sadly as he walked back toward his vehicle.

The inside of the little house was dark and cold and smelled of garbage, mold, dirty laundry and rotting carpets. Overwhelming it all was the rank, creeping odor of death. The walls were paneled in age-darkened pine and the floors were covered with a thin, stained, wall-to-wall carpet of an indeterminate color. Stacks of old pizza boxes, discarded packing materials and newspapers cluttered the walking area. The kitchen table and coffee table were covered with dirty dishes, paper plates and empty beer cans. Stained dish towels served as window coverings in the kitchen, and one blind hung crookedly from the front window. It was not the home of a man who took pride in his surroundings.

Two EMTs lingered in a corner beside the sofa, where someone had covered the body with a clean sheet. Buck nodded a greeting to them, and, bracing himself, lifted the sheet from the dead man's body. He was a big man, three hundred pounds or more, with a scraggly gray beard that reached his upper chest. He was wearing a stained gray sweatshirt and dingy track pants with wool socks. Buck saw no obvious wounds or ligature marks. No blood anywhere, no contusions that he could see. The details he would leave to the medical examiner, but he saw no reason to dispute Sam's conclusion about the cause of death.

Jolene came up behind him. "James Robert Beardsley," she said, "a.k.a. Smokey, age fifty-six. Eight years for armed robbery, three for assault, five for possession with intent to sell. You know him?"

Buck let the sheet drop carefully across his face again.

"Only in a usual-suspects kind of way," he said. "I sent him up the last time. Since he got out, I've interviewed him a time or two. Seems like anything that went wrong around here he had a hand in or knew the man who did. Never enough to take to court, though." He frowned a little, running over in his mind a list of the cases Smokey Beardsley had been involved in, however peripherally, over the years. He glanced over at the paramedics. "You guys were first on the scene?"

"Yes, sir."

"Was the heat on when you got here?"

"It was. We turned it off as soon as we got the carbon monoxide reading and ventilated the house to make it safe for entry."

"And what time was that?"

One of the men checked his logbook. "One thirty-six PM."

Buck glanced at his watch. It was the old-fashioned, stem-wound kind, and Jolene used to tease him about it until she found out it had belonged to his father, and he hadn't taken it off since the day his dad had died. She'd canceled the digital watch she had ordered for Christmas and had given him the fleece-lined jacket instead.

"Two hours ago," Buck observed. "Was the body cold when you got here?"

"It was. Rigor had started to set in. We called Sam out to declare." In Hanover County, death had to be certified by either the coroner or a medical doctor.

Buck nodded. "Okay, thanks, guys." He turned to Jolene. "Have you got everything you need?"

She answered, "We were just waiting for you."

He told the EMTs, "All right, then, he's all yours. Help Sam get him loaded up."

The two men went to work, and he and Jolene moved out of the way. "So, what am I doing here?" he asked her. "I'm guessing you have reason to suspect this wasn't an accidental death?"

She gestured him toward the back door, and they went

outside, where a deputy was standing guard near the corner of the house. "Hey, Pat," Buck greeted him. "What've you got?"

Jolene answered the question. "On a routine inspection of the premises, looking for the cause of the failure of the heating system, we found this."

The deputy stepped aside, and Buck saw a yellow evidence marker next to a rusted heat vent protruding from the wall. It wasn't particularly safe or even legal, but neither was it unusual to see heating systems vented this way when the homeowner was either too cheap or too lazy to install a proper chimney. A scrap of color protruded from the vent opening, and when Buck squatted down to examine it, he saw what appeared to be a grimy blue towel stuffed into the pipe.

"Well," said Buck, standing. "That would do it. Even in a house as leaky as this one, it wouldn't have taken long to build up enough fumes to kill a man."

Jolene told the deputy, "Get somebody to help you tape off the place. Make sure to get some clear photos of this vent pipe first."

"Yes, ma'am." He nodded to Buck. "Good to see you, Buck. Stay warm."

"Same to you."

Buck gazed around the yard while Jolene finished making notes. There was a tool shed with half the roof collapsed a few yards away, filled with a jumble of rotting crates, old oil cans, rusted tractor parts and a push mower with two flat tires. Buck walked over and found a work bench with a wad of towels, stiff with age and other substances, tossed in one corner. He pointed them out to Jolene. "This is probably where he found the towel he used to block the vent."

Jolene jotted that down. "So, we're calling this a homicide?"

"Or a suicide." At her steady gaze, he admitted, "All right. Probably not. An investigation is officially opened." He took out his own field notebook and wrote, *Beardsley Suspicious Death, Investigation opened at*—he checked his watch again—

3:50 PM Jan. 26.

"Sounds to me like you're not going to have much trouble finding suspects," Jolene observed.

"Yeah. The problem will be narrowing it down. Did y'all take the package that Carter delivered into evidence?"

"We did. We'll have it X-rayed and open it at the jail."

"Sure would be helpful if it contained something incriminating, like drugs. And a return address."

"Don't hold your breath," she replied. "It was from one of those home shopping television shows. Probably some kind of useless gadget that'll break after the first week."

"Well," Buck said, "at least he doesn't have to worry about returning it."

They started walking back toward the front of the house. Jolene said, "Are you coming for supper tonight?"

"Actually," Buck replied, "I was thinking we might go to my place tonight. I could pick up barbecue on the way home."

By unspoken agreement, they confined their intimate moments to Buck's place. Jolene's rental house was small, with only one bathroom, and her bedroom shared a wall with her son's room on one side and her mother's room on the other. It was not an ideal setup for romance.

She said, "Mama's making fried chicken."

He groaned softly. "You are not making me choose between your mother's fried chicken and sex with you."

Her lips twitched with repressed amusement. "Buttermilk biscuits and those corn fritters you like so much."

"And apple pie?"

Jolene said, "I'll tell her to set an extra plate."

Buck paused, looking around the desolate little yard again thoughtfully. "He used to have the meanest old dog," he recalled. "Some kind of pit bull killer mix. Kept him tied up right over there." He nodded to a leafless maple tree, where a length of green clothesline could still be seen trailing on the ground. "He had a girlfriend living out here with him for a while, too."

"What happened to her?"

"She found somebody that treated her better, is what I heard."

"Maybe we should talk to her."

"Yeah, maybe."

But Buck's tone was distracted, and so was his expression as he let his gaze wander inward and his thoughts take him backwards. He was starting to remember what had brought him out here the last time he had talked to Smokey Beardsley.

And what had happened afterward.

CHAPTER FIVE

Melanie regarded the shaggy creature in the grooming tub skeptically. "I don't know, Raine," she observed. "Are you sure it's a goldendoodle?"

Because Corny did not permit any rescue to cross the threshold of Dog Daze without the full spa treatment—the least we could do, he always said, after all the poor things had been through to get here—and because I refused to allow him to groom a dog with his arm in a cast, Melanie had been called in as his assistant. The truth was, she hadn't so much been called in as insisted on helping when she heard about the new dog, and I was glad to turn it over to her. Melanie did not like to be left out of any important life event, and an addition to the pack was a major life event. Besides, as she was quick to remind me, she needed the money.

I helped Corny fasten the dog into the bathing harness and replied, "We won't know what he is until we get some of the fur trimmed away from his eyes." The puppy wriggled and danced and nipped playfully at the straps. "Don't get your cast wet," I reminded Corny sternly. "Melanie is perfectly capable of washing a dog."

"Yes, ma'am," Corny assured me. "I have every faith in Miss Melanie. I trained her myself."

With her confidence thus plumped up, Melanie tied back her curly hair, adjusted the straps of her plastic-coated apron and placed her hands on her hips, regarding the array of grooming products with all the authority of a surgeon selecting an instrument. "Golden Sheen shampoo," she pronounced at last, choosing a bottle from the shelf.

"Excellent choice," agreed Corny. "And perhaps a Snowdrop facial?"

I left them to it and returned to the office, where Cisco, who also didn't like to be left out of major life events, was pawing at the door. I edged past him, and Mischief, Magic and Pepper all leapt off the sofa, where they had been sprawled out around Miles, and raced to greet me. I sat down on the floor and let them crawl all over me. Not very good training technique, I know, but I could use all the doggie hugs I could get right then.

Finally, I struggled to my feet, got all four of them to sit, and rewarded them each with a treat from my pocket. Miles watched me with amusement in his eyes for a moment, then turned the last page of the blue folder and closed it.

"It all looks good to me, hon," he said. He stretched to return the folder to my desk and held out an inviting hand to me. "So, you're a real estate baron now. What are you going to do with the property?"

"I'm not going to sell it," I told him, frowning a little as I came over to him.

"Agreed," he said, surprising me. Usually, Miles was all about the buying and selling of real estate, and, all things considered, I figured he would have made me an offer by now. "Given the location and the market up here, you're not going to get half what it'll be worth in another eight years. Your best bet is to keep it as an income property for now."

I sighed. "I never thought I'd be a landlord."

Cisco, seeing me about to sit down beside Miles, snatched a stuffed toy from the basket and leapt up onto the sofa in my place. Apparently, someone had been feeling a little neglected this morning. I gave him a stern look and he regarded me with thumping tail, big eyes and a toy racoon hanging from his mouth. I said firmly, "Off." He jumped down, but barely allowed me enough time to scoot in beside Miles before he leapt up onto the sofa again. He dropped the racoon in my lap and rested his head on my knees. I stroked his silky ears and sighed again. What in the world was I going to do with another dog?

Miles said, "The house is fifty years old. It's bound to need some work before you can rent it out. If you want, we can ride over there and take a look tomorrow."

"Can't," I reminded him. "We promised to take Melanie and her friends ice skating tomorrow."

"Right," he remembered. "Monday then. You don't want to put it off. The place might not be winterized, and you don't want to have to replace broken pipes and a well pump on top of everything else."

"I guess."

He put his arm around my shoulders and kissed my hair. His voice was gentle. "You okay, sugar?"

I nodded, twisting a strand of Cisco's curly ear fur around my finger. "It's just... it brought it all back, you know?"

Miles did know. He had been with me when Maude, whom I had trusted and depended upon all my life, confessed her decades-long affair with my father, the judge. My mother had been dying of cancer, and the two of them had been lying to her, to everyone. They had even allowed an innocent man to go to prison to cover up their affair. My father, the judge, a legend in this state, admired by one and all but no one more than his starry-eyed daughter—that revered man, that pillar of truth and justice, had even tampered with evidence and violated his oath of office in order to conceal his dirty little secret. My stomach filled with acid whenever I thought of it, which was why I tried very hard not to think about it.

I added uncertainly, "It's just... I don't know how to feel. I mean, Maude's gone, and I never got a chance to tell her I forgive her. Except..." I paused a moment and swallowed. "I'm not sure I do. I should feel bad about that, but... I don't know."

I looked up at him anxiously and saw nothing but understanding in his eyes. "I get it, Raine," he said, and I believed that he did. "But," he added, "did you ever think that maybe it's your father you really need to forgive?"

I tensed. "My father was a liar and a cheater who betrayed everyone who ever depended on him."

"Your father was a good man who did a bad thing," Miles corrected. "Both things can be true."

"Right." My tone was bitter. "Like Buck is a good man who did a bad thing when he cheated on me while we were married. Over and over again."

"In a way, yes," Miles said. "Everybody falls short of the standard now and then—their own, and everybody else's. God knows I've done some things I'm not proud of. So," he fixed me with a steady gaze, "have you."

I drew in a short breath. "It's not the same. My father was a judge."

"Raine," he began, but I couldn't hear any more.

I stood abruptly. "I'm going to help with the dog," I said and left the room without looking back.

CHAPTER SIX

Buck rinsed off a soapy dish and handed it to Jolene to dry. "Every town has one, I guess. The go-to criminal for all-purpose crimes. That was Smokey. He was pretty good at flying below the radar, though. We haven't heard a peep out of him in two, three years now."

"Well, whatever he was up to," Jolene said, "he must've been good at it. Ten thousand dollars stashed away in go-money is not something you get by selling bottle caps."

As soon as Buck had opened an active investigation into Smokey's death, deputies had begun a thorough search of his house. In addition to a stockpile of empty boxes with post office labels addressed to Smokey, ten thousand in cash, along with a collection of driver's licenses, credit cards and passports that did not belong to him, had been found in a canvas bag beneath a loose floorboard in the back of a closet. Definitely motive for murder.

He handed her the last dish and drained the water from the sink. "My best guess is he was involved in some kind of identity theft racket," Buck said. "Easy money if you do it right, I guess. That SUV Carter saw yesterday might have been one of his customers."

"We're keeping an eye out." Jolene stretched to place a platter on the top shelf, and Buck paused to admire the way her sweater rode up to reveal an inch or two of smooth caramel flesh just above her waistband. "But it's not like there aren't a few thousand dark-colored SUVs on the road."

"Right." Buck frowned thoughtfully as he began wiping down the sink. "I started running down the crew Smokey was known to hang out with. Some of them are dead, a couple are in prison. The girlfriend moved out of the area. No talk of any drug activity in a while. Whoever he pissed off it's starting to look like it was somebody unknown to law enforcement."

"I hate it when that happens." Jolene took a spray bottle from beneath the sink and started spritzing down the countertops. "I guess you saw the report about the package Beardsley ordered."

"Yeah. A dark-blue velour tracksuit, size medium. Unless he's got a girlfriend stashed somewhere, I'd say somebody clicked the wrong button on that one."

"Well," she pointed out, "you said you were getting tired of shoplifters and petty thefts. At least this one looks like a challenge."

"Yeah." His smile was a little distracted. "I guess." He put the sponge back in its holder and turned to her. "Listen, Jo, there's something I wanted to talk to you about."

She looked at him with a mixture of curiosity and trepidation in her eyes, but before he could say anything her mother appeared in the kitchen doorway.

"Well, look at you two," she declared, "in here talking shop and still working this late on a Saturday night. I swear, Buck, you keep a cleaner kitchen than I do."

"My mama raised me right," he assured her with a grin. "That was a fine meal, Miss Eloise, and I appreciate it. The least I can do is help clean up a little afterwards."

"Don't listen to him, Mama," Jolene said. "He's just trying to get on your good side for the next time you make fried chicken."

"Or anything else," Buck clarified.

"You're welcome here anytime, honey," Eloise told him. "But really…" She looked from one to the other of them. "Why don't you two go to a movie or something? I'll be here with

Willis. Go on and have a good time."

Buck and Jolene exchanged a look. Clearly, it was the "or something" that interested them both.

There was the clatter of running footsteps in the hallway, and Willis raced into the kitchen wearing pajamas printed with red fire trucks. "Buck!" he cried and flung his arms around Buck's knees. "You're not leaving, are you? We were going to play Chutes and Ladders!"

Buck glanced at Jolene, eyes twinkling, and then reached down and picked Willis up, hoisting him onto his hip for a hug. "Are you kidding? I've been looking forward to that all day."

"Where are your socks, young man?" Jolene scolded. "You'll catch your death."

"Sorry, Mama," he returned solemnly. "I was in a hurry to finish my bath and get dressed before Buck left."

"Tell you what." Buck set the little boy on his feet. "Why don't you go see if you can find some socks while your mom and I set up the game board?"

"And I'll make some hot chocolate," Eloise decided.

"It's a party!" cried Willis.

Jolene laughed and slapped his bottom lightly. "I guess it is. Go on, now."

He scurried away and Eloise bustled about at the stove, taking out the ingredients for the hot chocolate. Jolene slipped an arm around Buck's waist as they left the kitchen.

"Now," she invited with a perfectly straight face, "isn't this more fun than going to your place?"

He smiled and kissed her hair. "You know something?" he said. "It almost is."

CHAPTER SEVEN

The truth is, if it hadn't been for Miles I probably would have delayed going to Maude's house—my house now, I guess—until spring. Maybe not even then. Some people are good about confronting unpleasant tasks, truths or emotions; I am not one of them.

It's not that I had any particularly poignant memories of the place. I had known Maude all my life, it's true, but mostly as a fixture around my father's office or my house. Sitting at a table in the courtroom near the bench, bringing papers for my father to sign, leaning over to speak to the stenographer. Helping my mother give a party for county dignitaries or state court judges—white tablecloths, bone China, heavy crystal goblets, big, showy bunches of hydrangeas and roses everywhere. Later, of course, my memories of Maude revolved around the golden retrievers and the dog shows and the handling classes and obedience classes, field trials and agility trials. Between the ages of nine and eighteen, I probably spent more time with Maude than I did my contemporaries, but I didn't remember much about her house except that it was always graced by the most stunning, beautifully behaved golden retrievers I had ever seen.

I had not been to Maude's house on Deer Run Trail since she left town—probably long before, if I think about it—and I wasn't looking forward to going out there now and walking through cold, empty rooms that served as nothing but a reminder of what would never be again. Ever. Nonetheless, I bundled up in my puffy coat and knit hat and climbed into Miles's Lexus right after breakfast on Monday morning and tried not to act as unhappy about it as I felt.

Cisco, on the other hand, couldn't have been more delighted. He bounded into the backseat beside his best friend, Pepper, and I secured both dogs in their seat belts. As for Rags, well, I have to admit, I felt a little bad leaving Corny alone with him. All puppies are rambunctious, but this one—aside from being twice the size of a normal six-month-old golden *or* poodle—was something else. He had already shredded two of Cisco's favorite toys and one indestructible kennel ball, destroyed a remote control and a wicker porch chair, and had retrieved and eaten my sandwich from the kitchen counter before I even finished making it. And all of this had been while he was under supervision; I didn't dare let him out of his crate without at least one adult in the room. If Maude had been here, she would have reminded me sternly that all of this was my fault, not the dog's, and she would have been right. But I liked to give rescue dogs a couple of days to adjust to their new environment before I began training in earnest. Maybe I should reconsider that philosophy.

Miles thought it was amusing, but that was because so far all the damage had been done at my house. Not, of course, that I would ever let Rags anywhere near Miles's contemporary design-museum of a house. A twenty-year-old wicker chair is one thing; a thirty-thousand-dollar sofa is quite another.

"Just remember," Miles said when I'd finished telling him about Rags's latest misdemeanors, "you promised to find him a home. You didn't promise to keep him."

"I know." I sighed. "But he's Maude's last dog. He can't go to just anybody."

I should probably also mention that even Corny's skill with the grooming scissors had not been able to make Rags look any less like Chewbacca than he had before. Most potential adoptees would take one look at that shaggy, unkempt coat and see nothing but money, in the form of grooming bills, floating out the window. I hated to shave him in the middle of the winter, and Corny pointed out that a close-cropped coat might be even less attractive than the unruly golden locks he sported now. Bottom line: no one who was looking for an expensive designer dog would be remotely interested in Rags, and finding him an appropriate home this time of year, while all the big-hearted part-timers and tourists were wintering in warmer climes, would not be easy.

Miles said, "I talked to Mom last night. She's starting to pack up some of her stuff for the move. I thought maybe we could go up and give her a hand next weekend."

I knew Miles had talked to his mother because she had called me as soon as she hung up with him—first to express her sympathy over Maude, and then to enlist my support regarding Miles's plans for her future. Miles, who, like his counterpart the border collie, wanted to keep his entire flock under his watchful eye, had finally persuaded his mother to move here, for part of the year, at least. The other part—and on this she and I were in perfect agreement—would be spent in her house on the ocean in Myrtle Beach. The dispute came over exactly where she was to live when she got here. Miles was already remodeling a suite of rooms for her in his house. She had her eye on the cute little modular home in the woods where Miles had lived while waiting for his big house to be completed. The little house was less than a five-minute walk to his front door, had a gorgeous deck, hot tub, and yard for gardening, and—most important of all—privacy. I probably should have stayed out of the dispute, but she was right. She deserved her own place.

I said, "I can't next weekend. Uncle Ro's birthday."

"Right. Maybe the weekend after that."

The golden-retriever travel mug that Melanie had given me for Christmas was waiting in its cup holder, filled with Miles's special caramel latte concoction that was, quite literally, the best thing I'd ever tasted. I took a sip and closed my eyes in silent ecstasy. I would have married him for that alone. "Thank you," I remembered to say after the second sip. "This is heaven."

"No," he pointed out, "heaven is a beach in Cabo where it's 82 degrees at this moment." He winked at me and picked up his own mug. "But I guess drinking coffee with you on an icy road in 22-degree weather is the next best thing."

"You do have a way with words." I took another sip and remarked, as though the idea had just occurred to me, "Say, maybe your mother would like to live in Maude's house. I'd give her a real break on the rent, and it would save me having to look for a tenant."

"No way," he replied immediately. "It's too far out, and who knows what shape it's in?"

"You can fix it up."

He shot me an impatient glance. "What on earth would I want to do that for when there are two perfectly good houses on my own property..." He stopped in mid-thought, frowning. "You talked to her, didn't you?"

I sipped my coffee. "Come on, Miles, the woman has lived alone for decades, has all her faculties, looks better in a bikini than I do—not to mention probably has lower blood pressure— and she wants her own place. Set her up in the little house."

He was silent for a moment. "In the first place," he said, "no one looks better in a bikini than you do. In the second place, I'm not at all sure what that has to do with anything. Thirdly, I don't see what she needs her own house for. But I'll think about it."

"That's what you said about Melanie's horse," I reminded him.

"Still thinking."

"And yet I see no horse."

He shot me a dark look. "Are you really going to start with me about the horse again?"

Some couples show their affection by bickering; Miles and I happen to be among them. Of course, we also show our affection in lots of other, more constructive ways, which is a good thing because we have so much to bicker about it could go on forever.

I said, "I just think certain people ought not to make promises—"

"I never promised."

"Or say things that could be construed as a promise to a child—or anyone else—without following through."

Miles punched a button on the dashboard and said, "Call Delta Airlines."

The car responded, "Calling."

I said, "What are you doing?"

The car speakers relayed the sound of a telephone ringing. Miles said, "Booking a flight to the Caribbean. You need a vacation. And if you don't take it..." Another quick, dark look. "I will."

I pushed the button on the dash to disconnect the call. "Just do it, okay?" My tone was a little short. "Your mom is doing you a big favor by giving up her life in Myrtle Beach and moving here, and you don't know how much longer..." I didn't finish that, mostly because I had been obsessing all weekend about every person over the age of sixty that I knew, and I didn't see any reason to make Miles start doing the same. So, I took another gulp of coffee and muttered, "Just do it."

He rested his hand lightly on my knee for a moment and I knew I didn't have to explain. I leaned back in my seat and tried to relax, sipping my coffee in silence until we reached the turn-off for Deer Run Trail. It was only a seven-or-eight-minute drive from my house, and I felt a little bad that I hadn't taken the trouble to drive out here and check on the place before now. Not that anyone expected me to. Not that it was any of my business.

The road, like most in the mountains, was narrow and winding, but leveled off and widened somewhat when the asphalt gave way to gravel. The houses were mixed: some stick-built, some double-wide mobile homes, even a couple of log cabins built from kits. Some of the yards had barking dogs enclosed in chain-link runs, other had barking dogs running free. There was no leash law in our county. Pepper and Cisco, of course, turned their heads to follow the voice of each new canine, shifting their paws in excitement, and were more than ready to get out and explore by the time Miles turned in to the short, potholed dirt driveway that led to Maude's house.

"Looks like somebody's been here," he observed. "The ice over the puddles is cracked."

The ground was too frozen to pick up tire tracks, but he was right—the ice had been cracked recently. "Maybe Mr. Whitmire stopped by while he was here," I offered, not really interested.

"Could be."

Miles pulled the car up in front of the metal carport that was a few hundred feet away from the house. I got out and paused a moment, looking around while Miles released the dogs from their seat belts.

The house was a one-story bungalow faced in mountain stone. The shrubbery that lined the front of the house had taken a beating the past few winters and was now mostly dead sticks and tangled vines. There used to be a couple of brick-lined flower beds out front, but I couldn't see them now. The yard had deteriorated to patchy brown weeds and mud puddles, and blackberry vines had completely taken over the bank to the west of the house. On the east side there was a flat, cleared area where Maude had once kept her kennels, but nothing was left of them now but a field of winter-dead fescue grass. There was a small metal barn out back, and next to it a firewood shed filled with rotten split logs. It was all incredibly depressing.

Miles handed me Cisco's leash. "I'll take a look around and meet you inside," he said. Already he was squinting at the roof. "Looks like you might need new gutters, and some shingles are missing."

Cisco was already sniffing the ground to the end of his

leash, anxious to start exploring the new environment. I took Pepper's leash from Miles, and she came with me happily, checking my pockets for treats. Of course, I gave her one, which immediately attracted the attention of Cisco, who bounded over with eager eyes and a perfect sit. When both dogs were sufficiently treated and Miles had gone to inspect the rest of the exterior, I dug out the keys the lawyer had given me and unlocked the front door.

The house was cold and stale-smelling, dark and empty. I closed the door and unclipped the dogs' leashes, letting them clatter off to explore the deserted rooms and sniff out stray mice. I stood there for a moment, looking around, trying to find something of the woman who had once meant so much to me, something that would conjure a memory or an emotion.

All I saw were dusty floors and scuffed walls, a stone fireplace stained black with soot around the opening. The windows were thick with the haze of neglect and little of the bleak winter light seeped through. I peeked into the kitchen —old-fashioned yellow Formica countertops and white appliances—and the bathroom, which was similarly outdated. Maude, like most dog people, cared little about the aesthetics of her living quarters as long as her dogs were comfortable.

I checked out the three boxy bedrooms and was almost mowed down by two galloping golden retrievers when I came back out into the hallway. "Cisco!" I commanded sharply. "Pepper!"

The two dogs skidded to a stop as Miles came around the corner and returned to me when Miles, who was almost as well trained as the dogs, ignored them. I gave the two dogs a treat when they sat before me with tails wagging, and Miles remarked mildly, "Baby, have we ever talked about the fact that you might have a small control issue?"

I released the dogs to go play, and Cisco started sniffing the perimeter of the room again, pausing now and then to dig enthusiastically at a loose baseboard or random corner. I frowned. "What *is* he after?"

"Rats, probably," Miles said. "A house this old... I'd definitely get an exterminator out here."

I grimaced in disgust and snapped my fingers at Cisco. He looked up from his rat-chasing game reluctantly, then seemed to remember the treat and returned to my side.

"You're going to need a new roof," Miles went on, "new gutters and downspouts. They'll probably have to replace some of the siding and fascia board around the eaves."

I smothered a groan as we walked back to the front of the house.

"The kitchen is a complete gut job," he went on, "and the bathroom too. The floors will have to be refinished, interior and exterior painting, landscaping... you're looking at a good six weeks to get it all done. Do you have a key to the barn? It has a padlock on it. And, by the way, the lock on the back door is broken. I just walked right in. Doesn't matter, you're going to have to replace both doors anyway. Windows, too." He turned his gaze to the ceiling. "New lighting fixtures, and we'll check out the electric while we're at it. With a house this old, we'll probably have to pull new wire. And I'd definitely recommend a new energy-efficient heat pump..."

I threw up my hands in a gesture of surrender. "Miles, stop! It would be easier to build a new house. I can't afford any of this. How much is it going to cost, anyway?"

"Don't worry about it," he assured me. "It's the slow season. I can have a crew down here before the end of the week."

We had reached the living room. I turned to face him in the bleary light. "I said," I repeated sternly, "I can't afford it. Let's go home."

"And I said," he returned, equally as sternly, "don't worry about it. I'll take care of it."

"I don't want you to take care of it! This is my house, my problem, and I'll deal with it." I swung determinedly toward the door, but he caught my fingers and turned me back.

He countered with, "Did you ever hear that part of the

marriage ceremony that says, 'With all my worldly goods I thee endow?'"

"We're not married!" I shot back. "And I don't want your worldly goods! I just want to go home."

I saw the quick flash of irritation in his eyes, quickly subdued, and the tightening of a muscle near his mouth. He worked a little too hard to keep his tone mild with the next words. "I can't believe we're going to fight over me offering to do you a favor."

I bent to snap on Pepper's leash, mostly so I wouldn't have to meet Miles's gaze. "We're not going to fight," I returned grumpily, "and you're not doing me a favor. I can find my own handyman to fix the roof, and I like the kitchen the way it is."

His silence bored into me. Finally, I straightened up and looked at him defensively. "I can't do this now, okay? I've got a ton of things to do at home and a new dog to train. I'm freezing and..." I shot a troubled look around the room. "This place is depressing. Let's just go, okay?"

But Miles made no move to go. He just stood there looking at me, as though waiting for me to finish. He knew me too well.

I watched Cisco trot over to the window and look out, probably checking for squirrels. My gaze left him and wandered around the room, my tone a bit more subdued. "It's just that... I mean, I know we hadn't been close for a while, but I always expected her to be here, you know? In the world, I mean. It's so hard to get my head around. It makes me feel..."

But there I ran out of words. Miles supplied them for me. "Disoriented," he said quietly. "Vulnerable. Even old, wondering how much time you have left, or the people you love. Helpless. And afraid."

I nodded dumbly and went into his arms. He held me gently. "I know," he said. And he did. His ex-wife, Melanie's mother, had died not that long ago, and while there certainly had been no love lost between them, he had been deeply shaken. Perhaps no one could understand how I felt now better than Miles—not even me. Just knowing that took some of the ache away.

I said softly against his shoulder, "I love you."

"I know."

"I'll deal with the house. I just need a minute."

"I know that, too."

I could have stayed there, resting my cheek against the soft nylon of his padded jacket, for hours, just letting him hold me. But just then Cisco, who was still standing at the window, gave a sharp bark. We both turned to look at him, and as we did, heard the sound of tires on the rough dirt driveway. We exchanged a puzzled look and went to the window. Cisco, with ears up and tail wagging, barked a friendly greeting as a dusty gray camper van drew to a stop beside Miles's SUV.

The minute Miles opened the door, Cisco bounded through. He never would have tried that with me, but I had my hands full with Pepper, who wanted to follow his lead. And besides, it's not such a bad idea to let a stranger know there's a dog on the premises when he decides to make an unannounced visit to a deserted house in the country... even if the stranger was probably just a neighbor wondering what we were doing here, and even if the dog was more likely to cover an intruder with slobbery kisses than to deter him.

A young man in jeans and a windbreaker was squatting on the ground, chuckling and ruffling Cisco's fur by the time I got Pepper under control and came out onto the porch. "Well, aren't you the finest looking dog I ever did see!" he declared. "What a beauty!" Cisco wagged his tail so hard that his whole butt swung back and forth, and the stranger looked up at us, grinning, as he stood.

"How're y'all doing?" he greeted us as he approached. Cisco trotted along happily, as though the newcomer was a trophy he was proud to bring to us.

I said, "Hi," because it seemed rude not to, but Miles just nodded, watching him.

He was a pleasant-looking man in his late twenties or early thirties with curly blond hair that fell well past his jawline and deep blue eyes. His jeans were faded and well worn, and so were his cowboy boots. He moved with an easy confidence and an engaging smile. He reached the bottom of the steps and Cisco bounded up to Pepper and me, probably intending to invite the stranger in.

"Sorry to bother you," he said, glancing around. "I hope I've got the right place. I'm looking for Maude Braselton?"

I looked at Miles, hesitating, and he answered first. "I'm sorry," he said. "Ms. Braselton passed away a short time ago."

Shock, and then dismay, flooded the young man's face. He sank back with one hip against the handrail and seemed for a moment too stunned to speak. Cisco, sensing his distress, started back down the steps toward him, but I caught his collar.

"Wow," the stranger managed at last. "Oh, wow." He looked from one to the other of us, and he said, "After all this time... I came so far... Just, wow."

He drew a breath and seemed to regain his bearings. "Sorry," he said. "I'm Casey Macintosh. Denver, Colorado."

He came up the steps, hand extended, and Miles shook it. "Miles Young," he said. He gestured to me. "And this is Raine Stockton. She inherited the property from Ms. Braselton."

The smile that had started to form on Casey's lips froze in place and he stared at me. "Excuse me," he said. "Did you say Stockton?"

I nodded, a little distracted by the two goldens who were not showing their best manners as I tried to clip Cisco's leash on.

He persisted, "Are you any relation to Jonathon Stockton, the judge?"

I finally got Cisco's leash on and, with a single sharp tug, got him to sit. I regarded the newcomer warily. "He was my father."

Casey drew in a breath and let it out slowly. He looked at Miles, and then back at me. "Man," he said softly. He looked for a moment at a loss, then seemed to come to a cautious decision. "Listen," he said, "there's no easy way to say this, but... I think I'm your brother."

CHAPTER EIGHT

To be clear, I am not one of those girls who always dreamed of having a brother. In the first place, I practically had two of them already. Buck, our best friend Andy and I grew up together like puppies in a litter, the inseparable Three Musketeers roaming the mountains and leaping from one adventure to the other until we were grown. In the second place, I loved being an only child. Why would I want to share my parents' adoration with anyone else? It never even occurred to me to want a sibling. So, as I stood there on Maude's front porch staring at the person who claimed to be my brother, I honestly didn't know how to react. Or even feel.

I felt Miles's hand on my back, lightly, prompting me into speech. But all I could think to say was, rather stupidly, "What did you say?"

Casey pushed a hand through his sun-kissed curls, tangling them further. "Yeah, I know," he said, "it's a lot. I shouldn't have come here without calling first, but I was afraid if I did, my mother—Ms. Braselton, that is—wouldn't want to see me and I don't think I could've stood that, you know? Anyway, this is not your problem. I should go."

He actually turned to go before I blurted, "Wait!" and Miles, at the same time, said, "Hold on a minute."

Casey looked back.

I said, "You don't get to just drop a bombshell like that and walk away. Are you saying Maude Braselton is your mother?

Who told you that? How did you find me, anyway? What makes you think we're related? Was it one of those home DNA tests? Maude hasn't lived here in years. And why didn't Maude's lawyer mention you? He was just here. He would have known..."

Beneath my barrage of questions Casey just stood there, smiling a puzzled, regretful smile, probably waiting for an opening in which to respond. It was Miles who held up a staying hand to silence me. "Why don't we go inside out of the wind?" he suggested. "Some of the logs in that woodpile out back look like they'd burn. We can get the fireplace going and try to figure this out."

Casey looked relieved. "Do y'all like campfire coffee?" he said. "I've got a pot in the truck."

I've got to hand it to Miles: he knows how to defuse a situation. While he and Casey were busy gathering wood, breaking up kindling, inspecting the flue and starting a fire, there was no time for me to bombard anyone with questions. I did, however, take a good look at Casey's van while I took Pepper and Cisco for a walk, and confirmed that his license plate was indeed from Colorado, and that the van looked like it had a few miles on it. I couldn't see much of the interior without being obvious about my snooping, but it looked as though it was outfitted for sleeping, with a sofa that probably folded down into a bed, and even a little kitchen area.

"So do you live in your van?" I asked Casey bluntly when I came back inside.

They had a nice fire going, and Casey was pouring water from a jug into a cast iron camp percolator. I had one like it, but mine was aluminum and suitable for backcountry hiking. His was much nicer.

"Only since I started this trip," he replied. He separated the logs and got a nice bed of embers going beneath the iron grate, then set the coffeepot on top. "It's a pretty sweet setup. I'll show you inside if you like." He glanced over his shoulder at me, smiling at the dogs. "I snagged some jerky for them when I went for the coffee," he said. "Can they have a piece?"

Score one for him for asking. "Just one," I said. I unclipped the two leashes and the goldens scrambled over to him. He spent a long time chuckling and ruffling their fur while they snuffled his pockets for the jerky. "Okay, guys," I told them firmly. "That's enough. Sit and wait."

They did, and Casey knew enough to reward them with the jerky as soon as they obeyed. "What great dogs," he told me. "What are their names?"

"The big guy is Cisco, and the little one is Pepper. Cisco is mine. He's a certified Search and Rescue dog and a therapy dog. Pepper belongs to Miles's daughter, Melanie."

He gave them each a pat on the head and opened his hands to show them empty. Thus assured, the goldens began sniffing the floor for crumbs. "We had a yellow Lab when I was growing up," Casey said, dusting off his hands on his jeans. "Cheyenne. God, I loved that dog. Mr. Young…"

"Miles," Miles corrected, coming in with another load of firewood. "You can call me Miles." He dumped the wood on the floor beside the hearth and stoked up the fire with a few dry sticks. Already the room was beginning to smell like coffee.

Casey's smile was a little shy. "Miles," he said, "told me the two of you are engaged. Congratulations. Also, that you're a dog trainer. So was my birth mother, I guess. Maude."

"Maude taught me everything I know," I said. "She was amazing. She gave me my first golden retriever. We were very close. We started Dog Daze together, and she helped me run it until she moved to Florida. Everyone in dogs knew Maude."

But wait. Why was I doing all the talking? Shouldn't he be the one answering questions? I cleared my throat, but he seemed to read my mind. Before I could say anything, he reached inside his jacket and brought out an envelope. "I figured you'd want to see this," he said, handing it to me. "I've always known I was adopted, and when I turned eighteen my mother showed me my birth certificate. It was a privately brokered adoption. My birth mother chose my parents, but didn't want to, you know, be involved. My folks said it was because my father was a married man. That was all they knew."

Miles came to stand beside me, reading over my shoulder as I took the oft-folded paper from the envelope and examined it slowly. It was an official document from the State of South Carolina, County of Greene. I had to read it in small doses, and at this I looked up. "Greene County," I said. "That's not that far from here."

Casey nodded. "My dad didn't get transferred out west until I was three. Before that, we lived in South Carolina."

I swallowed, trying to lubricate my dry mouth, and turned back to the birth certificate. Infant Male Braselton, born on July 13 twenty-nine years ago. I would have been barely seven. Just finishing up first grade, catching tadpoles in the creek with Buck, playing fort with Andy, standing on a stepstool to brush the tangles of out the horses' manes. What would I have known of what was going on in the adult world back then?

"Looks like a private maternity hospital," Miles observed, pointing to the name of the issuing institution.

I glanced at him briefly and read on. Mother: Maude Elizabeth Braselton, Place of Birth: Surrey, England. Current residence: Greenville, South Carolina. Age: 32. Race: Caucasian. Marital Status: Single.

It felt creepy and intrusive to examine the private life from so many years ago of someone I knew. Thirty-two-year-old Maude Braselton, alone in a South Carolina hospital, about to say goodbye to her infant son forever. I had to force myself to continue.

But that was all there was. After the next line, *Father*, was written simply, "Unnamed."

I looked at Casey in confusion. "I don't understand. It doesn't say who the father of Maude's child was. What makes you think it was Jonathon Stockton?"

Casey said, "A few years back—two or three, I guess—I

finally tracked Maude down, found out where she was living, got a phone number... She wasn't—she didn't seem exactly overjoyed to hear from me, but maybe she was just surprised. Either way, it wasn't a very comfortable conversation, and I guess maybe..." He looked embarrassed. "I didn't handle it very well. She said I was the result of her affair with a married man and that she wasn't able to take care of a child by herself, that she had been out of work and not even sure she would be able to stay in the country, she wanted the best for me, the usual." He gave a dismissive shrug. "She did say my dad was a good man, a judge, and at one point she let slip that his name was Jonathon. Afterwards, I did a little more research and found out that she had worked for a judge named Jonathon Stockton for years, and I guess I put two and two together. But that was one of the things I planned to ask her when I saw her."

I didn't know what to say. I just stood there, staring at Casey, trying to make myself believe this stranger was my father's child. Trying to figure out how I was even supposed to feel about that. He didn't look a thing like me.

But he did look a little like Maude.

I said, "She, um... my father and Maude, they were involved for a time, as it turns out. But I never knew..." I cleared my throat. "I never knew it went back that far. Did you keep in touch?"

He shook his head. "Like I said, that conversation was pretty awkward. She didn't ask how to reach me, and I guess I took that to mean she wasn't interested in hearing from me again, so I didn't volunteer the information. I didn't want to risk messing things up between us even more with another phone call, so I thought the next move should be in person."

Miles took the birth certificate from me and examined it for himself. He glanced at Casey. "Do you mind if I take a photo of this?"

"No, of course not." Casey took his wallet from his back pocket and fished out his driver's license. "You'll probably want to see this too."

Miles showed the driver's license to me, but I barely glanced at it. There was Casey, there was his name, there was his date of birth. It was him, all right. Whoever he was.

While Miles took out his phone and started to photograph each document, Casey looked at me apologetically. "Look," he said, "I can see you're upset. I didn't mean to spring this on you. I didn't even know you existed, although, if I'm honest..." He gave me another quick, shy smile. "It's kind of cool that you do. That I have a sister, I mean. I'm not here to cause any trouble. I just wanted to meet my birth mother. I didn't know... Ah, crap!"

There was a hissing and a crackling as the coffeepot boiled over, filling the room with the smell of smoke and burned coffee. The dogs barked and rushed over to see what all the excitement was about. Casey lunged to grab the pot and burned his hand. He stepped back, shaking his fingers, and almost tripped over Pepper. I tried to corral the dogs out of the way while Miles grabbed a glove from his pocket and lifted the coffeepot from the fire. Somehow in the process the birth certificate fluttered out of his hand. Casey tried to grab it but so did Cisco who, since the beginning of his "reading" training, had developed an unreasonable attachment to all things paper. The birth certificate drifted into the fire, leaving nothing but a pale haze of blue smoke curling from the fireplace in its wake.

Of course, I sprang to try to save it from the flames, but Miles caught my arm, and so did Casey. "It's okay," Casey said, "it's okay, leave it! It's a copy. A certified copy," he amended, "but I can get another one from the state. It's okay."

"I'm so sorry," I gasped. "Cisco can be a little... I'm so sorry!"

"Well, at least your license survived." Miles bent to retrieve Casey's driver's license from the floor where it had landed, and he had a rather odd look on his face when he returned it to its owner. Probably no one would have noticed but me.

"Thank goodness," Casey said, tucking the license back

into his pocket. "That would be a little harder to get along without."

"Is your hand okay?" I asked, worried. "Did you burn it?"

He glanced at his fingers, which were rouged but didn't appear to be blistered. "Fine," he assured me. He smiled. "Now, let's see if the coffee was worth all this trouble. What do you say?"

Miles and I topped off our travel mugs and Casey filled a speckled enamel mug with the strong, hot brew. Miles spread his jacket on the floor and he and I sat on it, close to the fire, with a dog stretched out contentedly on either side of us. For a moment we all just sipped our coffee and warmed our hands around the cups, letting the tension in the room settle down to a more normal level.

Casey was the first to speak. "Hits the spot," he said of the coffee. "I've been driving all night." He took another sip of the coffee and looked at me. His voice grew more subdued. "Do you mind?" he said. "I'd really like to know how she died."

"Cancer," I answered. It was still a little hard to think about, even under these extraordinary circumstances. "It was only a couple of weeks ago, and I guess it happened fairly quickly. I just found out myself this weekend."

He nodded somberly. "I don't guess... she ever mentioned me."

I shook my head slowly, feeling bad for him even as I did so. "Not that I know of. If she did, no one ever told me. But there was a lot I didn't know about her. And about my father."

I lowered my eyes and sipped from my cup. Miles put a reassuring hand on my knee.

"She had a nephew though," I added helpfully. "Leon Whitmire. He's a lawyer in Tampa. You could reach out to him."

"I guess I could," said Casey, without much enthusiasm. "I'm not sure why, though. I just... wanted to see her, you know? Maybe apologize for some of the things I said before and... just see her."

I found myself nodding sympathetically. There was something about Casey that just made you want to be on his side.

Miles said, "So what did you do back in Colorado, Casey?"

Casey drew one leg up beneath him, settling in on the hearth. "My dad was a building contractor, and when I graduated college, I went home to help run the business. Then, a year ago this past Christmas, my folks hit an icy patch coming home one night, slid off the road into a ravine, the car burst into flames. Neither of them survived."

I said softly, "I'm so sorry."

He nodded in acknowledgement, staring into his coffee cup. "Most of their assets were tied up in the business, but after all the dust settled there was enough left over for me to take a year or so off and see the country. And of course, I guess I'd had it in the back of my mind that one day I'd like to meet my birth mom, so..." he took a sip of his coffee. "Here I am." Again, he shrugged. "I don't know. Maybe that was stupid. Maybe she wouldn't have wanted to see me even if..." He finished that sentence with nothing more than a shake of his head.

"I think she would have," I said. I had no idea if it was true or not, but it seemed like the right thing to say.

He looked at me hopefully. "What about Judge Stockton?"

I shook my head. "He died some time back of a stroke."

Casey's expression fell. "Oh."

I cast around for something to say, trying to be mature, trying to pretend my whole world hadn't just been spun around and landed on its ear. Trying, with all my might, not to think about everything Casey had just told me, and what it meant.

"I think I have her nephew's card at home," I said finally. "If you'll give me your number, I could text you his information. It might help to talk to him. Like I said, she'd lived in Florida the last couple of years, and we weren't that close. He'll probably be able to answer more of your questions than I can."

He nodded. "Sure. That would be good." He glanced around the room. "She left you her house," he remarked. "She must have thought a lot of you."

I said without thinking, "I think that was just because she didn't have any..." I broke off before finishing, my cheeks going hot, but it was pretty obvious what I'd meant to say. *Because she didn't have any children.* But she did. Apparently.

Casey gave an understanding smile and tilted his head toward a corner of the ceiling. "Looks like you've got a little water damage there."

I followed his gaze toward the stain near the front of the house. Miles said, "Yeah, I was going to try to get up in the attic and check it out. There are some missing shingles, probably snow or ice soaked through the decking."

"Could be," Casey agreed. "Or it might just be backwash from your gutters. The lock is broken on your backdoor, too," he added. "Looks like it's been jimmied. Has the house been vacant long?"

"I don't really know," I admitted. "I think Maude had a real estate company in town handling the rental for her."

"The last tenants might have left it like that," Casey said. "Or you might have had a vagrant break in while it was empty. I've got a lockset in the van that might work," he volunteered. "I can install it for you, if you like."

"Oh, no," I objected. "I couldn't ask you..."

"No problem." He was already on his feet. "It won't take ten minutes."

"I'll give you a hand," Miles offered, and I suspected it was because he wanted to inspect the quality of Casey's work.

It really did take the two of them less than ten minutes to install the lock, and while they worked, I made sure the fire was out and fastened the dogs into their seat belts in the car. I came around the back of the house just as they were finishing up. Casey turned the key in the lock, tested the door and then handed the key to me. "That should hold it," he said.

"Thank you." I tucked the key into my purse while Miles

gathered up the trash and the parts of the old lock. "How much do I owe you?"

Casey waved a dismissive hand and snapped his toolbox shut. "Don't worry about it. I had the lock left over from a job I did in Ohio or someplace. I don't even know how much I paid for it."

"But..."

"Maybe you'll buy me lunch sometime," Casey said with another one of his heart-melting smiles. "We'll keep in touch."

I said uncomfortably, "Look, this has all been a lot. I hope I haven't seemed... you know."

"Shocked?" he suggested. "Overwhelmed? Like you'd been hit by a truck?" He gave a wry grin. "My fault. Like I said, I should have called. I guess I'm a little impulsive. I've been told I should work on that."

Well, that much we had in common. I pulled out my phone with a quick decision and handed it to him. "Give me your number," I told him. "I'll text you the information about Maude's nephew."

"Where do you go from here?" Miles asked as Casey typed his cell number into my contacts list.

Casey handed my phone back to me. "I hadn't thought about it, to tell the truth. Maybe Florida, now that you mention it, if Maude—my mother's—nephew is willing to see me."

I sent Casey a message that said, *Hi, this is Raine*, and when his phone pinged I told him, "Now you have my number too. In case you need anything or... I don't know." Then I added, "Anyway, Mr. Whitmire isn't in Florida. He was on his way to Washington for a two-week conference. You could probably reach him through his office, though."

He looked disappointed. "Yeah. Maybe I'll try that." A gust of wind blew through his curls and he hunched his shoulders, tucking his fingers into his pockets. "Right now, I think I'll try to find a campground or someplace to bed down for the night, have a fresh go at it in the morning."

"All the campgrounds around here are closed this time of

year," I said. "But there's a nice motel back down Highway 197 four or five miles. It even has a Waffle House next to it."

"Yeah, I think I passed it coming in," he said. "Maybe I'll give it a try. A hot shower and a real bed would be quite an upgrade right now."

Another blast of wind made us all shiver and Casey said, "Well, I'd better get going." He stuck out his hand to me. "It was nice meeting you, Raine. I'm sorry if... well, about everything, I guess."

I shook his hand. "Yeah, me too. About Maude, I mean. I wish you could have met her."

His smile grew sad. "Me, too." He turned to Miles, who shook his hand. "Good meeting you, Miles."

He replied, "Take care, Casey."

We watched as he got in the van, backed it out of its parking space, and bounced down the driveway. It seemed like there was a whole world of things we hadn't said, questions we hadn't asked and questions we hadn't answered, and even now I couldn't seem to find the words. Miles let me have the silence, and finally I said, "Let's go."

CHAPTER NINE

When we exited the side street and were headed toward the main road again, Miles said, "I know you don't want to talk about it."

I gave a sharp shake of my head to stop him. It wasn't so much that I didn't want to talk. I just didn't know what to say, or even what to feel. The whole thing was just so incredible. Two days ago, my biggest challenge had been training my golden retriever to perform on cue. I worried about what to get my uncle for his birthday and how to stay out of the fight between Miles and his mom. Now Maude was dead. She had left me her house. My father, the man I'd idolized all my life, was a lying, cheating snake who had strayed, not just once, as I'd thought, but who had had a decades-long affair with the woman my mother loved like a sister. He had a son whom he'd abandoned. He'd virtually lived a double life.

I finally found the words as the truth came to me in a kind of horrible awe. "My whole life was a lie. It's like I don't even know who I am anymore. Everything I ever knew about my father—maybe about everyone—it was all a lie."

Miles said, "Maybe not. We don't have anything except Casey's word."

I darted him a sharp look. "And a birth certificate!"

"Which very conveniently fell into the fire before I got a photo of it," Miles pointed out.

I scowled. "That was an accident."

"Maybe." He didn't sound convinced. "Look, honey, you don't think it's a little bit of a coincidence that three days after you find out Maude is dead some stranger shows up claiming to be her son? He shows up *here,* not in Florida where she actually lived. And how about the timing on that, anyway? He drives across country and just happens to arrive at her house within minutes of us getting there?"

My frown deepened. The truth was, I had been bothered by that, too. "There was mud on the kitchen floor. I thought the dogs had tracked it in."

"And someone had driven on that driveway before we got there," he reminded me. "Not to mention the broken lock. Deer Run Trail makes a loop, you know, circling back out to the highway. He might have already been at the house, heard us coming, and left without us ever seeing him."

"Look," I said, "I'm not disagreeing with you. The timing is weird. But Maude and my father *did* have an affair. How could Casey even have known about a judge named Jonathon unless Maude told him? Nobody knew about them until..." I trailed off, reluctantly answering my own question.

Miles spoke my thoughts out loud. "After it came out about the judge tampering with evidence and sending an innocent man to prison to cover up his affair with Maude. The papers made a pretty big deal out of it. After all, the man he sent to prison tried to get his revenge by shooting up a fairground. It was a big case, lots of news coverage. And names were named."

How well I knew. My life had been a nightmare for months after it all came out. I rubbed my temple, where the tiniest of headaches was beginning to form. "But Miles, still... that's a pretty elaborate scheme, and what could he expect to get from it? Maude's house?" I shrugged. "As far as I'm concerned, he can have it. It'd save me a lot of trouble. Maude didn't have any money. Neither do I. So, what could he want?"

"Well, you know what they say. When you win the lottery, all kinds of relatives come crawling out of the woodwork."

"I didn't win the lottery," I objected, puzzled. "Not even close."

"Babe." Miles cast me a sidelong glance and hooked a thumb at his own chest, one eyebrow raised meaningfully. "You won the lottery."

I stared at him. "You?" I demanded incredulously. "You think he's using me to get to *you*?"

He made the turn onto the highway. "Look, hon," he said patiently, "in a few months your uncle is going to walk you down the aisle and your aunt is going to cry, and Melanie is going to toss rose petals everywhere and some preacher is going to say the words that make us legally responsible for each other. But in the meantime, legally or not, we're responsible for each other. If I had the nuclear codes and some terrorist said, 'We've got Raine,' I'd turn over those codes in a heartbeat, the rest of the world be damned. You'd do the same for me."

"Well," I muttered uncomfortably, "I might think about it for a minute." At his dry look, I assured him, "I would. Of course, I would. But—"

"Bad guys know that," he said. "So do con artists and other kinds of opportunists. So we have to be careful. I'm not saying this guy isn't exactly who he says he is. But I did manage to get a photo of his driver's license, and I'm going to have my people run a background check."

I sighed. "Of course you are."

Of the many things that had changed about my life since Miles had come into it, this was the one I liked the least. He was a man with deep pockets and important connections; enhanced security was second nature to him. I was accustomed to dealing with life's little ups and downs in a much more straightforward fashion.

I said, "Send me the photo of his license, will you?"

"Sure thing."

Not that Miles's detectives weren't perfectly capable, but I like to do things my own way. And most of the time, my way is better.

CHAPTER TEN

Buck tapped lightly on the frame of Sheriff Marshall Becker's open door. The other man beckoned him in without glancing up from the computer screen, and Buck took the hard wooden chair in front of the desk.

"Sorry," Marshall said, holding up a finger for patience. "If I don't finish this now, I'll never get back to it."

Buck, who had held the job of sheriff before Marshall, smiled. "I know the feeling."

He waited until Marshall finished his task, clicked the mouse to exit the program, and swiveled his chair to face Buck, giving him his full attention. "What can I do for you, Buck?"

Buck took a moment. He had made up his mind; he knew it was the right thing to do. Still, it was hard to get started. He had a sudden flash of himself sitting in Marshall's chair almost three years ago. He couldn't have imagined then that the day would ever come when he would be saying these words.

"When I took this job," he said, "I told you I'd give it a try. I said I wasn't making any promises."

Marshall must have known what was coming, but he kept his expression carefully neutral, listening.

"It was a good opportunity for me," Buck went on, "and I appreciate it. I've enjoyed working with you. I mean that. You run a good department. But I've given it a lot of thought, and I've decided it's time to move on. I wanted to be fair to you, and let you know I was looking."

Marshall nodded slowly. "I can't say I'm surprised," he said. "But I'm sorry to hear it, nonetheless. Is it because of the shooting?"

"In a way," Buck admitted. "It gave me some time to think, and if I'm honest, I look at things a lot differently now."

Again, Marshall nodded. "I've seen it happen before, after a trauma on the job. If it was anybody else, I'd try to get you to reconsider, give it more time. But I've got to believe that you know what's best. It's a damn shame, though. Law enforcement needs more good men like you. We sure can't afford to lose one. So, what are you thinking of going into? You're a young man, plenty of time to start a new career."

Buck chuckled ruefully. "I'm not nearly as young as I was eight months ago," he said. "Besides, I don't know anything but policing. I reckon I'll stick with it." He paused. "There's a fellow down in Georgia, retiring as police chief in July. He wants me to interview for the job."

Marshall sat back, surprised. "Georgia, huh?"

"A place called Mercy, not far from the Florida line. Looks like a sweet town, and the money is good."

Marshall shook his head. "Well, I've got to say, I never thought I'd see you leave the mountains."

"I haven't left yet," Buck assured him. "But I've got a long weekend coming up next month, so I thought I'd ride down there, see what this fellow is all about. It'll probably all come to nothing, but, like I said, I just wanted to keep you in the loop."

"I've got to ask," Marshall said, "do I need to be worrying about losing my chief deputy, too?"

Buck looked uncomfortable. "That I couldn't tell you," he replied. He wrestled with his conscience for a moment before adding, "But it might be on the table, yeah."

"Fair enough." Marshall regarded Buck thoughtfully for a time. "Meantime, I'm going to assign Harrigan to you."

Now it was Buck's turn to be surprised. "Harrigan?" Retired from the Charlottesville police force, Brett Harrigan had signed on with the sheriff's office less than three months ago. He'd barely had time to learn the roads.

"Is that a problem?"

"No, of course not," Buck said quickly, although he didn't really know whether it was or not. He'd barely met the man. "It's just that I'm the middle of a murder investigation, and I thought Harrigan was a part-time road deputy." There was also the fact that Buck did not have time to train a rookie, or to listen to an old-timer relive his glory days. That might have been harsh, but it was true.

"Let's just see how it works out," Marshall suggested. "He might be more help than you think. I'll have him report to you first thing in the morning."

"Yes, sir." Buck started to rise, but Marshall stopped him.

"How is the Beardsley investigation going, anyway? Any leads?"

"Yeah, maybe," Buck said. "We found about ten thousand in cash and a bunch of stolen driver's licenses, credit cards and bleached checks under a loose floorboard in the closet. I'm working the identity theft angle. Could've been one of his customers or one of his victims that Carter saw parked there the day he was killed. I'm on my way to interview Carter again now, see if he can give us any more details."

Marshall looked at him thoughtfully. "You know who else you might talk to? Ro Bleckley. He's the one that put Beardsley away the first time, back a dozen years ago, and it seems to me it was for credit card theft. He might have some contacts we haven't thought about."

"Good idea," Buck agreed. He tilted his head thoughtfully and added, "If I recall, Miss Mart does her baking on Mondays. Maybe I'll talk to Ro first."

Marshall grinned. "Bring me back something."

Buck rose and returned the grin. "Will do."

"And keep be updated," Marshall added as Buck turned toward the door, "about everything."

Buck nodded his agreement and left.

CHAPTER ELEVEN

Aunt Mart and Uncle Ro live in a brick house on two acres just outside of town, literally. The city limits sign is a hundred feet from their property line; the courthouse a three-minute drive away. They had bought the house right after Uncle Ro was elected sheriff the first time and had lived there now over thirty years. After my mother died, their house became the center of all family gatherings —birthdays, Christmas, Thanksgiving—and I never needed an invitation to stop by. This had become particularly true since my collie, Majesty, had decided a couple of years ago that she wanted to be Aunt Mart's dog. I would never dream of separating the two of them, but I did miss my beautiful girl, and I tried to see her as often as I could.

Truth be told, I couldn't blame Majesty for her choice. In Aunt Mart's house she was queen of the kind of domicile a regal canine such as she deserved. She slept on a velvet bed and had a collection of plush toys that she kept in pristine condition. She was groomed twice a month and always came home with pink-painted nails and bows in her hair, not to mention the fact that she dined every day on Aunt Mart's cooking. I should have it so good.

Twenty minutes after leaving Miles, I arrived at Aunt Mart's to a chorus of welcoming barks and delighted exclamations. I hugged Majesty first, who smelled like rose perfume, and offered her a gourmet treat that I had sneaked out of Cisco's stash. Only when Majesty took the treat delicately between her teeth and carried it to her fireside bed to enjoy did I turn to hug my aunt—who also smelled like rose perfume—and Uncle Ro.

"Well, now, sweetheart, what a nice surprise!" declared my uncle, helping me out of my coat. "What brings you out on such a cold day?"

"Perfect timing!" exclaimed Aunt Mart, clasping her hands together. "I just took a pan of cinnamon rolls out of the oven."

"Is that what smells so good?" I said, feigning enthusiasm I didn't entirely feel. Even Aunt Mart's cinnamon rolls couldn't tempt my appetite this morning.

"Come on in the kitchen and I'll put on some coffee."

Uncle Ro hung my coat on a hook by the door and I answered his question as we followed Aunt Mart into the kitchen. "Miles and I drove out to Deer Run Trail to look at Maude's house," I said.

Aunt Mart shook her head sadly. "I still can't believe she's gone," she said. "She was so young. But it only goes to show, no one is promised tomorrow."

We all allowed a respectful silence for that.

Uncle Ro said, "So what kind of shape was the place in? I heard the last tenant skipped out on his lease. Dale had to go out and clean the place out himself. Was there much damage?"

"No, not really," I answered, and added, "Dale?"

"Comstock. His real estate company was managing the place for Maude."

We came into the kitchen and Aunt Mart busied herself putting on the coffee while Uncle Ro put the sugar and creamer on the table. I took the cups out of the cabinet, needing a moment to gather my thoughts before I spoke. My back was to them as I said, "Something happened while we were there."

I told them about Casey, and by the time I finished we were all sitting at the table, coffee abandoned, cinnamon rolls forgotten on the counter, while I showed Uncle Ro the picture of Casey's driver's license Miles had forwarded to me. "He had a birth certificate, too," I said, "but we didn't get a picture of it." I saw no need to go into details. "It was from a private maternity hospital in Greene County... The mother was Maude Braselton, and the father was unnamed. But Casey said he'd talked to Maude on the phone, and she'd mentioned his father was a judge named Jonathon."

Uncle Ro passed my phone, with the picture of the driver's license, to Aunt Mart. Her troubled frown deepened as she looked at it. "Oh, honey," was all she said, sadly. She returned my phone to me.

There was something about their silence, their covert looks, that was more disturbing than either an admission of guilt or an outraged denial could have been. My heart was a leaden lump in my chest.

I said, "Miles thinks he's a scam artist."

"Very likely," agreed Uncle Ro. He deliberately avoided looking at Aunt Mart. Or me.

"I just," I said, stumbling, "I guess I just wanted to know whether... I don't know, whether it was possible. Whether you thought it was possible that Casey could be telling the truth."

The silence was long and weighty. Majesty wandered in, clearly wondering what had become of the cinnamon rolls, and I dropped my hand to her sleek head, tangling my fingers in her lush mane. Eventually Aunt Mart spoke.

"Honey," she said uncomfortably, "it was a long time ago. Your father wasn't even a judge then, just a lawyer thinking about running for election. But the fact is, about a year before this fellow says he was born... well, it was a tough time for your parents. They were having problems, like people do." She exchanged a glance with her husband, and he took over the narrative.

"It wasn't long after we bought this house," he said. "Your mom was... well, she was struggling. Your dad took a job teaching at the university in Greenville, and he was only home two or three days a week, sometimes not even that much. They argued about that, and about other things. If I'm being honest with you, we didn't know if the marriage would make it." His eyes were steady on mine. He knew not to sugarcoat things for me. I needed the truth. "You spent a lot of time at our house that year. I don't know if you remember."

I did, now that he mentioned it. Pancake breakfasts at Aunt Mart's. They were always a treat. "I was just a kid," I said. "I never knew anything was wrong."

"They worked hard to keep it from you." Aunt Mart picked up the story, her tone reluctant, her expression distressed. "It's just that... the timing. We never knew the full story, never thought it was any of our business. By fall they were reconciled, Jonathon was planning to run for district court judge the next year, and everything seemed fine. It wasn't until after he was elected that we even met Maude. We knew she was an old friend, but that was all."

Again, she consulted her husband through a silent glance, then looked back at me. "Raine, we were as shocked as you were when we found out what had been going on between them. Maude was practically a member of the family, and we all loved her." She shook her head slowly, her expression tinged with dread and disbelief. "It's still hard to imagine. But in retrospect... if you're asking if it was possible Jonathon had an affair and a secret child during that year he and your mother were separated... I suppose I have to say it's possible."

The silence settled like a weighted blanket around the table. Uncle Ro's chair creaked as he leaned back in it, his expression thoughtful. "If there was a child," he said, "and notice I say *if*, I can just about one hundred percent promise you Jonathon didn't know about it. The man had his share of faults, I guess we all know that now, and I don't mean to defend the man who cheated on his wife, my own sister. But nothing will make me believe he ever would have abandoned a child of his. If he even suspected the boy existed, he would have moved heaven and earth until he found him."

Aunt Mart nodded her head in such adamant agreement

that her blonde bangs fell over her eyes. She pushed them back impatiently. "I'd stake everything I ever knew or thought I knew on that, Raine. And I'll tell you something else. From what I knew of Maude, it's no stretch of the imagination to see her keeping the baby a secret from him. She had that whole British stiff-upper-lip thing going, and when she saw Jonathon was going back to his wife, she wouldn't have done anything to interfere."

I said, "What I don't understand is why Maude, if she knew she had this kid out there, and had even talked to him not that long ago, would leave her property to me instead of him."

"Could be she didn't get around to changing her will," Aunt Mart suggested, "or didn't want to. She felt so bad about the way you found about the affair, Raine, and the damage it did. I think this was her way of making it up to you."

She added thoughtfully, "Hard to imagine Maude working with Jonathon all those years, though, seeing him every single day, knowing they had a child together and not saying anything. But..." She lifted one shoulder helplessly. "She did have that strange British stoicism about her. Who knows what goes on in another person's heart?"

"I think you're making a pretty big leap there, Marty," said Uncle Ro, "assuming that there even was a child, or that the two of them were carrying on way back then. There are people who make their living studying the obituaries, researching the deceased, finding a way to profit off the family. Why, I remember one time..."

"Raine asked if it was possible that Jonathon and Maude had a child," Aunt Mart interrupted in that exasperated way long-married people have of dealing with each other. "I'm just saying it *might* have happened, not that it did."

With a series of sudden sharp barks, Majesty spun and raced toward the back door, jumping up with her paws on the window just as I caught a glimpse of a car passing by. It was all I could do not to command Majesty to get down; I tried to discourage that kind of behavior in my house. But she was Aunt Mart's dog now.

"That'll be Buck," Uncle Ro said, pushing up from the table. "He called a few minutes before you got here, Raine, and said he'd be stopping by. Said he wanted to talk to me about an old case."

Relief washed over Aunt Mart's face. "Well, that's good. He's the one you ought to talk to, Raine. I'm sure Buck will know what to do."

I wasn't sure of that at all. And the last thing I wanted to do was to get Buck involved in my personal life. But it would be rude to leave now, so as Uncle Ro and Majesty went out onto the back porch to greet the new arrival, I got up to help Aunt Mart plate the cinnamon rolls and pour the coffee.

"Did you know Buck was dating that pretty Black woman from the office?" she asked, innocent as could be, as she took a dish of butter from the refrigerator. "The one who used to have the drug dog?"

"Yes," I agreed neutrally. "I heard that." I took the platter of cinnamon rolls to the table.

"I ran into her mother the other day at Pins and Needles, picking out yarn," Aunt Mart went on. "She's the sweetest thing."

Not a quality she shares with her daughter, I thought, but said nothing.

"I invited her to join our knitting club, and she said she would. We're making afghans for the women's shelter."

"That's nice," I said, and even managed a smile.

The door opened with a sweep of cold air and Majesty trotted in between the two men, looking as pleased as though she had personally discovered them and shown them the way. The room seemed instantly smaller with the sound of male voices, the aroma of gun oil and leather and all of outdoors.

"Good morning, Miss Mart," Buck said, slipping off his jacket. He grinned as he kissed her cheek. "I was hoping I'd get here in time for some of your good baking."

"I'll be sure to pack you a box to go," she returned, patting his cheek fondly. "Come sit down and have some coffee. How's that leg coming along?"

"Not too bad," he answered. "It's a little worse with the cold." He nodded at me. "Hey, Raine," he said. "I was real sorry to hear about Maude. It must have been a shock."

I said, a little uncomfortably, "Thanks. It's... complicated."

Buck touched my shoulder lightly. "I know."

I smiled at him because I understood that he did, in fact, know.

Uncle Ro said, "As a matter of fact, that's what we were just talking about. Maude left Raine her house."

Buck lifted a surprised eyebrow as he pulled out a chair at the table. "Is that right?"

"There's more," Aunt Mart said, setting a cup of coffee before him.

I protested, "I don't think..."

But Uncle Ro interrupted me sternly. "It might not be a police matter now, Raine, but it doesn't hurt to have them onboard, just in case."

Buck looked interested as he helped himself to a cinnamon roll. "Oh, yeah? What's up, Raine?"

I took a cinnamon roll for myself and chomped down on it, leaving the explaining to Uncle Ro. By the time he finished, I had consumed my first roll and started on the second. Buck hadn't said a word; he'd just listened. That was his style. Also, there really wasn't anything to say. No crime had been committed, unless you could consider betrayal of one's wife a crime, and my father had committed that one thirty years ago.

It was an infraction with which I was sure my ex could sympathize.

Buck watched me alertly as he sipped his coffee. "Did he ask you for anything, Raine? I don't just mean money. Information, access, anything like that?"

I shook my head, frowning and feeling somewhat defensive of Casey. "Nothing like that. He just wanted to know about Maude."

Buck reached for another cinnamon roll. "No attempt at extortion, then. I'm not seeing a crime."

"I didn't *say* there was a crime," I replied, exasperated. "I didn't even say he was lying. Why does everyone assume he was lying? The only liar I see in this scenario is my father, and..." I drew a sharp breath, suddenly aware of everyone's eyes on me. I felt my cheeks go hot. "I just," I finished, mumbling a little, "wanted to get to the truth."

Uncle Ro covered my hand with his. "That's what we all want, honey."

I said to Buck, "Miles is having his people run a background check."

It sounded petty the minute I said it, as though I was trying to point out to Buck that it wasn't only people with badges who had the power to do such things, and I was embarrassed. But Buck did not appear offended.

"Probably a good idea," he said. "The timing is suspicious. Dude says he's been looking for his mother since he was eighteen, and shows up here right after she dies? Feels fishy."

"That's what I thought," agreed Uncle Ro.

I thought they both were missing the point. It wasn't Casey's mother that was the headline here, but his father. If, in fact, he was telling anything that remotely resembled the truth.

Aunt Mart refilled Buck's cup, and he stirred sugar into his coffee. "Do you know where he is now?"

"No," I said, defensiveness coming to the fore again. "I mean, he might have said something about getting a motel room, but what difference does it make? The poor guy was just trying to find his birth mother, and now he's going to think I called the police on him. He even fixed the broken lock on the back door for me, for free. Just leave him alone."

I saw both lawmen register the information about the broken lock the minute I said it, but neither of them commented. Buck said, "I don't suppose you thought to jot down his tag number?"

I scowled. "No. Why would I? But it was a Colorado tag. That's where he said he was from."

"What kind of vehicle was he driving?"

Reluctantly, I told him, "It was one of those converted camper vans. Gray. It looked fairly new, maybe four or five years old."

"And you got a picture of his driver's license?"

"Miles did," I replied. "He forwarded it to me."

"Mind if I take a look?"

Still struggling with annoyance, I brought up the photo on my phone and passed it to him. I watched as he sent the photo to himself and then, incredulously, as he tabbed over to my contacts. I knew immediately it was Casey's number he highlighted.

"Hey!" I snatched the phone from him. "That's unlawful search and seizure!"

"And you just lied to a police officer. You said you didn't know how to reach him."

"I did not!" I glowered at him. "I said I didn't know where he was."

"And do you?"

"I might," I returned petulantly.

"Are you going to tell me?"

"No. I told you to leave him alone and I meant it." Don't ask me why I was being so protective of a man I didn't even know—somebody of whom even I was suspicious—but I think it probably had a lot to do with the fact that it was Buck who was asking. And that he had gotten far too accustomed to protecting *me* over the years, especially when I didn't need it.

"Children," Aunt Mart put in mildly, "no fighting at the table. Does anyone want more coffee?"

"No, thank you, Miss Mart," Buck replied.

I said, still fuming a little inside, "I'll help you with the dishes, Aunt Mart, then I need to get back. I left Corny in charge of the new dog, and I don't want him to overdo it while his arm is still in a cast."

I started gathering up the cups and saucers while Aunt Mart searched for a plastic container for the cinnamon rolls. "You take him some of these rolls, honey, and tell him to take better care of himself."

"Thanks, Aunt Mart. That's sweet."

Buck said to Uncle Ro, "Marshall said I should stop by and ask you about Smokey Beardsley. You remember him?"

"Sure, I do," my uncle replied. "Heard on the police scanner he was found dead at his house out on Quail Pass over the weekend. Carbon monoxide?"

Buck replied, "It's starting to look like a little more than that. The heater vent was deliberately blocked off with a shop towel. And we found a bunch of cash and some stolen credit cards and checks hidden in the house."

Uncle Ro gave a thoughtful grunt. "I remember when I sent him up the first time he was hanging out with old Stunt Dirkson, Happy Waynesboro, Jimmy Tyler and a couple of other boys. They called themselves The Russian Mob. No reason, they just thought it would scare off the competition. Then I heard they ran afoul of a fellow on the inside from the real Russian Mob, and it wasn't so funny anymore. Happy's dead now," he reported, "Stunt's doing thirty years in Texas for manslaughter. Jimmy Tyler's doing eighteen months over in Culver County for possession, I think."

"Oh, for heaven's sake," Aunt Mart exclaimed, "how many times have I told you boys no shop talk in my kitchen?"

"I'm sorry, Miss Mart," Buck said. "I'm on my way out, I promise. Just one more thing." He asked Uncle Ro, "So what was it you caught him on the first time? Something to do with credit cards back then, too?"

"Yeah, he was planting scanners on gas pumps and ATMs to capture credit card numbers. You probably remember, that was all the rage in the bank fraud business ten years ago, but I always did think it seemed like a pretty clever operation for an old country boy. We were fairly sure there was somebody else behind it, somebody a lot smarter, if you know what I mean, but never found out who."

Buck said, "What about the rest of them, Tyler and the rest? They were part of the same operation?"

"Yes and no," Ro said. "We were able to pin the gas-pump scam on them with Smokey, but they branched out from there to mail theft. They had a whole little credit-card-for-sale racket going on between them. And get this. You won't believe who their accomplice was. The postmaster at the main branch out on Highway 10. He'd intercept credit card applications, payments, even cards themselves and pass them on to the boys for a cut. Matter of fact, we might never have broken the ring if we hadn't had so many complaints about missing mail."

"Huh." Buck frowned thoughtfully. "Okay, Ro, thanks."

He stood and brought his cup and saucer over to the sink. I took them from him and put them in the dishwasher. When I straightened up, he was still there, and he held my gaze. "So," he said, "we've got a possible identity theft racket going on, and we've got a man who might not be who he claims to be suddenly showing up with suspicious credentials. Does anything strike you as suspicious about that?"

I scowled. "His credentials are not suspicious," I returned. *Only his story was,* I thought but didn't say.

"Tell your friend when you see him," Buck said, "that I might want to talk to him in connection with this case."

"He's not my friend," I replied, "and I'm not going to see him. Also," I couldn't help adding a little acerbically, "not everything is connected to your case."

I could tell by the way he looked at me that he didn't believe me.

Sometimes he knows me too well.

CHAPTER TWELVE

"**G**ood news, Miss Stockton!" Corny greeted me cheerfully when I got back. "We have 80 percent compliance on the recall, and 90 percent on the sit!" He glanced down at a grinning Rags, who was maintaining a sloppy puppy-sit at his side. He lowered his tone a fraction, as though not wishing to offend his client. "We're having a bit of trouble with the down," he confessed.

I clapped my hands together in delight. "Good job, Corny!" I exclaimed. Maybe the poor dog wasn't as far beyond redemption as I'd thought. I dug a scrap of liver treat from my pocket and offered it to Rags, who gulped it down with one swipe of his tongue and immediately broke his sit. Corny did a quick correction, and I said, "How many reps on the recall?"

"Seventy so far," he said. "I was thinking we'd go for another fifty after this young fellow has a nap."

"Excellent," I said. "If he keeps this up, maybe I'll take him with me to the school program Cisco and I are doing next month." It's never a bad idea to show off an adoptable dog to a bunch of vulnerable kids. They fall in love with the dog, go home and tell their parents, parents get tired of listening to them beg, parents call me. I've placed more than one dog that way.

"We'll have to teach him a trick," Corny said, already ahead of me. "What shall we start with?"

Generally, I'd be all over this; there's nothing I like better than fully immersing myself in training a new dog. But in light of everything else, it was hard to concentrate on dogs today. I said, "Let me think about it. Aunt Mart sent you some cinnamon rolls. I left them in the break room."

His eyes lit up. "Say, thanks! Your aunt's sweet rolls are the best."

I took Rags's leash. "I'll get Rags settled in his kennel," I said. "Help yourself."

And so it was with all good intentions that I put Rags down for a nap in the quiet part of the kennel, then took Cisco, Mischief and Magic through their paces in the agility training room. I managed to fill up almost half an hour that way before I relented and returned to my office. I found lawyer Whitmire's card and texted Casey the information. When he replied with a *Thanks. I'll call him* barely ten seconds later, I didn't hesitate.

Have you had lunch? I texted.

I haven't even had breakfast, he replied.

How about I buy you a burger at the Waffle House?

You're on, he answered.

I typed back, *Give me half an hour.*

I called out a request to Corny to keep an eye on the dogs, grabbed my coat and my purse, and left before I could change my mind. I knew Buck would not approve of what I was doing. Neither, as a matter of fact, would Uncle Ro, or Miles.

Good thing I didn't care.

The Waffle House wasn't too busy—it was January, after all—and I managed to get a booth near the front so I could watch for Casey. Ordinarily, of course, I would have suggested we meet some place in town, but the food here wasn't too bad and I had good reasons for not wanting to be seen dining with a strange man, never mind if that man claimed to be my brother. In a town the size of Hansonville, gossip spread faster than a bad cold in a kindergarten class, and until I knew what was up with Casey Macintosh, I preferred to keep him to myself.

I waved at him when he came through the door, and he smiled as he made his way over to me. He looked freshly shaved and showered—his curls were still a little damp around the collar, and the light scruff of his beard had been neatened. He wore clean jeans and a Broncos sweatshirt beneath his windbreaker.

"Hey," he said as he slid into the seat opposite me. He shrugged out of his jacket. "I've got to say, this is a surprise."

"For me too," I said, suddenly awkward. "I mean... I didn't want you to leave town before we had a chance to talk some more." I glanced toward the window, gathering my thoughts. "So, did you decide to get a room at the motel?"

"I did." The waitress had already left glasses of water and silverware at our places, and he unwrapped the paper from his straw. "It felt good to get a hot shower. I was just about to go looking for something to eat when you texted."

"Well," I said, "that worked out then." I decided I might as well get to it. I folded my hands in my lap and said, "Casey, did you break the lock on Maude's back door?"

He didn't seem surprised by the question. I wasn't sure what that said about him. He looked at me with those calm blue eyes—Maude's eyes—and he said, "No. It was broken when I got there. But I did go inside and look around a little. I heard you guys coming—sound really travels on those gravel roads—and figured it was a neighbor coming to see what I was doing there, or even the police. I didn't want to be caught breaking and entering so I hightailed it out of there. I made the loop around to the highway and waited a little bit for you to leave. I figured you'd be gone by the time I came back around, but when you weren't I decided to go back and introduce myself." He smiled. "Glad I did."

I nodded. That, at least, made sense.

I said, "Listen, Casey. My ex-husband and my uncle are both cops. I might have mentioned you to them. I just wanted you to know."

He stuck his straw in his water glass. "Oh, yeah? What did they say?"

"They had… questions."

He looked amused. "I can just bet they did."

"Anyway," I rushed on, "that wasn't what I wanted to tell you. I asked my aunt and uncle about the year you were born and whether, you know, they knew anything. They said my parents were having problems back then and that my father was teaching Greenville, where Maude lived, the year before you were born. It's possible they met there, and then a couple of years later she moved to Hanover County and started working for my dad. It doesn't really mean anything, but we know Maude and my father were involved later in life, so I guess…" I shrugged uncomfortably. "It's possible."

He regarded me somberly. "I'm sorry to bring this trouble to you, Raine. I didn't mean to upend your life. All I really wanted was a chance to meet my birth mother face to face. I didn't give a lot of thought to, I don't know, collateral damage."

"So, have we decided?" The waitress appeared at our table, bright and efficient, notebook in hand.

I said, "We need a minute."

I handed Casey a laminated menu from the stack by the condiment holder, and the waitress disappeared again. Casey took the menu, and as he reached for it his sleeve slid up, exposing the tattoo of a chain encircling his wrist. In the center of the chain, on the underside of his wrist, was a blotchy red spot that looked like a pair of wings. I stared at it.

"Interesting tattoo," I said in a minute, taking a menu for myself. "What is it?"

He glanced up at me, and then down at his wrist. "Oh," he said, and smiled. "Funny story. This…" he held up his arm and pointed at the red spot, "is actually a birthmark. I wanted something to dress it up, you know, make it look intentional. So, I told the tattoo artist to add a vine or plant to make it look like the butterfly was sitting on something. But he thought he knew better than me and turned it into a chain. Chained butterfly, it's stupid, right?" He shrugged. "But what're going to do? Hardly seemed worth beating the guy up over."

My gaze fixed on the tattoo, the wings at the center of it. My voice was tight as I said, "My father had a birthmark just like that, on his shoulder. My mother called it his angel's wings."

Casey's expression went still, and he lowered his arm, and his eyes, to the table. "Well," he said quietly after a moment, "what are the odds?"

"Yeah," I agreed in a tiny, stifled voice. "What are the odds?"

He looked up at me and smiled. "I have a dragon on the other arm."

There was something about Casey's smile that made it impossible not to return. So, I did, however weakly. Then I said seriously, "Casey, I am one hundred percent sure—and so is my family—that my father never suspected he had another child. So if he was the father, Maude never told him."

Casey nodded. "I figured as much."

The waitress, ever vigilant, appeared at the table again with her pen poised over her notebook. "Are we ready?"

I was about to order a bacon cheeseburger with onion rings, not fries, and a Coke. But Casey spoke up first.

"I'll have a bacon cheeseburger with onion rings, not fries," he said. "And a Coke." He folded the menu and looked at me.

I smiled. "Same," I said.

"So," Casey said when the waitress was gone, "I Googled you. That's a pretty neat job you have. What is a therapy dog, anyway? Are those the ones that help people in wheelchairs?"

"No," I told him, "but a lot of people make that mistake."

I explained to him the difference between a therapy dog and a service dog. He laughed when I told him about teaching Cisco to put a basketball through a hoop and do a little dance routine to entertain people at the nursing home. He was fascinated when I told him how Cisco was learning to read to help children with reading challenges, and that Cisco's main job was wilderness search-and-rescue. By the time our burgers arrived Casey was telling me about a summer he had spent on a ranch helping to take care of horses in an equine therapy program.

"I've heard about equine therapy," I said, intrigued. "I'd love to see it in action. The horses actually bond with troubled kids, right, and help them work out their problems? I saw a documentary on TV."

"Yeah, it's pretty cool," he agreed. "I almost talked myself into becoming a horse trainer that summer."

"Why didn't you?"

He shrugged. "Life got in the way." He took a bite out of his burger. "Besides," he added when he'd swallowed, "the competition is pretty stiff for the best trainers, and if you're not one of the best you can't make a living. Do you ride?"

"A little. My dad had horses when I was growing up. He sold the last one when I went off to college."

He nodded, his expression pleasantly interested, but I thought I saw a faint wistfulness in his eyes. I wondered if he was imagining what it might have been like if he had grown up differently, if we had known each other as kids. I put down my burger.

"Casey," I said, "would you be willing to take a DNA test?"

He seemed to think about this as he finished chewing. He took a sip of his Coke, then dipped an onion ring in a puddle of ketchup on his plate. "Yeah," he said. "Okay, sure. I mean, I've got nothing to lose either way, right? The only thing is..." He popped the onion ring into his mouth. "I'm not exactly sure how to do that."

"Yeah, me either," I agreed, frowning a little. Then I shrugged. "But I'm sure I can find out. Can you hang around for a while?"

Now he hesitated. "I don't know, Raine. I'm not really on a schedule, but I had thought about going on down to Florida as long as I'm here, maybe meeting that lawyer cousin of mine.

And it's a lot warmer there than it is here. Besides, someday pretty soon I've got to think about looking for a real job."

"What if," I said suddenly, "you had a job? That house of Maude's needs a lot of fixing up and you could live there while you're doing it. I could have the utilities turned on by the end of the week."

He looked skeptical. "Are you sure? You don't even know me."

That was the thing, I realized. I *wanted* to get to know him. If there was any possibility at all we were related, I would never forgive myself if I let him leave now. I said, "I know you're pretty good at fixing broken locks."

"What about that fiancé of yours? He seemed to know his way around a builder's square, and I got the impression he was planning to have the work done himself."

"Maybe," I agreed. "But it's my decision, not his." Then I hesitated, wondering if I had been a tad impulsive. It wouldn't be the first time. "Um, how much do you charge?"

He grinned. "I'll give you the friends and family discount."

I grinned back and offered my hand across the table. "Deal," I said.

After only another moment's hesitation he shook my hand with a single firm, up-and-down pump. "All right then," he said. He leaned back in his seat and took up another onion ring. "When do I start?"

CHAPTER THIRTEEN

Buck ran Casey Macintosh's driver's license, and it came back clean: no outstanding warrants, no priors, no moving violations. As a matter of fact, it seemed a little too clean to Buck. A guy that age ought to have had at least one speeding ticket in the past three years, or even a DUI. But lacking any evidence against him, Buck's hands were tied for further investigation. Besides, he had a real lead to follow up on.

Buck sat on Carter Frank's green floral-colored sofa and made conversation with his wife for twenty minutes while he waited for Carter to get home. During that time, he noticed a few interesting things: a seventy-inch television set hanging above the fireplace, for one; a new minivan in the garage for another. And that was not to mention the way his wife, who was a plain woman at best, kept nervously twisting the ruby and diamond ring on her finger. When Buck noticed, she explained, "It was our anniversary last month. Thirty years. Carter always promised me a nicer ring than the one he could afford when we got married, and he finally managed it." She looked down at the ring fondly. "Don't tell Carter, but I liked my old ring better. Memories, you know? And this one is a little..." She clenched her hand self-consciously. "Showy."

"Thirty years, though," Buck said. "That's really something." He smiled. "I'd say you deserve something showy."

She laughed uneasily and glanced at the clock for what must have been the fifth time in the last ten minutes. "I don't know what's keeping Carter. He's usually…" Her face sagged in relief at the sound of tires on the driveway. "There he is."

Carter Frank looked curious, but not alarmed, as he hung his coat on a peg by the door and came forward to shake Buck's hand. "I saw your deputy outside," he said, nodding toward the door. "She's welcome to come in out of the cold. Honey…" he turned to his wife. "Did you offer the man some coffee?"

"She did," Buck assured him, "but I'm good. I won't be here much longer, and neither will the deputy."

Carter nodded and rubbed his hands together, which were chapped with the cold. "I reckon this is about what happened the other day."

"It is," Buck said. "I just had a few more questions for you."

"Well," his wife said, standing quickly, "I'll leave you to it, then. The whole thing is just so upsetting, finding a dead body like that. Carter hasn't slept through the night since it happened, and I'm not doing much better."

"Yes. ma'am," Buck agreed gravely. He gestured Carter to be seated as she hurried out of the room. "This won't take long."

Carter took the leather recliner a few feet away and Buck sat on the edge of the sofa, his notebook in hand. "I've been going over some of Smokey's old arrest records," he said, watching Carter's face carefully. "It probably won't surprise you to know he's run afoul of the law once or twice before."

Carter replied, "I might have heard, but it's my job to deliver the mail regardless."

Buck went on, "One of Smokey's illegal enterprises was a credit card fraud and identity theft racket that I think Smokey might have kept going on up until he was killed. Might even be the reason he was killed."

Carter's expression remained frozen in a mask of polite interest, but Buck noted the fast throbbing of a vein in the other man's neck, and a slight shininess to his forehead that hadn't been there before.

Buck said, "Apparently the way they pulled it off—back in the old days, anyway—was they enlisted the help of the local postmaster, paying him to misdirect certain items like credit cards and such so that Smokey and his gang could sell them on the black market. This would have been oh, ten or twelve years ago. Maybe you remember that case? The postmaster went to prison."

Carter shook his head, but his face was tight. "I might've heard of it, but I've only been with the post office six years."

Buck nodded. "Right. But still, I was wondering if you might be able to give me some insight into how easy you thought something like that would be to pull off these days? Stealing mail, I mean, and repurposing it, so to speak."

Carter pretended to consider that. Buck saw him swallow before he spoke. "I don't know, Buck. Sounds pretty wild to me. There are a lot of checks and balances all along the way, you know. And mail tampering is, well, that's a federal offense. We swear an oath. A person could go to prison."

Buck nodded gravely. "True enough, as that former postmaster found out. But for the right price, you'd be surprised at what a man would do." He looked deliberately at the seventy-inch television hanging over the fireplace, then back at Carter.

Carter wiped a hand over his face, shifting his weight in the chair. "I don't know, Buck," he said again. "Like I said, sounds a little far-fetched to me."

Buck consulted his notes. "So, I was trying to figure how a person might do that, you know, deliver a bunch of stolen mail to an address and exchange it for a bunch of cash. Maybe he'd put the mail in a box or an overnight envelope and deliver it to the target—in this case, Smokey—then pick up a box containing his payment. We found a whole bunch of empty boxes that had been delivered to Smokey with official US Postal Service labels at his house, but when I checked with the Post Office, they didn't have a record of any boxes being delivered to Smokey's address—not a single one—in the past six months. Which makes sense, I guess, since none of the boxes we found actually had postage on them. Except that one, of course," he corrected himself. "The one you delivered Saturday, when you found Smokey dead. But here's the funny thing about that. That package had a US Postal Service label on it, just like all the others, with Smokey's address handwritten on it. But it was covering up another address. That package was addressed to Mildred Beckett, and she reported it missing this morning."

Carter swallowed hard once again. "I don't follow."

Buck asked quietly, "Did you kill Smokey Beardsley, Carter?"

The other man's face went an oily, sickly shade of yellow, his eyes frozen in a horrified stare. For a moment he seemed unable to speak. "No!" he managed at last, hoarsely. "No, God, no! Why would you even say that? I thought he died of carbon monoxide poisoning. It was an accident."

Buck said, "It looks like somebody might have helped that accident along by blocking off the heater ventilation with an old rag he found in the workshop. Did you go to the workshop for any reason?"

"No. You can't be serious about this! I told you, I went to the door, I saw him through the windows..."

"Why did you go to the door?" Buck inquired mildly. "It wasn't to deliver a package. The only package you had in your truck was the one addressed to Mildred Beckett, so you slapped a new label on it and left it on the porch so it would look like you had a legitimate reason to go to the door. But what was the real reason? Was it to collect your payment?"

Carter wiped his face with a shaky hand and blew out a couple of breaths between his lips. "Look," he said, "I didn't kill him. He was dead when I got there. I swear to God. Why would I have called 911 if I killed him?"

Buck waited patiently, silently.

Carter glanced frantically toward the back of the house, where his wife could be heard moving about, rattling pans, closing cabinets. "Thirty *years*, Buck. The woman deserves some nice things. And it wasn't really stealing—the mail was returned, wasn't it? It was just borrowed. Most of it anyhow. And it wasn't me, not really. I was just the delivery man."

Buck said, "What do you mean?"

Carter pushed a hand across his face again, wet his lips, and leaned forward a little in his chair. "Every Thursday there'd be a Priority Mail envelope left in the drop-off box in front of the post office addressed to George Brewer General Delivery. I'd pick it up before my shift and take it to Smokey. I don't know what was in it, could have been money, could have been more pieces of mail from somewhere else, I don't know. But I got the idea it was a whole operation, you know? And Smokey, he was just a little cog in a big wheel. He would sort it all out and send it on up the line to some fellow he called Deacon. Then it would get copied and put back in the mail and nobody'd be the wiser."

Buck jotted down the name. "Any idea where this guy Deacon was located?"

Carter shook his head. "I only pieced together this much from what I overheard. The guy had a real fancy printer is all I know. Like 3-D or something. He could duplicate credit cards and driver's licenses that would fool the government, even key cards and ID badges. There's a big market for that kind of thing, I guess. What Smokey was doing with birth certificates and social security cards and credit applications was small potatoes to him." He looked at Buck helplessly. "Don't you think?"

Buck took out his phone, sent a brief text instructing Jolene to stand by, then put it away again. "You said there was a dark SUV parked at Smokey's house the day before you found him dead, is that right?"

He nodded. "I'd seen it there before, usually on Fridays. I always figured it had something to do with Smokey's, you know, business."

"Did you ever get a look at the tag?"

"No. It was always parked facing the street."

"Okay, Carter." Buck put away his notebook and got to his feet. Carter stood uncertainly as well.

"The deputy outside is going to give you a ride down to the detention center," Buck said. "Somebody there will take your statement, and I'll probably be by to talk to you some more later today. Better get your coat."

"But..." He cast an alarmed glance toward the kitchen. "But I told you everything I know! Does Kathy have to find out about this? Isn't there something you can do?"

Buck walked over to the coatrack and retrieved Carter's coat. "I'm real sorry, Carter," he said. "I'm afraid there's not."

CHAPTER FOURTEEN

Casey walked Raine to her car and lifted his hand as she drove away. Shoving his hands into his pockets, he started across the parking lot back toward the motel, feeling pretty good about the way things were going. That was, at least, until a man in a parka and blue knit hat fell into step beside him. Casey had seen him, out of the corner of his eye, get out of a black SUV when he passed in front of it, but by then it was too late. What was he supposed to do, run?

"Crap," he muttered, not looking up as the man drew up beside him.

"Good to see you again, too, Casey," returned the other man easily. "Although I've got to say I wish you'd picked someplace warmer." He glanced at the sky. "Looks like snow."

"What do you want?"

"Oh, the usual. Just one old friend checking on another. Making sure you stay out of trouble, you know."

"This is legit, man," Casey returned. "It's got nothing to do with you."

"Is that a fact?" He jerked his head back toward the restaurant from which Casey had come. "Who's the chick?"

Casey scowled. "Leave her out of this. She's a sweet kid. She raises golden retrievers, for God's sake. Leave her out of it."

"Yeah, she's also surrounded by cops, not to mention a boyfriend who's got more contacts than a CIA operative. You need to stay shy of them."

"I told you, this is legit. I'm just a guy tracing his roots. My mother used to live here."

"We're aware. So did another person of particular interest to us both. What's going on here, Casey?"

They had reached the door to Casey's motel room. He kept on walking. The other man stepped in front of him and stopped. "So, here's the deal, Casey," he said. "We're in the middle of a pretty big operation here, as you know very well. We've got one man missing and another man dead and all of a sudden you show up, right smack dab in the middle of it, when here is the last place you're supposed to be. Out west, remember? Out west where nobody knows you and nobody has you in their sights. So, what do you know that I don't know? And you'd better talk fast because I don't know how much longer I can keep this nice."

Casey made sure none of the surprise he felt showed on his face. This was the first he was hearing about a dead man. Fortunately, he was an expert at making his expression reveal exactly what he wanted it to; no more and no less. He said shortly, "I told you I would handle it. Do you trust me or not?"

The other man chuckled completely without mirth. "About as far as I can throw you." He nodded back the way they had come. "You passed your room," he said. He took a phone from his pocket and dropped it into Casey's. "You want to talk, call me. My number's programmed in there. Meantime, I know how to find you. You take care, now. And..." His eyes were dark marbles as they fixed on Casey's. "Don't even think about screwing me over. You know what will happen if you do."

Casey, unfortunately, knew all too well.

CHAPTER FIFTEEN

Miles and I have what some people might call an unusual relationship, particularly regarding our living arrangement, but it works for us. In fact, I can't think of anything else that would work. We're both adults with more than one failed marriage behind us; we had established very different lives and businesses that demanded our attention long before we met, and we always knew merging those two lives together would not be easy. So, we just made a bigger one.

His glass-and-cedar contemporary house on the hill looks down on my nineteenth-century farmhouse in the valley, with the colorful Dog Daze building in the back and its multiple fences and play yards. The two properties are linked by a half-mile trail through the woods which, in the summer, is great for jogging and dog walking and, in the winter, for sledding and snowmobiling. Before the bad weather set in, Miles had started enclosing the entire property—his and mine—in a cedar-board fence. I had hated it, of course, and we'd had lots of fights about it. He called it a family compound, and I made snide remarks about prison yards. He pointed out that the dogs would now have over fifteen secure acres in which to run—a somewhat compelling argument, I admit—and I pointed out that the deer and bears and foxes would now have fifteen less acres in which to traverse freely. At any rate, the argument went on long enough to prevent the fence from being completed before the ground froze, which was a minor victory for me. However, Miles did score one point: a very nice private road now branched off from my driveway on the west and his driveway on the east, breaching the distance between our two houses without either of us ever having to get on the highway. I hate to see a natural environment disrupted almost as much as Miles likes to build things, but I've got to admit, this I like. It was all very symbolic, of course, and he had gotten his family compound after all. We are separate but together, surrounded by what we love, connected by what we value, and even when we're an ocean or two apart, we're never really alone.

All this is to say we basically share two houses, his and mine, and this is the way we have decided to live even after we're married. We come and go as we need to and adapt when we have to. It takes a lot of trust to live this way, very limited expectations, and a good deal of flexibility. Until I met Miles, I wasn't particularly good at any of those things. Now I am.

So Miles didn't lift an eyebrow when I arrived at his door that afternoon lugging a folding dog crate, a backpack filled with toys and treats, and a ten-pound bag of puppy food. Joining the fray were two gorgeous Australian shepherds, who trotted across the threshold and into Miles's marble-floored kitchen with all the ease and familiarity of a couple of princesses returning home, a bouncing Cisco, and Rags the puppy.

"I thought we'd better go ahead and get set up over here," I said, handing over the crate and the backpack to Miles. I kissed him and added, "I've got some bedding in the car."

He was wearing jeans and one of those silky sweaters I love, and bare feet. Bare feet, in the middle of winter in the mountains; imagine that. But Miles had heated floors, which was just another thing I loved about him. I kicked off my boots and left them in the mudroom while he gathered the rest of my gear.

"I'll get it after I get this set up in the puppy room," he told me. "Then I'll pull your car into the garage. The forecast is for sleet tonight."

Yes, that darling man has turned an entire 20x30 room of his house into a puppy room, complete with the same colorful puzzle mat flooring I have at Dog Daze, luxury beds for each of my dogs, monogrammed dishes, and a multitude of toys that include a puppy slide and a wading pool filled with colorful foam balls that Cisco loves to plunge into and roll around in. Granted, the design was courtesy of Melanie, and the room provided a perfect way to keep the dogs from destroying Miles's Ming Dynasty vases and whatever other ridiculous artifacts his designer had furnished the place with, but still. It was nice. And my dogs loved it.

Cisco bounded past me in search of Pepper, who could be heard bounding toward him down the hardwood floors of the hallway, and I opened the French doors in the dining room to let them both out to play on the deck. Rags tugged at his leash, eager to join them, but he was in training.

My preferred way of training a new dog, puppy or rescue, is to keep him tethered to my belt for the first two weeks. He goes everywhere I go; he does everything I do. He learns to pay attention, he learns to walk by my side, he learns to respect human authority, and he gets lots and lots of treats. Most importantly, he learns to trust and bond with another species —namely, me. Of course, the key to this kind of training is to make it fun for both you and the dog with lots of happy-voiced encouragement and treats. When he gets tired, he goes to his crate. When I get tired, he goes to his crate. When I'm working on the computer or talking on the phone, he's lying by my side, chewing a bone. Except for training sessions, potty breaks and meals, we're together, learning each other's habits and eccentricities. And, as a side benefit, with this kind of training, there is absolutely zero opportunity for Puppy to have an accident on the rug.

I distracted Rags with some bits of cheese and some quick, happy power walks and about-turns through the football field that was Miles's kitchen while the other dogs got settled and

Miles pulled my car into the garage. As he tossed me my keys, he pointed out, "You know, if the fence was built, you could leave your keys in the car. Complete security."

"Because you'd have guards with AR-15s at every corner," I replied dourly and pocketed the keys.

"Like I said, complete security." He liked to tease me about things like that. "Mrs. Banks left some gingersnaps, and I've got cider in the fridge. Want some?"

Aunt Mart—in careful consultation with Miles's mother, Rita—had scoured the county for weeks, interviewing every possible candidate, before finally settling on Eugenia Banks as a suitable housekeeper for Miles and Melanie. She worked from 8:00 to 3:00 five days a week and was available to stay over with Melanie in case of emergency. Except for her sequined jeans and logo tee shirts, she was straight out of central casting: plump, rosy cheeked, curly haired and ineffably cheerful. The only fault Miles could find with her was that her apple pie was better than his.

I took a glass jug of artisanal cider from the refrigerator and commented innocently, "So if you finish the fence this spring..."

"If?" he returned with lifted eyebrow, placing a pot on the stove.

I ignored that and handed him the cider, Rags trotting along attentively at my side. "Does that mean Melanie can have a horse?"

"Not at all." He poured the cider into the pot and turned the gas on low.

Mischief and Magic skidded into the kitchen, a toy rabbit caught in a tug of war between them. Rags immediately lunged after them, but because he was tethered to me, I was able to turn his attention back to me with a treat almost before he finished the motion. "Girls!" I said sharply. "Go to your room!"

Mischief rolled her eyes toward me, giving Magic the opportunity to snatch the rabbit and run with it. The two of them galloped back up the stairs toward the puppy room. Rags started to leap after them, but I stopped him with a snap of my fingers and a morsel of cheese. Miles winked at me and ruffled the top of Rags's curly head. "You're my hero," he said.

I hated to ruin the moment, but I had gone to some trouble to set this up. So, I plunged on innocently, "Casey used to work at an equine therapy facility."

Miles slanted me a look that told me I wasn't fooling him for a minute. "I take it that means you finally got around to Googling him?"

In fact, I had, as embarrassed as I was to admit I hadn't thought of it before. I didn't find much. A three-year-old family photo on the Macintosh Construction website, *Family owned and operated for 30 years, see us for all your home building and remodeling needs,* a few Facebook posts of him with friends, Instagram photos of scenery. He wasn't big on social media, but neither was I. Who has the time?

"Also," I went on casually, "I took him to lunch." This time the look Miles gave me wasn't so tolerant, and I returned impatiently, "Oh, please. Don't pretend you didn't know I would."

He snapped open a plastic storage container and started transferring cookies to a plate. I could smell the ginger from across the room.

"Also..." I figured I might as well get right to it. "I hired him to do the repairs on Maude's place. Come on, Miles," I rushed on when he didn't reply, "he seems like a perfectly nice guy. He has the tools and the experience and he's only charging me $20 an hour. Plus, if you think about it, the house should probably be his anyway. I told him he could stay there while he's doing the work," I finished, and waited.

Miles finished putting the cookies on the plate and leaned against the countertop, arms folded across his chest, regarding me with the same steady, carefully controlled look he gave Melanie when she pushed him to the edge of his patience. I guess between the two of us, that happened more than it should have, because I saw that look a lot.

"What?" I demanded defensively. "Can you think of a better way to find out what he's up to? If he's up to anything at all, which I doubt."

I figured he must be counting to fifty, at least. He knows I hate it when he does that; I'd rather go ahead and have an outright fight any day.

"I like him, okay?" I said. I turned the heat down under the cider, which was beginning to simmer. "Even Cisco likes him. I don't know why you have to make everything so hard."

He said, "I seem to recall you said the same thing once about a terrorist you met in the woods. You and Cisco are the worst judges of character I've ever met. Tell me you didn't pay him in advance."

I scowled sharply at him. "We're going tomorrow to pick out the materials. I'll pay him when the job is done. He said it would take a couple of weeks if the weather holds. He also said you're welcome to supervise. I said over my dead body."

That made his lips twitch a little with repressed amusement. "It'll take more than a couple of weeks if he does it right."

"He will or he won't," I said. "That's not the point. I don't care about the house."

"I can see that."

I took a breath. "He offered to take a DNA test. This is hard for me, Miles. But I need to know the truth."

His face softened with understanding, and he closed the space between us to kiss me gently. "Do you want me to set it up?"

I nodded.

"Okay," he said. "I know a couple of labs that can probably get results to you quicker than one of those home DNA companies. But it still might take a while to hear back."

"Which," I informed him, "is why I wanted him to hang around."

He smiled wryly. "All right, Sherlock, got it. I should know better by now than to underestimate you."

Pepper and Cisco started barking from the deck, and he glanced toward the window. "That's Melanie. She took the shuttle home from school today."

Most of the time, Miles drove her back and forth to the fancy private school she attended, but shuttle service was also provided for those few students who did not board there. The difference between the yellow school bus that I used to ride and the shuttle that Miles paid a small fortune for her to use was that the "shuttle" was basically a stretch limo outfitted for kids with a chauffeur who served juice boxes instead of champagne and who was trained in evasive driving. Nonetheless, Melanie preferred the shuttle, because, she said, it was more "egalitarian." Egalitarian was her new favorite word. I'd had to look it up.

"Hi, Dad! Hi, Raine! I'm home!" Melanie clattered into the mudroom, dumped her belongings and bounded into the kitchen with Pepper and Cisco at her heels. She scooped a couple of gingersnaps from the plate and declared, "You won't believe what happened to me today."

There followed a predictable amount of chaos while Cisco and Pepper tried to tempt Rags to break training and Rags was more than happy to oblige, lunging and play bowing on his leash and completely forgetting that the leash was attached to me. It took a minute, a few sharp words, and a considerable number of treats before order was restored. When it was, I looked at Melanie meaningfully and returned, "You won't believe what happened to *me*."

"I'll bet mine's better."

I turned to take down the mugs from the cabinet, and she came over to pat Rags on the head, making sure he was sitting first. "You'd lose that bet," I told her.

For once, I was right.

CHAPTER SIXTEEN

You can believe me when I tell you I'm no expert on the subject, but here's my take on the love match: it's the little things that make a relationship work, not the grand gestures. I mean, you don't fall in love with the guy who rescues you from a fire or holds your hand at the scene of a traffic accident or stands beside you at the funeral of a relative; any decent human being does that, am I right? No, it's the guy who knows how you take your coffee, who always orders an extra cruller even when you say you don't want one, who lets your dogs sprawl all over his Italian leather sofa and who rubs their tummies absently while he checks the stock exchange. It's the guy who repurposes his bonus room into a puppy room without even asking you and who has a his-and-hers bathroom built into the master suite before he even asks you to marry him… that's the one you want to spend the rest of your life with, in my opinion. But like I say, I'm no expert.

I was thinking about this as Miles, Melanie and I settled with the dogs into the only part of the house that is ever really used, aside from the bedrooms—the big family room that adjoins the kitchen. He has a media room with a projection TV and theater seats, but the novelty wore off of that after one or two screenings. This is where we watch television. He has a game room with a billiard table and video gaming stations that he never uses because this is where we put together puzzles and play video games. This is the home of the giant, aforementioned Italian leather sectional sofa where dogs are as welcome as humans and crumbs of popcorn and cheese doodles litter the carpet until Mrs. Banks vacuums them up. There is a cubby with an L-shaped desk where Melanie does her homework. There are dog toys on the floor. This is where we live.

Miles turned on the television and started scrolling through his phone, which used to make me crazy but doesn't anymore because even when he's doing two things at once most of his attention is always on me. I started to scoot in beside him on the sofa, but before I could do so Cisco hopped up to take my place. Miles's arm, which had reached to embrace me, embraced Cisco instead, and he chuckled.

"I think the big guy is jealous," he said.

"Of you?" That hardly seemed likely, since Miles had won his heart forever on our first non-date with a box of imported dog biscuits.

Miles shook his head and pointed to Rags, who was munching a Nylabone at my feet. He was doing a pretty good job of maintaining the down, as long as he had the bone to chew on and I kept the leash wrapped around my fingers. I said, "I can't imagine why. He's been around plenty of puppies. Besides, he likes Rags."

"You know, Raine," Melanie said from her homework station across the room, "you're never going to find a home for that dog if you don't give him a better name."

Her father said, "Headphones." She was supposed to wear noise-cancelling headphones while doing her homework in the family room, and most of the time she did. But she also liked to eavesdrop on our conversations, a tendency of which we were both perfectly aware.

She said, "I'm almost done."

"Good. Because you've only got ten minutes of screen time left."

She pulled her headphones back over her ears and concentrated on her laptop. I glanced down at the pile of curly fur at my feet and said, "I don't know. I think Rags suits him." I gave Cisco's ears a rub and said, "Okay, Cisco, off." He just looked at me with happy brown eyes, pretending he had never heard the word "off." I glared back at him. "Don't make me repeat myself."

Just as genially as he had ignored me, Cisco leapt down from the sofa, circled around Rags, and jumped up again on my other side. Cisco rested his head in my lap, and I slid closer to Miles's shoulder. "He's not jealous," I told Miles, stroking Cisco's ears.

"Fearful of being displaced, then," Miles said, typing out a text. "It's a common condition among males."

I looked at him with interest. "Are you fearful of being displaced?"

He gave a small grunt of laughter and draped an arm around my shoulder, drawing me close in a brief hug. "Oh, hell, no. I happen to know I'm entirely irreplaceable."

"Well," I said noncommittally.

He went on, "But I can't help wondering if that's why you don't want my mother to move in here. Because you're afraid she'd be taking your place."

I stared at him accusingly for a moment, then said firmly, "Absolutely not."

"Good," he said.

"For heaven's sake, Miles, I can't believe you," I continued, my irritation rising. "You've already got your whole family tucked in behind a gate like a bunch of sheep, does it really matter what pen we live in? Can't you just..."

He shut me up by holding his phone in front of my face. I scowled at it for a moment, then snatched it up. Displayed on the screen was an e-mail to his mother.

Hi Mom, it read. *Thought it might be good if we talked about renovating the modular home for you when you get here. Send me your ideas and I'll get somebody on it. Yes, this was Raine's idea. Love you-- M*

I punched him in the leg, just for good measure, then

returned the phone to him.

"Finished," Melanie declared. "E-mailing." Miles required that she e-mail him her homework every night before turning it in, and he actually checked it over, even when he was out of town. "Six minutes left."

"Good job," he said. "What'll it be tonight, Master Chef or The Great British Baking Show?" Because he was something of a television addict himself, he did not count television as "screen time" as long as they watched together. I'm not that much of a television person myself, mostly because there aren't any good shows starring dogs, but I've learned to broaden my horizons for their sake.

"It's cupcake night on Master Chef," she said.

"Cupcakes it is." He picked up the remote control and changed the channel, volume on mute.

I like cupcakes as much as the next person, but I knew they wouldn't be able to hold my attention tonight. I said thoughtfully, "Casey had a birthmark on his wrist just like one my father had. It was a little spooky. Are birthmarks hereditary?"

"I don't know, baby. Are you sure it was a birthmark?"

From across the room, Melanie read, "'While most birthmarks are not hereditary, there have been incidences of a port wine stain or strawberry birthmark being passed down from parent to child—often in the same place.' So, which was it, port wine or strawberry?"

I twisted around to look at her. "You have six minutes left and that's what you choose to look up?"

"Five," corrected Miles.

"It was red," I said. "Might've been a strawberry birthmark."

"Or it could've been a tattoo," suggested Miles.

"Or a drawing," said Melanie. "They make theses rub-on stamps with food dye, you know, and they wash off after a few weeks. Can I get one, Dad?"

"No," he said.

Remembering Casey's tattoo, I frowned irritably and said, "It wasn't any of those things. Anyway, how would he even know what kind of birthmark my father had?"

Miles replied, "I didn't say he would."

Melanie said, "Must be weird, having a brother you never even knew about. Do you think I'll have a brother some day?"

"No," said Miles.

At the same time, I said, "No chance."

She shrugged. "Probably just as well. I'm pretty overscheduled as it is. I don't know how I'd make time for a brother."

"Speaking of time," her father said, "you've got five minutes to brush your teeth and get ready for bed if you don't want to miss the cupcake competition."

She snapped closed her laptop and scampered toward the stairs, Pepper at her heels.

When she was gone, I said, "Casey admitted he got to the house before us and went inside. So those were his tire tracks we saw."

Miles put down his phone and looked at me.

"He didn't break in," I clarified. "He said the lock was broken when he got there."

Miles said, "And you believe him?"

I shrugged. "Why tell part of the truth?"

"Because that's what con artists do. They tell just enough of the truth to make themselves sound convincing, to get you to open the door. Once they have your trust, you do the work for them."

I scowled, shifting uncomfortably beneath the weight of Cisco's head in my lap. "Oh, please. I know how con artists work."

"I don't want you out there at that house alone with him," Miles said. "At least not until we know more about him."

I stared at him. "You don't *want*?"

"I didn't tell you to stay away from him," Miles replied impatiently.

"Damn straight you didn't," I interjected shortly.

"Just use some common sense until we get more information, can you do that?"

I sat up straight, glaring. Cisco lifted his head, alert to the sudden change of tone in the conversation. "Let me ask you something, Miles. When has telling me what to do ever worked out well for you?"

Instead of replying, he unmuted the volume on the television.

You know all those warm and fuzzy things I said about the love match earlier? Well, they're all still true—right up until the point Miles pisses me off. I moved away from him and flopped back hard against the sofa, crossing my arms over my chest. Cisco, who had apparently had it with both of us, jumped down and made himself comfortable in Pepper's fluffy dog bed beside the fireplace.

"You are *never* getting that fence," I muttered.

He just smiled. "I love you, Raine."

And of course, the worst thing was that I knew he did. No, the worst thing was that I loved him back. But right at the moment I wasn't in the mood to say it.

CHAPTER SEVENTEEN

Jolene came in on a gust of frigid air that caused the candles Buck had lit on the mantle to waver. "Sorry I'm late," she said, shrugging out of her coat. "At the last minute Willis told me it was his turn to bring cookies for snack time tomorrow, which normally wouldn't be a problem but we were down to one stick of butter, wouldn't you know? So, I had to run out and get some." She paused to kiss Buck and then laid two fingers across his lips, wrinkling her nose. "Pizza breath," she said.

"Sorry, I was starved. I started without you."

She lifted an eyebrow. "I certainly hope that's the last time I hear that tonight."

He grinned and reached for her, but she brushed his lips with another kiss and slipped away, heading for the open pizza box on the coffee table. "Anyway, I left Mama and Willis baking four dozen chocolate-chip cookies, which will probably be a waste of time because it's starting to sleet, and they'll close the schools if the roads ice over." She sat on the sofa and took up a slice of pizza.

"Well, damn," he said. "I wish you'd stayed a little bit longer and brought me some cookies."

"Heads-up," she said and tossed him a zippered bag filled with chocolate-chip cookies.

He smiled as he caught it. "Baby, you are the light of my life."

She tossed him a kiss and he turned for the kitchen. "I don't think it will ice," Buck added. He opened the refrigerator to pour her a glass of Chardonnay. He'd never dated a woman who drank Chardonnay before, and every time he looked at the bottle in his refrigerator, he felt a little spark of awe. "But I'm glad you're here. I was starting to worry."

She lifted a finger for patience while she chewed and swallowed her pizza, then said, "By the way, we found that camper van you were looking for, parked at the High Point Hotel on Highway 197. I got the message just before I went off duty. Do you want us to keep an eye on him?"

Buck handed her the glass of wine and sat down beside her, reaching for the bottle of beer he had left on the coffee table. "No, I'll stop by and have a chat with him in the morning. Did you run the tag?"

"It came back clean. Registered to a Casey Macintosh out of Denver. What's the deal?"

"I'm not sure yet." He reached for a slice of pizza. "He showed up here a couple of days after Raine found out she'd inherited that property out on Deer Run Trail, claiming to be her half-brother. The illegitimate son of the woman who left Raine the property, to be exact."

"Oh, that's not suspicious at all," noted Jolene sardonically, taking another bite. "That ex of yours sure does know how to get herself in some situations, doesn't she?"

He lifted one shoulder in tacit agreement. "Let's just say I would very much like to know what this guy's relationship with Smokey Beardsley is. Was."

"So how did your interview go with Carter Frank after we booked him? Do you make him for our killer?"

"I don't know," replied Buck thoughtfully. "He's what you might call the most likely suspect, but none of the prints we took from the workshop or the back part of the house match."

"It's the dead of winter," she pointed out. "He was wearing gloves."

Buck nodded. "He kept talking about some kind of

organized crime involvement, and some fellow they called Deacon. But from what I hear, those folks aren't usually that subtle when they want to get rid of somebody. Whoever killed Smokey wanted it to look like an accident." Again, he shrugged. "I'm taking it to the prosecutor tomorrow, and he'll probably want to turn the case over to the feds. Either way, Carter is screwed. He's looking at federal fraud, racketeering and mail theft charges just to start the list."

"You've got to admit," Jolene said, "the whole thing was pretty clever. I mean, a rural community like this, using the postman as your bagman, a 3-D printer, for God's sake." She shook her head in muted admiration. "Clever."

"Oh, I don't know. Sounds like a lot of hard work to me. Seems like it'd be easier just to steal numbers off the internet. Let the computers do the work."

"It's also a lot easier to get caught," she pointed out, "and a lot more expensive to set up—unless you've got an in with the Russians, that is. Sometimes the old-fashioned way is the safest. Slow and steady wins the race."

"Maybe you're right." He put down his beer and turned to her, changing the subject. "Listen," he said. "How'd you like to go to the beach for Valentine's weekend?"

Jolene tucked one foot beneath her and sipped her wine, lifting an interested eyebrow. "Tell me more."

"Do you remember that little town in south Georgia that was looking to replace their retiring police chief?"

"The one that was offering an obscene amount of money? Boy, talk about your organized crime."

He said, "According to the web site, it's two hours from the white sand beaches of the Gulf of Mexico. And the guy seems really eager to talk to me, so I figured we could drive down there on Thursday, see what he's got to say on Friday, and spend the rest of the weekend at the beach. We'd be back here for change of shift Tuesday morning."

She put her glass down slowly, staring at him. "You're joking. Is this a serious job interview?"

He answered, "I won't know that until I get down there. But I told Marshall I was looking. I wanted to give him plenty of time to replace me."

"You're leaving?" She got slowly to her feet, her eyes glinting, her fists closed. "You're *leaving*?"

There followed the biggest fight of their lives, and when it was over, the last thing on Buck's mind was his case.

CHAPTER EIGHTEEN

There is a reason the FBI likes to execute raids before sunrise. Sometimes it's just showboating, of course; sometimes it's plain meanness. But for the most part it's for the same reason other predators attack at night: to catch their victims off guard.

When Buck banged on Casey Macintosh's motel room door at 6:00 the following morning, he told himself it was simply a matter of convenience. He had a long day ahead and he wanted to get this last interview out of the way on his way to work so he could start compiling his report. He probably wouldn't have woken a neighbor at 6:00 AM for the same purpose, but he didn't owe this guy anything. So, if he was completely honest, there might have been a little bit of meanness behind his actions, after all.

The fight with Jolene had been brief and intense; the making up had lasted a lot longer than the fight, as it always did. Despite the fact that he had gotten less than five hours sleep, Buck should have been in a pretty good mood because, in the end, things with Jolene had turned out very well indeed. But in the process, he had come to realize a few disturbing things about himself and the way his life was going that he didn't yet know how to resolve. He therefore wasn't at his most patient when he knocked on the door of room 103. When there was no immediate response he knocked again, louder, and called, "Sheriff's Office! Open the door!"

A light appeared through the crack of the drawn draperies in the room next door, and then in the room on the other side of 103. Buck started to bang on the door again when it opened to the width of the safety latch and part of a face appeared in the crack. Behind him, the room was dark. Buck held up his badge. "Casey Macintosh?"

A bleary voice replied, "What do you want?"

"Just to talk. It won't take long."

The door closed, and a light went on in the crack of the curtains. The door opened again, all the way this time. Casey Macintosh was wearing sweatpants and a rumpled tee shirt with sneakers over his bare feet. They were the kind with Velcro fasteners, so a man didn't have to waste time tying laces when he needed to run. His blond hair was tangled, his eyes squinting a little in the light. Behind him was an unmade bed and an open duffle on the chair beside it. A crumpled take-out bag in the trash, a Coke can on the night table.

Buck said, "Can I come in? Or do you want to do this standing in the cold?"

Casey hesitated, then stepped away from the door with a short sweep of his arm. Buck stepped inside.

"What's this about?" Casey asked, stifling a yawn. He closed the door behind them, but Buck noticed he did not move far from it.

Buck said, "My name is Buck Lawson, and I'm an investigator for the Hanover County prosecutor's office. I'm also," he added, watching Casey closely, "a friend of Raine Stockton's. Her ex-husband, in fact."

"Ah, Christ." Casey gave a grunt of resigned amusement and sank back against the door. "I've heard about these small-town bully cops, but never thought I'd meet one. Are you really here to tell me to back off from your ex? Because, let me tell you, you've got it all wrong."

Buck just smiled. "You look a little bit like her, you know. Maude, not Raine."

Casey's gaze sharpened. "You knew Maude?"

Buck nodded, moving into the room. He noted the half-open bathroom door with a shaving kit on the vanity, towel on the floor. Nothing else out of place, nothing unpacked. "As well as Raine did."

Buck said, "When did you get to town, Mr. Macintosh?"

"Yesterday," said Casey. "I would've thought your ex had told you that."

"First time you've been here?"

Casey said impatiently, "Look, I'm trying to be nice about this, but it's not even light out. If you're not going to get to the point, I'd really like to go back to bed."

Buck said, "I'm investigating a homicide, and I hope you might be able to shed some light on a couple of things."

Casey stared at him. "Me? I haven't had time to get mad enough at somebody to kill them. What are you talking about?"

Buck nodded and took out his phone. "Do you know this man?" He held up a booking photo of Smokey Beardsley, and Casey stared at it blankly.

"No," he said. "Should I?"

Buck said, "He was found dead under suspicious circumstances on Saturday."

"I was in Mississippi Saturday."

"Got any proof of that?"

"I guess. Maybe a gas station receipt out in my van. You're not really going to make me go out in the cold and look for it, are you?"

Buck said, "Not just yet. The evidence so far shows that Smokey was involved in an identity theft racket. Credit cards, social security, birth certificates… You wouldn't know anything about that, would you?"

Casey shook his head. "Man, I told you. I just got here. I don't know anything, and I don't know anybody except your ex. And," he added innocently, "her boyfriend."

"Fiancé," Buck corrected easily. He put away his phone.

Casey said, "So this guy, Smokey, the one that's dead. What

happened to him?"

"That's what we're trying to find out."

"Are you questioning everybody in the motel about him?"

Buck replied pleasantly, "No. Just you."

Casey looked at him, unblinking, for a long time. "So, I'm guessing this is your way of saying welcome to town," he said at last.

Buck replied, "Something like that." He took out a card and handed it to Casey. "If you think of anything that might be of assistance in this case, please give me a call," he said. "And don't throw away that gas station receipt. Have a good day now, you hear?"

Buck left, and Casey bolted and double-bolted the door behind him.

CHAPTER NINETEEN

Casey sat on the edge of the bed, his face in his hands, swearing profusely under his breath. "Son of a bitch," he muttered. "Twenty-four hours. Twenty-four hours and already you've got the cops on your tail. That's got to be a new record, even for you. Damn it. Damn it."

Because the hell of it was, this time he was innocent. This time he hadn't done anything wrong. Yet.

But Smokey was dead. Smokey was dead and the cops were looking at him, and what were the odds of that? He thought for a minute about walking away. That girl with the golden retrievers, she didn't deserve to be sucked into this. But wasn't it just his luck that she'd be married—or formerly married— to a cop? It was starting to look like he couldn't catch a break with both hands and a butterfly net.

Except that this *was* his break. It was the last one, the biggest one, he was likely to get. Did he really think he could walk away now? Seriously?

He slid open the drawer of the bedside table. Nestled next to his Ruger was the burner phone Detweiler had given him. He looked at it for a long time. Every time he talked to the guy his life got more complicated, not that it could get more twisted than it was now. But what was he supposed to do? Had he really ever thought he'd be able to slide by on his own?

He picked it up and hit "dial."

"Okay," he said, when the other man answered. "Let's

talk."

This time Casey chose a booth at the back of the Waffle House. He also wore a heavy jacket and tucked his hair up beneath nondescript baseball cap. It was habit, really. He wasn't particularly worried about anybody spotting him; no one knew he was here. Then again, that's what he'd thought when Detweiler walked up beside him the other day, too.

The place was redolent of maple syrup and bacon, and sounded like clanking spoons and cranky babies as the breakfast crowd grew thicker. The waitress had just finished filling his coffee cup when Detweiler slid into the seat opposite him, shrugging off his coat. "Man, it smells like old times in here, huh, Case?"

Casey curled his fingers around his coffee cup. "Smokey is dead," he said lowly. "You might've mentioned that."

"Didn't think you'd be interested." Detweiler lifted a hand for the waitress and when she paused by the table he said, "Hey, honey, bring me a couple of waffles with scrambled and sausage. Same for my friend here. On my tab," he added with a wink to Casey.

"Coming up." She turned his coffee mug over and filled it. Casey didn't speak until she was gone again.

"Smokey's dead and the cops are talking to *me*," Casey said in a hissing whisper. "You know damn well I didn't have anything to do with it. I wasn't anywhere near here when it happened! I haven't even done business with the dude for years. So what the hell's going on?"

The other man shook his head regretfully. "Sounds to me like you picked a really bad time to go visit Mama, Casey."

"My mother," Casey said coldly, "is dead."

For a moment he thought he saw an actual flicker of humanity across the other man's face. "Man, I'm sorry to hear that," said Detweiler. "That's rough."

"Yeah," said Casey stiffly, "it is. She seemed like a decent person, and I blew my one chance to meet her."

"Well, that's the way of the world though, isn't it?" Detweiler picked up his coffee cup, took a sip. "Actions have consequences."

Casey released his hands from around the coffee cup with an abrupt gesture and started to rise. "See you, Detweiler."

Detweiler waved him back into his seat impatiently. "Look, man, you know I wouldn't be here if I wasn't trying to help you out, so let's stop playing games. You're the one who set up this scam with Freddie and I went to bat for you. Nobody believed you could do it. Not even me, if I'm being honest. But I'll be damned if you didn't go and stir up some kind of hornet's nest, so how about just cutting the crap and telling me what the hell is going on?"

Casey picked up his coffee cup and took a sip, looking around the restaurant casually. He said, "Freddie did it."

Detweiler stared at him. "What did you say?"

"He broke in," Casey said. "He got the info. And..." He drew a breath. "I think he got caught."

Detweiler sat back against the booth, looking at him, saying nothing.

Casey put down his coffee cup and took out his phone. He tapped a few buttons, then pushed the phone across the table to Detweiler. He pushed play.

A tight, slightly breathless voice came through. "Okay, bro, we did it. Mission accomplished. We're golden. Only problem is..." in the background there was a clattering, as though the speaker was doing more than one thing at once, and his voice grew muffled, hurried. "I think I might have tripped a wire. And this particular wire might have a location tracker on it. So, I'm outta here. I'm leaving the key in the lock, and if you don't hear from me in two months you use it to get me out, you hear? That was our deal. We're in this together. Only..." Now a nervous, half-hysterical cackle of laughter. "We both know what you're going to do if you don't hear from me so screw it. Knock yourself out. This has been the biggest rush of my life. Almost worth it. Later, man."

Casey retrieved his phone and put it away. Detweiler picked up his coffee cup. They were silent for a moment. Then Detweiler said, "What did he mean, he left the key in the lock?"

Casey lifted one shoulder. "Don't know. My guess is he left something that he could use to negotiate with the cops if they caught him, or even with the old man. "

Detweiler regarded him steadily. "And what do you suppose that something is?"

Casey answered with a small smile and another shrug.

Detweiler said, "You should have called me."

A flash of something very close to anger crossed Casey's eyes but melted quickly into mere annoyance. "Called you? That would've blown the whole job and you know it. Everything depended on absolute anonymity. That's why I set him up here, in the middle of damn nowhere, put him in touch with Smokey so he'd have the means to make a quick getaway if he needed it, and left him alone. Even after he called, after he said he'd struck gold, I stayed put and I stayed quiet. He said two months and I gave him two months." He took another sip of coffee, his expression shuttered. "How the hell did you find me, anyhow?"

"Smokey," replied Detweiler. "The minute I heard he was dead I knew something was starting to unravel. Not the sharpest knife in the block, but he was key to operations in this sector. Now Freddie's missing, and one of the couriers, that mailman, got busted yesterday. He won't make it out of prison alive. They're not the only ones. At least three other ground soldiers have dropped off the map since Christmas. Not to mention the fact that the Feds are getting closer by the day to wrapping up a ten-month RICO investigation that will put the whole operation on the skids." He sipped his coffee. "So, here's my theory. The old man has figured out there's a fox in the henhouse, and he's going after it with a machete even if it means cutting off the heads of every man, woman and child who ever crossed his path. Maybe he's already figured out the fox is Freddie, maybe not. Either way, things are not looking good for you, my friend."

The waitress returned with two platters of waffles, eggs and sausage. The sweet-hot aroma of syrup and grease turned Casey's stomach; nonetheless, he cut off a bite of sausage, speared it and managed to chew and swallow. All the time he was thinking, weighing options, making choices. He watched Detweiler dig into his eggs, and he felt the walls closing in. That was never a good thing.

Detweiler said, "Let me ask you something, kid. This key Freddie was talking about. Is it what I think it is?"

Casey, unblinking, nodded once.

Detweiler sank back against the booth again, staring at him hard. "Then you'd better get off your ass and find it, huh?"

Casey picked up his coffee cup.

"Are you going to keep the cops off my tail?"

Detweiler scraped up another forkful of eggs. "I'll see what I can do. Are you going to keep me in the loop?"

"I'll see what I can do."

Detweiler smiled. "Come on, kid, eat up. You're going to need your strength."

After a moment Casey picked up his fork, and he finished his breakfast in silence.

CHAPTER TWENTY

O f course, the first thing I did the next morning—given the fact that Miles had done everything but forbid me to do so—was text Casey and tell him to meet me at the house at noon to start putting together a materials list. He didn't reply immediately; I figured he was in the shower or something. Eventually the reply came, Sounds good. See you then.

As soon as I finished my chores and had given Corny enough paperwork to keep him off ladders for the rest of the day, I packed up Rags and Cisco and headed to town. Perhaps the one good thing about winter in the mountains is that it's almost always cool enough to leave your dogs in the car while you run errands, and I thought this would be a good time for Rags to practice good traveling habits. Cisco, who had excellent travel habits, rarely let me leave the house without bounding into his place in the backseat. That was another thing Miles was wrong about, by the way. Cisco wasn't in the least bit worried about being displaced.

I stopped by the power company to have the electricity turned on in Maude's house, which they said could be managed in two days. Then I crossed the street to my insurance agent's office to have the house added to my policy while Cisco watched me alertly from the half-open back window of my car and Rags snoozed in his crate. I couldn't help wincing when I heard the amount the new house would add to my yearly premium, and I hadn't even gotten the tax bill yet. I know, I know. Why should I wince at anything when Miles could have paid all my bills out of petty cash and had already volunteered to take care of the house himself? But that's just not the way I work. And as comfortable as we were together, we weren't married yet.

Which, in a nutshell, also summed up my objections to the fence.

As I was leaving the insurance agent, I ran into Dale Comstock, who was on his way to his real estate office a few doors down. "Raine," he said, coming toward me when I waved at him. "I was going to call you later this week. I got the message about Maude while I was out of town, but I just heard she'd left her house to you. I'm so sorry for your loss." He gestured toward his office. "You want to come in out of the cold and talk for a minute?"

I glanced over my shoulder where my car was parked in the nearly empty street. "I've got the dogs in the car," I apologized. "I shouldn't leave them much longer."

He nodded understanding, shoving his hands into his pockets. His cheeks and nose were already chapped with cold, as were mine. "I just wanted to let you know that I'd be happy to go on managing the rental for you, if that's what you want to do, or list it for sale. But I've got to tell you, a house that old, and not in the best of shape, is not going to command much on the market. And the best we can hope to do is a month-to-month rental, like we've been doing. Have you been out there yet?"

I nodded. "I've got a guy who's going to help me with the repairs, but I can't afford to put a lot of money into it."

"I understand. But you might want to think about that." I'm sure he was wondering, like everybody else did, why I would use words like "can't afford" when I wore an engagement ring that cost more than the average yearly salary of most people in this county. He went on, "The vacation rental market is really picking up in this area, and if you were willing to do a few upgrades—new floors, new kitchen, maybe add a bathroom and hire a landscaper—you'd probably net two, three times what you could get now. Not to mention you'd avoid the problems like the one we had with the last renter. They're not only expensive, they can be a real headache."

The day was damp and gray, and I shivered, wanting to get out of the cold. But I had to ask, "What about the last renter?"

He said, "A fellow by the name of Frederick R. Thompson. Seemed a decent enough type, kind of brainy looking, if you know what I mean, said he did computer work from home. I thought for once we had a stable tenant, but no such luck. He signed a rental agreement in October, paid a month in advance and a month's security deposit, and I never heard from him again. Legally with a month-to-month lease, you're supposed to give thirty days' notice before vacating, but most of them never do. So, at the end of December, after multiple attempts to reach him, I went out there and the place was deserted. Utilities turned off for nonpayment, pipes frozen—I had them repaired, don't worry, that's my job—dishes in the sink, trash can overflowing; it was a mess. One of those midnight moves, if you know what I mean. A few pieces of junk furniture, a pretty nice television set, all of which we're allowed to keep for nonpayment of rent, but I donated it to the women's shelter on Maude's behalf. I had a cleaning crew out, but without water or electricity they couldn't do much except sweep out the place. Anyway, the upshot is it cost Maude—or her estate, I guess I should say—more than she made on that deal. So, I'm just saying, Raine. Think about it."

My breath frosted as I released a puff of air. This was definitely starting to sound like more of a burden than a gift, and more importantly—and to my great frustration—it looked like Miles had been right about the house in the first place.

I said, "Thanks, Mr. Comstock. I'll let you know what I decide."

"Always happy to help," he assured me, turning toward his office with a wave. "You take care, now."

I started toward my car, then called after him, "Mr. Comstock?"

He looked back at me.

"I don't suppose, when you went out there to check on the tenant, you had to break the lock on the back door to get in, did you?"

He shook his head. "No, I had a copy of the key, but the door wasn't even locked when I was out there. Naturally I locked up after we finished cleaning the place out, though."

"Huh," I said. "Okay, thanks. I'll be in touch about the house."

I walked back to my car and the waiting dogs, wondering why anyone would want to break into an empty house.

CHAPTER
TWENTY-ONE

Buck rounded the corner to his office, a cup of coffee in one hand and a couple of break-room donuts in the other, and stopped short. A man he didn't know was sitting at his desk, calmly scrolling through his computer.

"Who the hell are you?" Buck demanded, striding into the office.

The other man sprang to his feet and extended his hand. "Major Lawson," he said. "I'm Brett Harrigan. The sheriff told me to report to you this morning."

Buck stifled a groan as he set the coffee and donuts on the edge of the desk. "Harrigan, right. Sorry, it slipped my mind."

"No problem, sir." He was in his early fifties, not more than ten or fifteen pounds overweight, dark hair in the regulation crew cut. His handshake was firm, his gaze steady. "I was just familiarizing myself with some of your open cases, if that's all right."

Buck glanced around the tiny, cluttered office. "We need to find you a desk somewhere."

"Already requisitioned, Major," he said. "I think somebody said they were getting one from the old school warehouse building, and they're sending over a computer and some office supplies. It shouldn't take long." He glanced around the room with a pleasant smile. "Not a lot of room for two grown men, but I expect we'll do okay. Meantime…" He pulled out the guest chair from the corner and set it up near the desk, across from Buck. "Where would you like me to start?"

"Look, Harrigan…" Buck sat in the chair the other man had recently vacated and closed the open file on the computer. It was, of course, the Beardsley case. "By the way, forget all that Major stuff. You can call me Buck. You want a donut?"

"No thanks, I'm good."

Buck was glad. He was starved. He picked up a donut and took a big bite. "Listen," he said gesturing him to sit down, "I didn't get a chance to go over your personnel file. Maybe you can give me the short version."

"Twenty-five years with the Charlotte-Mecklenburg Police Department," Harrigan said, sitting comfortably in the guest chair, "the last fifteen in the investigative division-- financial crimes, gang violence, homicide, in that order."

Buck lifted an eyebrow, impressed. "Interesting resume. Those three units don't sound like they have much in common."

He just smiled. "You'd be surprised."

Buck reached for the next donut. "So, what in God's name brought you here?"

"Retirement," he admitted. "We built a cabin out on one of the lakes, and I thought I'd spend my days fishing and working on my boat. That was fun for about eighteen months." He shrugged. "I missed the routine, and small-town policing is something I always thought I'd like to do. Signing on as a part-time deputy here seemed like the perfect opportunity."

Buck said, "Well, I can see why Marshall thought you were wasted on the road. But I've got to be honest with you…"

Buck's desk phone rang, and he raised a finger to excuse himself while he answered the call. He listened for a moment, then said, "Okay, get him ready. I'm on my way down."

Buck picked up his coffee cup and stood as he told Harrigan, "Well, nothing like jumping in with both feet. We've got a suspect in custody, and he wants to talk. Let's go."

The Hanover County Public Safety building housed the sheriff's office, the dispatch center, the prosecutor's office—which included the county's chief investigator, Buck Lawson—and the detention center. It was less than a six-minute walk across the corridor, down the stairs through the security checkpoints, and into the interview room where Carter Frank waited. While they walked Buck brought Harrigan up to speed on the case, realizing he probably wasn't telling the other man anything he didn't already know from reading the case file.

"Has Carter had any visitors since I talked to him yesterday?" Buck asked the guard who escorted them to the interview room.

"His wife," the guard replied. "And his lawyer came by after supper. It was past visiting hours, but you know we have to let them see their lawyers if they get here between 6:00 AM and 11:00 PM."

Buck said, "Who was it? David or Henry?" There were only two criminal lawyers in town, a father-son team whose caseload consisted mostly of DUIs and Failure to Appears.

"Neither one," replied the guard. "Some fellow from out of town, I figure the wife must've brought him in. I can look up his name in the log if you want."

"That's okay," Buck said, "I was just curious."

They entered the small interview room where Carter sat with his hands handcuffed to the metal table, looking shrunken and worn after a night in a jail cell. He looked up when Buck came in but there was nothing but despair in his eyes.

"Carter," Buck said, "this is Investigator Harrigan. He'll be working with me for a while. I understand you wanted to talk to me."

Carter nodded and cleared his throat. He had never seen a man look more defeated, and he couldn't help feeling a little sorry for him.

Buck walked over to the camera and turned it on. "Okay,

you understand we're recording this?"

"Yes."

"Are we waiting for your lawyer?"

"No." His eyes darted around the room uneasily as Buck and Harrigan pulled out chairs and sat down. "No, it's okay. I want... I want to confess."

Buck was too well trained to give away his surprise, and so was Harrigan. Buck made an absent note on the legal pad in front of him, and said, "Are you sure you don't want to wait for your lawyer?"

"I'm sure."

"All right, then, go ahead."

He twisted his cuffed hands together so tightly the knuckles were white. "Smokey owed me money, a lot. Over $10,000. He'd been putting me off for weeks. When I came by to collect on Friday, like I told you, somebody was there. I went around back and looked through the window. I saw this man count out rolls of money and put it on the coffee table. That was when I got the idea to block the vent—I was standing right by it—just long enough to make Smokey fall asleep, then I could go in there and get what was mine. So, I got a rag from the workshop and stuffed it in the vent. I remembered that article the health department puts in the paper every year about carbon monoxide poisoning, how it takes a couple of hours for you to feel sick, but almost six hours for it to kill you. I knew where he stashed his money—under the floorboard in the bedroom closet—so I figured I'd come back in an hour or two, get my money, and unblock the vent and open some windows. I'd even planned how I would call 911 if he didn't come around and pretend I'd found him like that. Only... when I got back an hour later, he was already dead. I didn't know what to do, Buck." He looked at Buck with desperate eyes. "It was an accident, you see that, don't you? I never meant to kill him! So, I went home and the next day started my route as usual, but I couldn't leave him like that, I just couldn't. So, when I got to his house, I slapped a label on the nearest package I saw, just like you said, and pretended to go to the house to deliver it, and then I called you guys." He dropped his head onto the table, atop his folded arms. "I never meant it to happen like this. It all went wrong, just so wrong."

Buck exchanged a look with Harrigan. He said, "What happened to the money, Carter?"

Carter straightened up, his expression bleak. "I don't know. I didn't even look. Once I saw Smokey was dead... I didn't even look."

Harrigan said, "How much money would you say you saw that other fellow put on the coffee table?"

Carter shook his head. "Usually the rolls were hundreds, amounting to ten thousand each. I saw five, six, before I stopped looking."

Buck said, "Can you describe this guy, the one you saw with Smokey?"

Carter said shakily, "Tall, well groomed. Salt and pepper hair. One of those overcoats that you see in the magazines, dark wool, hit below the thighs. I never saw his face. But I figured he was that guy I was telling you about, that Deacon, just because he looked expensive. And I didn't want to cross him."

Buck felt Harrigan stiffen beside him, and he cast him a curious look. The other man's face remained expressionless.

Buck said, "Who was the lawyer who came to see you last night? He wasn't local, was he?"

Carter shook his head. "It was a name I got from Smokey a long time ago when this all started. He said we didn't ever have to worry about getting in trouble because this guy could fix anything. Said he had our backs. I kept his name and number on a sticky note in the back of my desk at home. Leonard Albright out of Asheville. I told Kathy to call him. He said if I told the truth about what happened it would only be second-degree murder and he could probably get me off with time served. So that's what I'm doing. I'm telling the truth."

Buck and Harrigan exchanged a longer look this time.

Buck said carefully, "I think he also probably told you not to talk to us unless he was here."

"Maybe," Carter gulped. "Yeah, okay, but what difference does it make? The truth is the truth, and this is killing Kathy. I need to get out of here."

Harrigan said somberly, "Mr. Frank, right now I think jail is the safest place for you to be."

Buck took a breath but did not disagree. He said, "Okay, Carter, let's go over this one more time. Be real specific about the timeline. You got there on Friday when?"

Two hours later Buck walked with Harrigan back to his office. "I've got a feeling that out-of-town lawyer didn't mean for Carter to tell *that* much of the truth."

Harrigan agreed, "Yeah, well, most perps will hang themselves if you give them enough rope. It's no more than he deserves."

Buck remembered sitting on the green flowered sofa, watching Carter Frank's wife nervously twist her new ring around her finger. He said carefully, "You know, Harrigan, things here in Hansonville are handled a might different than they probably were in a big city like Charlotte. Carter Frank has lived in this county all his life. His wife teaches Sunday School. His mama and mine were in the Women's Club together. Most of the time the people we deal with are good folks who just made a mistake. I've found things always work out better if you treat the people inside the jail with the same respect you give them on the outside."

Harrigan acknowledged, "I guess you're right. It'll take a while to get over the big city thinking."

They were silent for a while, then Harrigan said, "Y'all found how much money at the scene? Ten thousand?"

Buck nodded. "And, if Carter was right, there was at least fifty or sixty thousand on the table when he left."

"He was pretty clear about only being gone an hour after

he blocked the vent."

"I'll have to look at the report again," Buck said, "but the EMTs seemed fairly sure the CO2 was at a level it would have taken eight or ten hours to kill him. Not one."

"You don't do autopsies here?"

Buck shook his head. "It'll take a couple of days to get the report back from Asheville. But it'll be interesting to see what it says."

When they reached the office they noticed a new desk, chair and laptop had been squeezed into the corner adjacent to Buck's desk, but neither man did more than glance at it. Buck said, "I need to talk to Dan about this. He's the county prosecutor, have you met him?"

Instead of answering, Harrigan said, "Before you do that, you should know a couple of things. That name, Deacon, it's the street moniker for a guy called Dimitri Petrova. He made a name for himself, so to speak, as The Decontamination Man—D-Con, get it?—for the higher-ups in the organization. He took care of snitches, cheats, the little guys who tried to take more than their share, that kind of thing."

"Ah, come on." Buck sat down slowly, staring at him. "You don't mean to tell me it really *is* the Russian mob?"

Harrigan, not getting the reference, shook his head absently. "More likely, the Dixie Mafia or one of the other syndicates that've popped up over the past couple of decades. I'm not sure his exact association was ever nailed down, at least while I was involved. All I can tell you is that this Deacon person came to my attention when I was working financial crimes. By then he'd moved up in the organization to money laundering—buying flea market junk and selling it online through legitimate vendors for outrageous prices. A twenty-five-cent used paperback book going for $8000, a $2.00 VHS tape selling for 15K... pretty hard to prosecute, since people are allowed to be as stupid as they want with their money in this country. Anyhow, I know he was the target of a couple of federal investigations, and they even took him in once or twice, which is my point."

"His fingerprints are on file," Buck said softly.

Harrigan nodded. "So, if that *was* him at the scene, and now that you've got a reason to look for a match..." He shrugged. "You might not be able to get him for murder, but you've sure got enough to get a search warrant, and if you don't find a whole lot of evidence indicating bank fraud, racketeering and identity theft, well, sir, my badge is yours."

"Wouldn't take it if I could," Buck replied, already dialing the phone. "Harrigan, you've earned yourself a donut. Take a break. And..." He glanced up as the line on the other end began to ring. "Welcome aboard."

CHAPTER
TWENTY-TWO

It was just after 11:00 when I left town, so I picked up a bucket of fried chicken and headed out to Maude's house. I was early, so I was surprised to see Casey's van already there. The barn was open, and as I parked, I saw him come cautiously to the door, his arm held at an odd angle behind his back. When I got out of the car, he waved and disposed of whatever it was he held behind his back, coming forward.

"Casey," I said, puzzled, "was that a gun you were hiding?"

He gave an embarrassed shrug and a little smile. "Not hiding," he said, "I just didn't want to freak you out. I travel through some pretty rough places out west, and it's a habit."

I said, in my best imitation of a good-old-boy drawl, "This is North Carolina, son. It's gonna take more than a concealed weapon to freak me out."

He chuckled. "I guess that's right."

I handed him the take-out bag and the aroma of crispy fried chicken wafted out into the cold air. "I brought lunch. Let's eat before it gets cold. How did you get the barn open? Miles said it was locked."

"Nah, it just looked like it. I thought I'd start cleaning it out while I waited for you."

I opened the side door and unbuckled Cisco, who

scrambled past me and raced toward Casey, tail swishing madly.

"Hey, big fellow." Casey bent to greet him, carefully holding the bag of take-out food out of reach. As he squatted down to pet Cisco, laughingly ducking both his sloppy kisses and the inquiring nose that sought out the chicken, I saw the holster clipped to the back of his jeans, and the grip of the gun stowed neatly inside it. "Did you miss me? I sure missed you."

"Cisco," I commanded, slapping my thigh. I don't like my dogs to display overly affectionate greetings, especially when there's food involved. "Get over here."

"Ah, he's fine," Casey said, giving Cisco's ears a final good rub before standing. Cisco, apparently acknowledging the fact that he was not about to be the happy recipient of a piece of falling fried chicken, came over to watch as I opened the back of my SUV and opened Rags's crate.

"Who do we have here?" Casey asked.

Rags bounded to the ground with puppy-like enthusiasm, and I tightened his leash before he, too, could lunge toward the fried chicken. The two dogs greeted each other with sniffs and wags, but immediately returned their hopeful attention to the man with the food.

"This is Maude's dog," I said. "One of her last puppies. I thought you'd like to meet him. His name is Rags."

He looked at me with mild surprise. "Is that right? One of her dogs, huh?" He extended a hand to Rags, who happily licked it. "The name sure suits him. He is a funny-looking thing." He clucked Rags under the chin, grinning. "Hey, bud. Are you going to grow up to be a good dog like my man Cisco, here? Because you're off to a real good start."

I say you can always tell a person's character by the way he talks to dogs. No wonder I liked Casey. Of course, liking someone and trusting him are two different things. You'd think a man as smart as Miles would know that.

"Say," Casey said as he straightened up, "you should teach this guy to count. Then he can go on the road with the Cisco the

Reading Dog."

I grinned at him. He totally got me. "That's a good idea," I told him. "Maybe I will."

"And don't forget you promised to show me that reading trick."

I kept that promise then and there, transferring Rags's leash to Casey while I scrambled for paper and a bold marker from my car. Casey laughed out loud with delight as Cisco demonstrated his remarkable ability to read "sit," "down," "paw" and—his newest accomplishment— "up," in which he stood on his hind legs.

"You guys are going to wow the crowd," Casey assured me, returning Cisco's leash. "It must be fun to be you."

"Most of the time," I agreed. Then, as we started toward the house, "What did you find in the barn?"

"I didn't get very far. A bunch of boxes you might want to go through, some wire fencing and folding gates, some other stuff that looked like it might have to do with dog training."

"I'll look at it," I said, although I wasn't particularly looking forward to that—going through Maude's things, remembering how she used to be, how much she taught me. Just remembering.

I unlocked the door with frozen fingers, and we went inside, where it wasn't much warmer than it was outside. Casey got a fire going with the wood he and Miles had brought in yesterday, and I went back out to the car to get Rags's crate. By that time the food was ice cold, but Casey reheated it in a camp skillet, which filled the house with mouthwatering aromas and—in my opinion, at least—made the chicken taste twice as good.

"The power will be on tomorrow afternoon," I said, doling out paper napkins and plastic forks, "so maybe this will be the last time you have to cook over an open fire."

"I don't know," he said, "I kind of prefer it."

"Yeah, me, too." I grinned as I plucked a piece of fried chicken from the skillet with my fingers and dropped it on a paper plate. Cisco, lying obediently a few feet away, watched me avidly while Rags, who thankfully hadn't yet learned the fine art of separating humans from their lunches, noisily chewed a bone in his crate.

Casey glanced around the room. "So, what happened to the last tenant?"

I shrugged. "Don't know. The guy who was managing the place said he just up and left. I guess they do that sometimes."

"How long has the place been empty?"

"A few months, maybe. At least since December. Mr. Comstock—that's the rental guy—said he had the furniture hauled off, but there wasn't much. Too bad. You could've used some of it if you're going to stay here."

"That's okay. I've got everything set up in my van. I'll just park it here and sleep there, if that's okay. But it'll be nice to have a real bathroom, and if that microwave in the kitchen works, I can warm up a pizza now and then." He took a bite out of a chicken leg and glanced around again. "So, what did he do with the stuff that was here? Put it storage in case the guy comes back?"

I shook my head. "Apparently, if you skip out on your rent, the landlord takes possession of whatever you leave behind. I think Mr. Comstock said he donated it to the women's shelter."

Casey nodded and took another bite. "There probably wasn't anything much of value. No computers or televisions or anything."

"I think he said there was a television. But..." I shrugged apologetically. "No cable or internet. I didn't think about it."

"That's okay. I'm not much for television, and I've got my phone."

We sat on the hearth and concentrated on our food for a minute, pausing only to comment on how good it was or how we might have discovered the secret to an even more successful fried-chicken franchise. Then Casey paused to sip from his Coke cup and said, "I almost didn't come today."

I wiped my fingers on a napkin. "How come?"

He lowered his gaze briefly. "Your ex came to see me this morning," he admitted.

"Damn it," I said. I put my plate aside, my appetite abruptly gone. "I told him to leave you alone."

"He wasn't an ass or anything," Casey assured me. "It was more of a welcome-to-the-neighborhood-and-I'll-be-watching-you kind of thing. Something about a case he was working. But it just seems like, I don't know, I'm making everything more complicated for you, upsetting a lot of people, and maybe I should just move on."

I picked a piece of crust off the remnants of a chicken breast, then dropped it back to my plate. "So why did you change your mind?"

"I don't know, really. It seemed important to you to get the DNA test, and I told you I would. I didn't want you to think I'd skipped out or had something to hide. Also…" He looked at me with those clear blue eyes. "Hell, I guess I want to know too. For sure. I mean, it's not that it makes any difference, with both of them being dead. It's not like I could talk to them, or ask them questions, or any of the things I always imagined I'd do if I found my birth parents. But I think there's something inside everybody that needs to know where they came from, who they're part of. It helps you know who *you* are, you know? Or at least who you're supposed to be." He shrugged self-consciously. "Maybe it's something you can't understand unless you've never known who your parents are."

"Yeah, I guess I get that." I absently pushed coleslaw around on my plate with the back of my fork. "The name Stockton is a pretty big deal around here," I said. "I guess in a way I've kind of taken it for granted, and in another I think I grew up knowing it was something special. The Stocktons were one of the first settlers of Hanover County, and they owned a lot of land around here. I'm not saying they were all upstanding citizens. I mean, we had our share of swindlers and horse thieves and even a killer or two, according to legend. But there were a few war heroes, too, community leaders, church builders, that sort of thing. You open any history book about this area, and you'll see the name Stockton a couple of dozen times. And I'm the last one. The name dies with me. It's weird to think about."

I shrugged self-consciously. "The thing is, my dad—he was one of the most respected men in the county, maybe in this part of the state, or at least it seemed that way to me, growing up. I worshipped him. I mean, all my life people would look at me and see Judge Stockton's daughter, and that meant something. And then a few years ago, long after my dad died, it came out that he had destroyed evidence and betrayed his oath in order to conceal that he was with Maude on a night when he was supposed to be somewhere else. It was... shattering. It made everything I thought I knew about my father seem like a lie. Maybe even everything I thought I knew about myself. But now..." I looked at him uncertainly. "If something good can come out of this mess, if I'm not the last Stockton after all... well, I just want to know. For sure."

He nodded thoughtfully, silent for a while. Then he said, "It must have been something, growing up like that, in a place like this. Where everybody knows you, and you know everybody. All those roots."

"Yeah," I admitted, "it was."

"You'll always have that."

I smiled. "Yeah."

He dropped his gaze again. "Raine," he said quietly, "I need to tell you something." He looked at me. "All that stuff I told you yesterday... well, I might have exaggerated a little about how great my life was. My dad's business started going downhill when I was six or seven, we lost our house, he started drinking. My mom was working two jobs, I started hanging out with the wrong crowd, ended up doing time in juvie for being in a stolen car where drugs were found. I made a lot of bad choices after that and ended up on the street for a while." He looked at me steadily. "I never went to college. I never helped run a contracting business. I wasn't a counselor at that equine camp; I was a student. Most of my social media posts —photoshopped to make me look normal to any clients or employers that might want to look me up. By the time my dad drank himself to death there was nothing left of his business, and my mom overdosed a few years later. That's when I found my birth certificate, stored away in her things, and decided to try to find my birth mom. I don't know why. Maybe to *ask* her why, who knows? Anyway, when I finally called Maude, I was pretty rough on her, blaming her for stuff that wasn't her fault. So, if you're wondering why she never tried to keep up the connection, that's why. I came here to apologize. And all that stuff I told you about my folks leaving me the business, it was total BS. Since my mother died, I've been living in my van, making ends meet doing odd jobs and signing on to construction crews when I can. I just thought you'd want to know what kind of person you might be related to."

I said, "Why did you lie?"

Cisco, with his eyes on the uneaten chicken, was belly-crawling his way toward us, paw by paw, inch by inch, while still making sure to technically maintain his down. Casey noticed him and smiled fleetingly. "Instinct, I guess. I've had this whole fantasy life going on in my head for so long, and then when you guys showed up and I realized who you were, it just seemed easier to tell the lie. You were driving a Lexus, for God's sake. Your fiancé's boots cost more than I make in six months doing handyman work. I didn't want you to think I was out to rip you off. So, I told you what I wished was true, instead of what was."

I lowered my gaze to my paper plate, which was a mess. I said, at length, "I stole a car once. Or at least, Buck and I did. It was my dad's Buick, and it broke down about 120 miles from home. All we could think to do was call Maude. She came and got us, had the car towed, and never, as far as I know, said a word to my dad. I guess she knew that our own guilt—and terror—was punishment enough, and she must've been right, because we both stayed on the straight and narrow from that day on. More or less. The point is, Casey, Maude was a good person. She would have been a good mom. I think if she had known what was going on with you... she would have come and brought you home."

Casey didn't say anything for a long moment, and then he abruptly swiped a hand across his face. I realized it was to hide tears. "Okay," he said gruffly. "Well. It's been nice to meet you Raine, and thanks for lunch. But I guess I'll get out of your hair now."

"Oh, shut up." I wadded up my paper plate and tossed it into the fire. Cisco looked at me in dismay as the aroma of crispy fried chicken bones filled the room. Casey's expression was more one of perplexity. "Can you run a power saw?" I demanded.

He said, "I can."

"Can you fix my roof?"

He started to smile. "Yeah, I can."

"Then let's get busy," I told him. "The building supply closes at 5:00 and you've got a lot of work to do."

DONNA BALL

PART TWO

CHAPTER TWENTY-THREE

The weeks between New Year's and Easter are so desolate around here that we will latch on to any reason to party, so Uncle Ro's birthday was always a big hit. Aunt Mart baked a ham with all the fixings and invited all the deputies who'd ever worked for Uncle Ro to drop by for a giant buffet with coffee and birthday cake afterwards. It was a big, raucous, joyous celebration with gag gifts and jokes—some not entirely suitable for mixed company--and stories about "the time when." I gave Uncle Ro a fleece-lined fishing vest, and Melanie gave him a cap with the slogan And fish fear me… embroidered on it. He wore it proudly the rest of the day. In keeping with the fishing theme, Miles gave him a fly-fishing reel that Uncle Ro couldn't stop admiring and showing off to everyone who came by. Yes, we'd done our shopping at the sporting goods store.

Marshall was there, and so was Buck. I couldn't help noticing that Jolene did not come, but I heard something about her being on duty. Of course, the big story of the day— this being a law enforcement crowd—was the way Buck had broken a major case. I picked up bits and pieces of it here and there between helping Aunt Mart in the kitchen and tossing the flying disk with Melanie and Majesty in the backyard and waiting, with growing impatience, to have a sharp word or two with Buck alone.

"The medical examiner's report didn't come in until Wednesday," Buck was telling Uncle Ro when I came into the living room with my slice of birthday cake, "and that was all we needed. Smokey died of asphyxiation, all right, but not from carbon monoxide. There was a ligature mark around Smokey's throat, fairly deeply embedded so Sam didn't notice it on his initial exam. Not his fault," Buck was quick to add. "Smokey was a big man with a thick beard and something like that wouldn't be obvious unless you were looking for it. The ME thinks it might've been done with a soft fabric, like a tie, maybe. But he was definitely strangled to death from behind."

I sat down on the arm of Uncle Ro's chair, and he patted my knee absently. He was used to me sitting in on these conversations; after all, I'd grown up around law enforcement. "So, you figure that fellow—what did you call him, Deacon?" Uncle Ro said. "You take him for the killer?"

Buck nodded. "His real name is Dimitri Petrova, and he's pretty high up in this crime syndicate. He's been in lockup a couple of times and always made the most of it, recruiting some of the guys with special talents to come work for him on the outside. He called them his Chain Gang, and the FBI has been trying to track them all down for years now. Anyhow, we found Petrova's fingerprints on more than one surface in the house, and we never did find the cash that Carter saw being laid out."

Buck paused to take a bite of his own birthday cake, and Marshall picked up the narrative. "So, the working theory is that Petrova, for whatever reason, was sent to dispose of Smokey and the cash was the bait. Carter Frank was just in the wrong place at the wrong time."

"Or maybe the right time," Buck put in, "since the carbon monoxide muddied the waters just enough that we might not have even looked at Petrova if it hadn't been for Harrigan recognizing the name."

I put in, "Who's Harrigan?"

Buck glanced at me. "A retired detective out of Charlotte. He's new to the force."

"And seems to be working out quite well," Marshall put in a little smugly, "if I do say so myself."

"So did you pick him up?" Uncle Ro asked. "This Deacon character."

"We didn't," Buck said. "But the police in Raleigh, where he's based, were awfully glad to have an excuse to go knocking on his door. Not to mention the Feds, who've been trying to break up this syndicate for years. Based on the evidence we provided, they executed a search warrant and seized all kinds of illegal money-making machines, card duplicators, and a whole slew of fake passports and driver's licenses. Last I heard Mr. Petrova was resting comfortably in the Wake County detention center." He grinned. "Say, Ro, tell Marshall what you told me about the Russian mob."

But I interrupted, "What will happen to Carter Frank?"

Buck glanced at me. "He'll do time. Maybe not for murder, and given how much help he's been on this case he might negotiate a reduced sentence, but he broke a half-dozen federal laws and he's going to go down for it."

"At any rate," Marshall said, looking pleased and proud as he picked up the coffee cup on the end table at his elbow, "this bust is going to look mighty good on your resume, Buck."

Buck seemed embarrassed by the praise. "In the first place, I didn't break the case, Harrigan did. In the second place, you know Petrova will probably be out inside a month. People like him usually are."

I forgot about the scathing remark I had been about to make to Buck about harassing Casey and said curiously, "Resume? Are you job hunting?" Since Marshall, his boss, had brought it up, I figured it was okay to ask.

"Not really," Buck said. Then, "Maybe." He turned to Ro. "Do you know anything about the law in a place called Mercy, Georgia?"

Uncle Ro grew thoughtful. "Sounds familiar. Yeah, if I recall, a man by the name of Aikens is chief down there. Seems like a decent enough fellow, good lawman..."

I gathered up the empty dessert plates and went back into the kitchen, where Aunt Mart was chatting with some of the officers' wives in the breakfast nook over coffee and cake. The buffet was set up in the dining room, and Melanie could be heard greeting some of the latecomers with, "Hello, I'm Melanie Young and I'm considering a career in law enforcement. What's the toughest case you ever had?"— just as she had been doing, off and on, all day. Fortunately, most of Uncle Ro's friends were family men or retired with grandchildren, so they found her more amusing than annoying and kept their stories on the tame side. Still, Miles didn't usually allow her to risk wearing out her welcome like that, and I looked around for him as I finished putting the dessert plates in the dishwasher.

Noticing this, Aunt Mart said, "Are you looking for Miles, honey? He had a phone call and took it out on the porch."

"Thanks, Aunt Mart."

Lettie Summers called from the table, "Raine Stockton, get over here and let me see that ring."

I was pleased and a little embarrassed to show off my engagement ring to the group gathered around the table. It was a gorgeous piece of jewelry, and I liked to tell the story about how Miles had had it custom made in Belgium, but even as they oohed and aahed and turned my hand this way and that, I couldn't help feeling like I was cow showing off her brand.

"So, when's the date, honey?" Bryn Rogers wanted to know.

I confessed that we hadn't exactly nailed one down yet, and Mary Walker looked appalled. "Raine, you'd better get busy." She turned an alarmed look on Aunt Mart. "Mart, something like this takes months and months—sometimes a year—to put together. Why, at the very least you should have sent out save-the-date cards by now. These A-list celebrities and such have to clear their schedules, and that's not so easy to do on short notice."

I almost choked at the thought. "Oh, we're not planning anything like that," I assured her hastily. "Just family."

A look of incredulity mixed with profound disappointment went around the table, and Aunt Mart put in quickly, "Well, of course we'll have a reception."

I stared at her. This was the first I was hearing of it.

"Rita and I have been talking," Aunt Mart explained. "We know you don't want anything showy, but really, Raine, a few friends, some cake and champagne? A small band?"

She and Miles's mother had become best friends over the past year or so, first on Facebook, then in real life. I shouldn't have been surprised they were up to something behind my back.

I managed a smile, wondering how much Miles knew about this. "Sounds lovely," I said. "Maybe you'll catch me up sometime. But now I've got to go find Melanie before she gets herself arrested for being a pest. Nice to see you all."

I left with a small wave, and almost made it to the dining room when I met Buck coming into the kitchen with his plate and coffee cup in hand. We stood awkwardly for a moment in a face-off, and then I took the dishes from him and turned to put them in the dishwasher. "Hey," he said, following me, "I didn't mean to cut you off a minute ago. It was just a little awkward, talking about looking for a new job in front of Marshall. He knows, but still. I just didn't want you to think I'd do something like leaving town without letting you know."

I closed the dishwasher and turned to look at him curiously. "You're not really thinking about Georgia, are you?"

He shrugged. "Probably not. I was hoping something would turn up on the coast—Wilmington, maybe, Nags Head, even Virginia Beach, but so far, no luck."

"Wow." I rested my hip against the sink and folded my arms across my chest. Buck had talked about leaving before and had even moved to Asheville for a couple of months a few years back, but nothing serious had ever come of it. I doubted this time would be different. "That's quite a leap."

"You know I've always liked the water," he said. "And I told you last year I was looking for a change."

He had, but he had been recovering from a traumatic injury at the time. I'm not entirely sure what I thought he'd meant by "change" but didn't think moving out of state was on the agenda. I still didn't.

"Yeah," I admitted, only half-teasing, "but I thought you meant joining a rock band or something."

He grinned and reached around me to take a soft mint from the bowl on the counter. "Still not off the table," he said and popped the mint into his mouth.

I frowned a little, remembering why I'd wanted to talk to him in the first place. "Listen, Buck, Casey told me you came to his motel room the other day and were harassing him about something or another. I hope you're not planning to make a habit of it, because he's going to be around a while and I already told you to leave him alone."

"I wasn't harassing him," Buck replied, annoyance showing in his eyes. "I was legitimately questioning him about this case."

"And?" I demanded.

"And you can relax." He took another mint from the bowl on the counter. "Automatic tag scanners picked up his vehicle in Mississippi when Smokey was killed so he's off the hook. Which doesn't mean," he added pointedly, "that he is who he says he is or that he's not guilty of something else. Are you still going through with the DNA test?"

The DNA test had been simpler to arrange than I'd thought. Miles got the test kit via overnight delivery, and we each ran a cotton swab over the inside of our cheeks and popped the swabs into separate test tubes. Miles watched the whole thing, although how he thought anyone might cheat on a DNA test is beyond me, then signed a form as a witness and sent the kit back to the lab. It would take two or three weeks to get the results back.

"Of course I am," I told Buck. "Why wouldn't I?"

Instead of answering, he said, "So where is he staying now?"

I saw no reason not to tell him; he'd find out anyway if he wanted to know. "His van is parked at Maude's house, and he's using the electricity and water there to cook and shower with while he works on the house. Is that okay with you?"

"No need to get hostile," he returned mildly. "I was just curious."

"You're never just curious," I replied, disgruntled.

We were getting some stern looks from Aunt Mart and some interested ones from the ladies at the table, so Buck made an obvious attempt to mollify me. "How's the house repair going?" he asked. "Have you decided what you're going to do with it yet?'

"No, not yet," I told him, rearranging my features into something resembling a pleasant birthday-party demeanor. "But the work is coming along nicely. Casey already patched the leak in the roof and replaced the front gutter. He does good work, even Miles says so. He wants to replace the kitchen sink and put in ceiling fans, but I think it's a waste of money."

The back door opened, and I turned to see Miles, his face and hands raw with cold, tucking his phone into his back pocket. He hadn't put on his coat before he went out, naturally. He came toward us, rubbing his hands together to warm them, his expression grim.

Buck said, "I've got to get going. See you later, Raine." He wasn't that wild about Miles and avoided him whenever he could, which was fine with me. Interestingly enough, Miles's opinion of Buck was completely neutral.

Buck started to leave but stopped and looked back with interest when Miles said, "That was Ron Diaz, the guy I hired to look into Casey McIntosh's background."

I could tell by the expression on his face that the news

wasn't good, and I braced myself for it. "And?"

"And nothing," Miles said.

Buck came back over to us. "What do you mean, nothing?"

"I mean there's no information about this guy anywhere beyond what you can find on Facebook," Miles said, "and nothing going back any further than five years."

"Well, that's good, isn't it?" I said, relieved. "Weren't you trying to find out if he had a criminal record or anything?"

"Everybody has a digital footprint, Raine," Buck said, frowning. "You sign a lease or buy a car or apply for a credit card, you graduate high school or go to the doctor... anything that can be traced back to your social security number leaves a trail."

"Unless," Miles said, unsmiling, "you hire somebody to deliberately erase that trail. And my guy said it looked like Casey McIntosh had been professionally scrubbed prior to five years ago."

I stared at him. "Why would anyone do that?"

Miles replied with the obvious. "Because he has something to hide?"

Buck said thoughtfully, "The more important question is *how* anybody would do that." He looked at Miles. "Something like that is expensive, right?"

"For a job good enough to block out somebody like Ron Diaz," Miles said, "you're looking at upwards of fifty grand."

I would very much like to know how he knew that, but now was not the time. I turned on Buck. "It's not illegal to erase your own personal online history, is it?" I demanded.

"No," he admitted. "What might be illegal is how you did it, and why." He glanced at Miles. "Let me put out a few feelers. I might be able to get further than you did through law enforcement."

"Oh, for heaven's sake, Buck," I exclaimed, "he hasn't broken any laws! Can't you leave the poor guy alone?"

"No," Buck replied simply. "I can't."

He went over to say goodbye to Aunt Mart and to get his

coat, and Miles and I were left looking at each other. "Raine," Miles said, "you've got to admit…"

"It's suspicious," I agreed glumly. But what I didn't want to admit, at least not to Miles, was that it was also infuriating.

CHAPTER TWENTY-FOUR

I banged on the window of Casey's van with both fists, shouting his name. Cisco, eager to do his part, put his paws on the van window and barked. When there was no answer, I cupped my hands around my eyes and peered in. Finding it empty, I spun around and marched to the house.

After the party, I'd had Miles drop me off at my house, telling him I planned to make a sandwich from the leftover ham Aunt Mart sent home and get a head start on my spring training class schedule. I'd see him in the morning. He looked at me sternly, not believing a word of it. "Don't make me follow you," he said.

"All right," I returned impatiently, "I'm going to talk to Casey. I want to hear his side of it, don't you? I'll be back before dark."

From the backseat, Melanie said plaintively, "Raine, hurry *up.* I've got to pee!"

Miles said, "Text me when you get there."

I said, "I'll text you before I leave."

He said, "If I don't hear from you before 7:00 I'm calling the sheriff."

Melanie said urgently, "Raine!"

I opened the car door. "She has to pee," I said.

"I have a tracker on your phone," he called after me as I got out.

"I know!" I returned a dismissing wave and ran toward the house through the cold.

Naturally, there was no way Cisco would let me leave again without him, so that's how we both ended up banging on Casey's van window. By this time, it was past 4:00, twilight in the mountains, but there were no lights on inside the house as I mounted the porch and pushed open the door. "Casey!" I shouted. "Where are you?"

Cisco galloped ahead of me, skidding on the wood floors, as I made my way through the shadowed house. "Casey!"

I heard a muffled reply, and when I turned on the kitchen light, I saw the attic stairs were down in the hallway. Cisco stood at the bottom of them, watching with interest as a pair of sneakered feet appeared in the opening, then a pair of legs. Cisco barked and stepped back in surprise as Casey descended from the attic. "Hey, buddy," he greeted Cisco. He skipped the last couple of steps and leapt to the floor, switching off the flashlight he held as he said, "What are you doing here? I thought you had a party today or something. There's a bunch of boxes of Christmas decorations and stuff up there. You want me to bring them down?"

I glared at him, hands on hips. "Who are you?" I demanded.

He looked baffled. "What?"

I swung out my foot and kicked him hard in the ankle. He yelped and staggered back, reaching to clutch his leg. "Damn it, Raine! What was that for? That hurt!"

I looked into his angry eyes and said, "You don't even exist before five years ago. You turn up here claiming to be Maude Braselton's son and then conveniently destroy the only evidence you have of that. There's no adoption record, no birth certificate, no credit application, no *nothing* about you online. So, who the hell are you? And what do you want?"

He straightened up from rubbing his bruised ankle,

staring at me accusingly. "You had me investigated?"

I felt like kicking him again. I probably would have, but Cisco had—accidentally or on purpose—placed himself between us. He looked from me to Casey with alert brown eyes as we faced each other down, obviously wondering who to defend.

"Do you know who my fiancé is?" I demanded.

He scowled at me. "You mean the dude with the Lexus?"

"Don't mess with me, Casey."

I took a menacing step forward and he put up his hand in self-defense. "All right, yeah, I know. He's some rich guy that builds resort hotels or something. Why?"

"Do you really think he'd let me hire you out of nowhere without checking you out?" I demanded. "How stupid can you be? And speaking of stupid, couldn't you have at least covered your tracks better? I told you I was married to a cop. Damn it, Casey, I stood up for you! I made excuses for you, I gave you a chance, and you played me for a fool! Why? Could you just tell me *why*?"

He glared back at me with churning eyes and compressed lips, and as we stood there in a face-off for a long moment, I felt a little chill tickle the back of my neck. I knew exactly where I'd seen that expression before. On my own face, in the mirror.

"Let me get this straight," he said coldly at length. "You're mad at me because your fancy-ass boyfriend had me investigated for no reason at all and he didn't find anything. Is that about right?"

"No," I spat back. "I'm mad because you're hiding something, and you won't tell me what it is. Don't you think I at least deserve the truth?"

He made an angry half turn and I thought he'd walk away, then he swung back. "I'm not hiding anything," he said shortly. "If your guy didn't find anything, it's because he was looking under the wrong name."

I stared at him. "What?"

"Casey Macintosh is not my real name," he said. Then he

pushed an aggravated hand through his curls and added, "I mean it is, but it's not the one I had all of my life."

I'm not sure what I was expecting, but that wasn't it. I said carefully, "What is it, then?"

He sighed. "Kevin Christopher Kinsey. K. C.," he repeated deliberately. "People have called me Casey all my life. Kinsey is the name I was adopted under and all my school records, everything, are under that. My mom divorced her first husband and when she remarried, she took his name. MacIntosh. So did I."

I said skeptically, "You can't just change your name without leaving a record of it. Not legally, anyway."

"It was legal, okay?" he replied irritably. "I don't know why your guy couldn't find any record of it. There are protections in place for adopted kids, maybe that has something to do with it. Maybe he's not as good as he thinks he is. Maybe there's a glitch in the system, I don't know and I don't care. I've told you what I know. You can go on wasting your boyfriend's money trying to prove me a liar if you want to, but I've got work to do. Unless..." His scowl sharpened. "Is that why you're here? Am I fired?"

I barely thought about it. "No," I said curtly. "If I fire you, you'll leave, and I'll never find out what's going on with you."

"Damn it, Raine, I told you..."

I threw up my hands. "Just shut up already. You're not fired."

He glared at me. "All right. Are you going to put in ceiling fans or not?"

"Yes," I told him, my tone just as a short as his.

"Good. You should be able to get them half-price at the hardware store this time of year. They'll keep last year's inventory in the back. And don't forget the light kits."

I took out my phone. "I'm texting Miles your real name," I told him and slanted him a dark, warning look. "And I'm copying Buck."

"I don't care what you do." Again, he swung away. "You want a beer?"

I looked at him warily, still not quite ready to be friends. My tone was grudging as I agreed, "Yes."

"And no more kicking," he told me resentfully, rubbing his foot. "I think you broke my ankle."

"Poor baby." I finished the text to Miles and followed Casey into the kitchen. I was quite sure he exaggerated a limp for my benefit.

Cisco bounced along between us, tail waving happily, having deduced by the fact that we were no longer shooting daggers at each other with our eyes that everything was probably going to be fine, after all. He followed Casey to the refrigerator and poked his nose in when Casey opened it. I saw a six pack of beer, some take-out Chinese food containers, and a bottle of milk. Cisco saw something much more important.

"I picked up one of those market bones when I was at the grocery today," Casey said, and pulled it out. "Okay if he has it?"

Cisco sank to a sit and eyed the bone worshipfully. I was a harder sell, or at least I tried to be. I don't usually allow my dogs to have those grocery store baked bones; in the first place, the fat content is too high, and in the second place who knows how well they are really sterilized? But watching the drool puddle on the floor from Cisco's jaws and seeing the look in his eyes, I had to relent. Whoever and whatever Casey Kinsey Macintosh was, he definitely knew the way to my heart.

"It's a little close to his supper," I conceded reluctantly, "but okay."

Casey stripped off the plastic wrapping and gave the bone to Cisco, who made us both grin when he did a little spin of joy before taking the bone to the corner by the back door to chew. Casey took a couple of beers from the refrigerator and brought one over to me. He had placed a piece of plywood between two sawhorses which apparently served as both his workspace and a dining table; I pulled up the only available chair—a lawn chair scavenged from the barn—and sat down with the beer on the makeshift table before me. Casey upended a cooler and sat on it across from me.

He said, "I guess if we'd grown up together, we would've killed each other by now."

"If our parents didn't do it first," I said, which wasn't as funny as I thought it would be. "I have a little bit of a temper," I admitted.

He gave me a sour look. "You think?"

"You're no cream puff," I shot back.

He opened the beer and took a sip. "Yeah, well," he said. "Something we have in common."

I twisted the cap off my beer and spent a moment or two wiping moisture off the rim. "So, what were you doing up in the attic?" I said, lacking anything better to say.

"Checking the wiring for the ceiling fans," he replied. "I knew you'd cave."

I scowled at him. "I did not cave. I changed my mind."

He shrugged and drank from the bottle again. "Anyway, it's not going to be a problem. The junction boxes are where we need them, and you've got plenty of structural support."

We were making small talk and both of us knew it. I took a sip of the beer and put the bottle down on the plywood table, turning it around in small circles just for something to do. In a moment I said, without looking up, "Miles's little girl was kidnapped a few years back. It was okay," I added hastily, glancing at him. "She was only gone a few hours and she wasn't hurt. But not long after that, her mother was killed. Murdered, actually."

Casey let out a slow breath. "Jesus," he said softly. "That poor kid."

I nodded, picking at the label on the beer bottle with my fingernails. "So, you see Miles has good reason to be careful about strangers. It's not personal. It's just smart."

Casey nodded and lifted the beer bottle again. "Okay," he said. "I get that."

I said, "There's something else. I told you about my father destroying evidence to hide his affair with Maude. What I didn't mention is that the guy he sent to prison in order to hide his adultery–a real scumbag, so don't waste your time feeling sorry for him—anyway, this guy spent his whole time on the inside plotting revenge. When he got out, my father was dead, so he turned his anger on me. He walked into a dog show with an assault rifle at a fairground where Cisco and I were competing and started shooting up the place. He would have killed me if Miles hadn't pushed me out of the way, and he almost killed Cisco. And Miles."

Casey paused in the process of lowering the beer bottle, staring at me. "Christ," he said. "And I thought I had problems."

I managed a faint, fleeting and completely unconvincing smile. "Melanie and I were also held hostage at camp one time by a group of terrorists," I said. "One of them later tried to shoot me and"—I pushed back my hair to show him the scar where the bullet had grazed my forehead—"didn't quite miss." I swallowed hard. "The point is, Miles is the bravest man I know, just for having me in his life. So, if he wants to vet the people I come into contact with, or his daughter does, I'm one hundred percent behind that. And..." I met Casey's eyes and held them steadily. "You'd better come back clean, because if you don't, I'm one hundred percent behind whatever he wants to do to you. And you don't want either one of us for an enemy, Casey. You really don't."

He held my gaze, then he inclined his head once in acknowledgement. "Got it," he said.

"Also," I said, taking a long draw from my beer. "I really hate it when Miles is right. So don't make me have to apologize to him."

We drank our beers without speaking for a time, the only sound that of Cisco's enthusiastic crunching of the bone in the corner. Then Casey said quietly, "I've got some things in my past I'm not proud of. Things I'd rather not talk about, if it's okay with you. But you said my mother was a good person, and I'd like to think there's a little bit of her in me. So, I want you to know..." He looked at me with a gaze so steady it almost hurt to hold it. "I would never, ever do anything to bring harm to you, or that little girl, or even to the big guy over there." He tilted his head in Cisco's direction, and Cisco looked up briefly from his bone, panting happily. "This I swear to you on my mother's grave."

I nodded slowly. "I believe you," I said. And I did—at least about that.

He took another sip of his beer, watching me thoughtfully. "You know, Raine, I don't know whether to hope you do turn out to be my sister, or to pray to God you don't."

I said, "I feel the same way about you."

Our eyes met, and we smiled, both of us reluctantly. We leaned forward in unison and clinked our beer bottles together, then drank the toast and finished our beers in companionable silence.

CHAPTER TWENTY-FIVE

Miles took me skiing in Vermont for Valentine's Day weekend. I'm not entirely sure why he felt we had to go to Vermont when there are perfectly good slopes here in North Carolina, but I have to admit it was heaven. We had an amazing chalet with a hot tub on the deck and one of those roomy outdoor sofas that curved around a gas fire pit where we cuddled together beneath a cashmere blanket and counted stars. I came home with a winter tan and aching knees, because I have to admit it had been a while since I'd skied.

I heard Buck took Jolene to the beach. But of course, I didn't hear it from him.

Rita came down to stay with Melanie, and Corny moved into the house with my dogs, who—just like anyone else—much prefer to sleep in their own beds. We were only gone three days, but I was glad to be back. Naturally, I missed my dogs and I hated to break the routine of Rags's training, which is so crucial at this stage, but I trusted Corny implicitly and knew he'd do a better job with Rags than I probably would have. My real concern was leaving Casey. I texted him surreptitiously once or twice just to make sure he was still around, which he was. It was too wet to paint the front steps, but the building supply had delivered the new windows, he reported. I really didn't see how anything could go wrong in three days, but it was Miles who worried me. He hadn't mentioned Casey once, and silence, with Miles, is never a good thing.

Miles had long ago made a vow never to lie to me, which is not as virtuous as it sounds. If I ask a question whose answer he knows I won't like, he simply changes the subject. If there is something he thinks I'm better off not knowing, he doesn't bring it up. The whole thing was infuriating more often than not. The fact that he studiously avoided the subject of Casey meant only that he was up to something, and that made me very nervous.

But, like I said, it was great to be home. Melanie, in anticipation of our arrival, had brought my three canines and Rags up to the "big house" (as I was coming to think of it), and Miles and I were greeted with a stampede of thundering paws and wagging tails when we came through the back door. Aunt Mart, Melanie and Rita were all gathered at the kitchen table with pictures, magazines and open laptops taking up most of the surface, and the next few minutes were a chaotic conglomerate of human hugs and doggie kisses, delighted greetings and "welcome homes." When Rita hugged me, she whispered, "Thank you, thank you, thank you!" and I had to grin because I knew she was referring to Miles's decision on the modular house. Aunt Mart exclaimed, "Raine, you look gorgeous! Is that a spray tan?" and Melanie tried to tell us everything that had happened in the last three days in one long sentence that ended with a breathless, "So what did you bring me?"

Miles, who had sent all three of them roses for Valentine's Day—and my aunt couldn't stop gushing about that—now passed out boxes of chocolates from the gourmet shop in the little village in which we'd stayed. Naturally, I'd picked up a few gourmet dog biscuits as well, and shared them with all four good dogs and one intractable puppy, Rags, who really was desperately trying to behave. When all the treats were distributed and tricks performed, I could tell the sheer magnitude of canine presence in the kitchen was starting to get on both of the older ladies' nerves, so I suggested Melanie take Rags and the Aussies up the stairs to the playroom. Pepper apparently decided the playroom was the place to be and raced after them, but Cisco knew very well whose hand his treats came from and stayed with me.

Some people might think I play favorites with my dogs, but it's really not true. Everyone has his or her own role in my family, including special talents and preferences. The two girls excel at outdoor sports and most often prefer each other's company over any else's. If there is an agility trial or an obedience match, they definitely get preferential treatment. Cisco is my Number One Guy all the rest of the time, and he knows it. As for Rags... well, I hadn't exactly determined what his talents were yet, but I was still sure he'd make someone a wonderful dog.

Only when the dogs were settled did I take time to remove my coat. "Something smells wonderful," I remarked as I returned from hanging my coat on the rack in the mudroom.

"Chicken divan in the Crock Pot," Rita replied. "Of course, it won't compare to the kind of gourmet meals you've been having, if I know my son."

I returned a dismissing wave of my hand. "Oh, please. If I never see another truffle, it'll be too soon." But I winked at Miles as I said it because—little known fact—it turns out I actually love truffles. Caviar, too. And to think, I never would have known that if I hadn't met Miles.

"I'm making Death by Chocolate for dessert," Melanie pronounced, clattering back down the stairs. "It's a welcome-home present."

I grinned and gave her a one-shouldered hug. "Thank goodness. I was worried I might have to go without dessert tonight." I glanced at all the pictures spread out over the table. "What's all this?"

"We're planning your wedding," Melanie said. "I think you should wear a white dress, but Aunt Mart says you don't want to. How come, Raine?"

"White dresses are for first weddings," I replied absently, turning a magazine photo of a gorgeous peach and white bouquet of roses toward me. "I've been married before. I already had my white dress."

"You can wear a white dress when you get married, Mellie," Rita assured her.

"Oh, I'm not getting married," Melanie replied airily. "I don't believe in marriage. It's like putting a collar on a dog."

My dismayed gaze flew to Miles, who returned my look wryly. We both knew there was only one place Melanie could have picked up that sentiment.

The silence that followed was uncomfortable, and my aunt tried to break it with a bright, "We were just having fun, Raine. There's no point in planning anything until you set a date, is there?"

I probably should have mentioned that, in the midst of all the romantic Valentine's Day splendor, there had been one small incident that was less than a perfect memory. On our last night at the chalet, as we were curled in each other's arm beneath the cashmere blanket, watching the fire pit and the snow that fell in dizzying sheets through the velvet night beyond our deck, Miles said gently, "You don't want to get married, do you, sugar?"

I twisted in his arms to look at him, alarmed. "What makes you say that?"

He responded dryly, "Aside from the fact that I know you well enough to play you on Broadway…"

The image made me laugh, and I slapped his arm playfully. But his next words were serious.

"You won't pick a date," he said. "You're not interested in looking at dresses or flowers. I know the girlie stuff is not your thing, but even your aunt is worried. If there's a problem, I'd just like to know, that's all."

I chose my next words carefully, turning to rest my head on his shoulder, fixing my gaze on the dancing flames. "I don't like being married," I admitted. "It's like putting a collar on a dog, or a brand on a cow. The whole thing just feels... I don't know, awkward to me. Not to mention that the only thing I know about marriage is that it usually ends in disaster. Look at my dad. Look at Buck. When I think about being married, I think about all the men who hurt me. Which is why..." I looked up at him, untangling my arm from the folds of the blanket to cup his face. "I could never marry anyone but you."

Looking at him now, I saw a man who sent roses to my aunt for Valentine's Day, who made sure his daughter knew no one would ever love her more than he did, who treasured his family so much all he wanted was to have them all under the same roof with him. A man who knew me well enough to play me on Broadway. How much luckier could one woman get? And why on earth was I hesitating?

"October 15," I blurted, and everyone stared at me. I took a deep breath and turned to Miles. "October 15," I told him firmly. "Save the date."

A slow smile curved his lips. "I'll be sure to do that," he said and brushed my lips lightly with a kiss. He squeezed my shoulder and added, "Right now I'm going to unpack and grab a shower." He glanced at his mother. "What do you need me to do for dinner, Mom? Wash the vegetables? Make the salad?"

She waved him away. "We've got hours yet, and it's all taken care of. But Mart..." She looked at my aunt, her mind clearly on more urgent matters. "Didn't you tell me the first frost is October 15? That wisteria we planned for the wedding arch is not going to make it through a frost. We could use silk, but I really don't like silk. You can always tell it's fake, I don't care how much you pay for it."

Aunt Mart was already searching through the pictures on the table. "We can always use ivy as a base," she said. "Ivy will stand up to anything. But the roses are definitely out."

Melanie rolled her eyes at me. "They've been like this

all day," she confided. "And they're completely forgetting the most important thing—the cake."

"We didn't forget the cake, sweetheart," Rita assured her. "But that decision is usually made by the bride."

That, I thought, trying not to feel overwhelmed, *would be me*.

Miles winked at me as he turned toward the door. "Have fun."

There was a certain smugness in his tone that suggested I would soon be lost in the world of ribbons and flowers, hors d'oeuvres and lace. That was all it took to ignite my competitive spirit.

I swung back to the two ladies—and Melanie—and declared firmly, "Orange."

At their surprised looks I expounded, "Orange cake with walnut date filling and lemon icing." I'd casually seen mention of it somewhere online and it sounded good. "And my colors are peach and chocolate. And yellow. I'm wearing a peach dress. Like this one..." I spun around the photograph I had glanced at earlier. "Only peach. Daisies on Pepper's collar and in Melanie's hair. Daisies on the wedding arch. How's that?" I will admit there was more than a touch of smugness in my own voice as I finished.

Rita and Aunt Mart looked at each other thoughtfully. "Glads," pronounced Aunt Mart decisively. "They come in the most luscious peach color..."

"Perfect!" Rita clapped her hands together. "And we can always use chrysanthemums to accent."

Melanie demanded, "What's Cisco going to wear?"

My phone buzzed in my pocket, and I gratefully wrestled it free. "His birthday suit," I replied, and Melanie giggled. Cisco, who had stretched out beneath the table, looked up at me with interest.

The text was from my friend Sonny. *In town and thought I'd drop by. Are you home?*

I practically sagged with relief. *Meet you at Dog Daze,*

I typed and stuffed the phone back into my pocket. "Sorry, ladies," I said, "I have to skip out. Sonny is back from Charleston, and I have her key." I turned to Melanie. "Tell your dad I went home to meet Miss Brightwell. Back in a jiff."

"Oh, cool," exclaimed Melanie. "Can I go? Ms. Brightwell has a service dog," she informed her grandmother. "He can do everything. Even pay with a credit card and dial a telephone! Also," she added with an air of deliberately casual superiority, "Ms. Brightwell can talk to animals."

Rita lifted her eyebrows, and I gave her a half-grin and a shrug that assured her I'd explain later. "It's starting to rain," I told Melanie, "and your dad will kill me if I let you go out in it. Besides, I need you to stay here and help your grandmother clean up all this stuff before supper."

"Oh dear," exclaimed Aunt Mart, "I didn't realize it was getting so late. I'd better run, too, before Ro has the sheriff's patrol out after me. Wait up, Raine, I'll give you a ride down the hill."

If you have ever tried to separate two female friends of a certain age who haven't seen each other in a while, you will appreciate my frustration as I urged for the third time, "Aunt Mart, I really have to go. Sonny is waiting."

Aunt Mart gave me a chastising look, the two women hugged goodbye for the second time and promised to have lunch tomorrow, Melanie pouted, and Aunt Mart huffed as she shrugged into her coat, "Really, Raine, I don't know why you young people have to be in such a hurry all the time." Then she hugged me and beamed, "I'm proud of you, sweetheart. And peach is a lovely color for fall!"

Rita called after me, "You'll be home for supper, Raine?"

I assured her I would and hurried out into the cold drizzle, where Cisco was already waiting by Aunt Mart's car. Honestly, it would have been faster to walk.

CHAPTER TWENTY-SIX

S onny was, in fact, waiting as I hugged Aunt Mart goodbye and thanked her for the ride. Cisco bounded out of the backseat and past Sonny's car, waiting with his paws on the gate until I hurried to open it for him. He raced up the walkway to Dog Daze, where Corny opened the door for him, and there was the predictable happy reunion. I had brought Corny a ski hat from Vermont knit in bright orange and yellow stripes with a red beagle worked into the fabric, and his response was, as always, over the top. He had to try it on, admire himself in the mirror, show it off to Sonny, and take a selfie for his social media.

All the while Sonny and her service dog, a yellow Lab named Hero, waited patiently in my office. Her border collie, Mystery, however, knew nothing of patience. The minute Cisco entered the building she sailed over the gate that separated my office from the reception area and flew down the hall, inviting Cisco to chase her, which he happily did. The two were old friends.

Sonny is an environmental lawyer who retired here from the coast to establish an animal sanctuary at the top of a very rugged mountain. There are goats and chickens, sheep and cats, racoons, possums, squirrels and deer, all with one handicap or another that prevents them from joining their own tribe in nature. Unfortunately, Sonny has a degenerative joint disease that occasionally keeps her confined to a wheelchair and makes it very dangerous to spend the winter in isolation at the top of a virtually inaccessible mountain. She therefore turns the operation over to her caretaker, Henry, and spends the worst part of the winter with her sister in Charleston. I am her emergency backup key holder, although, thank goodness, so far my services have not been required.

I apologized for keeping her waiting, and Sonny told me she'd been having a nice catch-up with Corny. She added somberly, "I'm so sorry about Maude, Raine. I've never known a woman more dedicated to dogs, except maybe you. I really liked her."

I smiled a little awkwardly. It was hard to know where to begin with the story that grew more convoluted each day. "She left me her house," I said.

"And a perfectly delightful young fellow named Rags." Corny came in, still wearing the colorful knit hat and bearing a tray with three mugs of tea and a plate of cookies that looked homemade—courtesy, no doubt, of Melanie and Rita. "He's a Labradoodle, we think," he added, setting the tray on a corner of my desk. "Still under six months old and very trainable. We're trying to find a permanent home for him."

He looked at Sonny hopefully and she laughed. "Sorry, my kennel is full. As"—she spoke just as Mystery rounded the corner and leapt effortlessly back over the gate and into the office again—"you can plainly see," she finished as Mystery skidded under the desk, pretending to hide from Cisco.

Cisco slammed into the gate, found it locked, and leapt up with his paws on the handrail, panting happily as he searched for Mystery. Hero, completely unmoved by this, barely glanced up from his resting position with his head on his paws at Sonny's side.

I told Cisco to get his paws off the gate and went to let him in. "No playing," I warned him sternly. He gave me a sheepish look and then wagged his way over to greet Sonny.

Sonny, of course, devoted her full attention to Cisco, rubbing his ears, scratching his chest, and murmuring things like, "Is that so, beautiful?" and "Well, I can just imagine!" and "Good for you!"

Melanie was right: Sonny *does* talk to dogs, and I admire that in a friend, as anyone will tell you. The issue is that Sonny thinks the dogs talk back. Of course, she claims this in only a half-serious manner, but some of the things she has been right about have sent chills down my spine. For example, she once claimed that Hero was trying to warn me to watch out for snakes. Mere days later, a man wearing snakeskin boots tried to burn down my kennel with me inside it. I'm just saying.

Corny, settling down in the chair across from us with his tea, was enthralled by the interchange between Sonny and Cisco. "What did he say, Ms. Brightwell?" he asked eagerly. "Unless, of course," he added quickly, "it's confidential, and then I wouldn't presume…"

Sonny smiled at him, and Cisco, who had just discovered where Mystery was hiding, scrambled over and play-bowed to her. "Cisco was just telling me he made a new friend," she explained. "He really likes him because he searches for things, just like Cisco does."

"My goodness," said Corny softly. His eyes were big as he sipped his tea. He glanced at me. "What do you imagine he's searching for?"

That, of course, was my cue to tell Sonny about Casey, who was searching for his birth parents, one of whom might well be my own father.

"Oh, Raine," she said, her expression rich with compassion. "That must be… very difficult for you."

I shrugged, because I was quite sure Corny—who, as much as I adore him, is a terrible gossip—had already told her the story. "Honestly," I said, "I can't decide. I like him well enough, and if I do have a half-brother, of course I want to know about it. At the same time, there's something a little dodgy about him. He probably thinks the same thing about me," I admitted. "Anyway, we took a DNA test, and he's fixing up Maude's house for me while we wait for the results. The lab said it should take two or three weeks, so I guess any day now."

Corny gulped his tea and lunged to his feet, spattering drops on the floor. "Oh, Miss Stockton!" he exclaimed. "The lab —I didn't think, but I should have—there was an envelope for you! I think that's it. It's on your desk, it came yesterday. I think—I mean, do you think it could be... the lab results?"

With a quick apologetic look to Sonny, I went to my desk and pawed through the stack of junk mail there until I found the overnight envelope. I picked it up uncertainly. Corny was right. It was from Synogen Laboratories, where Miles had sent our DNA samples. I stared at it for a long time.

Sonny said in a subdued tone, "Aren't you going to open it?"

I was surprised to find her standing beside me, leaning on her cane, and Corny on my other side. I looked from one to the other of them, took a breath, and tore open the envelope.

I pulled out the cover letter, scanned it once, and then read it again, more slowly. For the longest time, I wasn't sure how I even felt.

Corny, taking his cue from me, said uncertainly, "Miss Stockton?"

And Sonny placed a comforting hand on my arm. "Is this what you wanted?"

At last, I released the breath I had not been even aware I was holding. "I'm not sure," I said. I added, "But I'd better tell Casey. I'm sorry, Sonny, I have to go. We'll have lunch, I promise."

Our departure was much less protracted than Aunt Mart's and Rita's had been. Sonny assured me she had to leave anyway, and I promised to call, and I'm sure much more was said, but to be honest, I wasn't paying much attention. I think Cisco and I were already in the car before Sonny even got her coat on.

CHAPTER TWENTY-SEVEN

C asey had looked through every box in the barn. He had even swept the rafters, dislodging a couple of rat's nests and half a dozen abandoned wasp's nests, but absolutely nothing else. He'd naturally checked the freezer and the toilet tank, even the well pump house, although that was a long shot. The attic had been even less promising, but he'd dutifully pulled up insulation and unpacked boxes of Christmas decorations, even going so far as to shake the ornaments, listening for unexpected rattles, and pull apart Styrofoam wreaths.

He'd found a loose brick in the fireplace and pulled it out, momentarily hopeful, but the cavity behind it was filled with nothing but dust. He'd sealed it up with fresh mortar and caulk, so Raine wouldn't have to worry about doing that later. Similarly, a couple of floorboards in one of the bedrooms looked newer than the others, so he'd prized them up, only to be disappointed again. He'd even taken apart all the door handles, just in case Freddie had been literal with his "key in the lock" reference. The whole thing was an exercise in frustration, and he knew deep down that he was going about this the wrong way.

Freddie was smart, but he wasn't clever. He was too smart

to hide anything of value in a piece of furniture, for example, although Casey had checked out the thrift store at the women's shelter just in case. But he wasn't clever enough to create a hidey-hole behind a sheetrock wall and then patch it up like new, which was good, because Casey had a feeling he'd have a hard time convincing Raine to start tearing down walls. The problem was that Casey didn't know how to find that in-between space of smart and clever; he didn't know how to think like Freddie.

He knew his time here was limited and getting shorter every day. Detweiler had told him Deacon had been arrested, which gave him a little breathing room, but that man wouldn't stay in jail long. He never did. And then there was Raine, who had already proven she was neither stupid nor gullible. Who knew what she was up to behind his back? Or how much longer he had before she *really* turned that cop ex-husband of hers loose on him?

The problem was that life here wasn't half-bad, and he was starting to get used to it. He'd found a futon at the dump, dusted it off and dragged it back to the house, where it was a comfortable place to sit at night in front of the fire, watching videos on his phone or reading one of the paperbacks he'd found in a box in the barn. He made a table out of scrap lumber and started keeping more than takeout in the fridge. He even found a mattress at the recycle store for $25 that was a lot more comfortable than sleeping in the van, especially when the temperature dropped below zero at night. He was settling in. It was stupid, but he was.

He liked getting up in the morning with something to do. He spent a couple of sunny days clearing out brush and mowing down weeds, and he liked seeing the place change as he did it. He replaced the sagging front steps and painted the front porch; it looked good. He salvaged the wood from a couple of locust saplings he'd cut down and made a pair of simple log end tables that looked as though they'd always belonged on either side of the front door. Already he was thinking about sanding down and refinishing the hardwood floors, although he knew he wouldn't be here long enough to finish the job. Sure, he liked to see Raine's pleasure at the way the house was coming along, but mostly he just liked doing it. It had been a long time since he'd been able to visualize a project and see it through to completion. He'd forgotten how good it felt.

Raine texted him on a rainy afternoon as he was taping off the trim in preparation for painting the living room. *On my way over*, she said. *Are you there?*

Welcome home, he replied. *What did you bring me?*

She answered, *News*.

He frowned a little at that and put the phone away. He did a quick mental scan of possible incriminating things she might have discovered about him while she was in Vermont, but since he'd never been there, the results were negative. With his threat radar thus neutralized, he relaxed and went back to work, unscrewing the outlet covers and storing them in a plastic bag so they wouldn't get spattered with paint. He had gotten to the third cover when everything changed.

Almost at the same moment he heard the crunch of tires on the driveway. He quickly replaced the cover and went to the window, expecting Raine's red SUV. What he saw was the last thing he wanted.

Well, maybe not the last. But very close.

Casey went out onto the porch as Detweiler got out of his vehicle and splashed across the yard, tracking mud onto Casey's freshly built, as yet unpainted, front steps. "You need to get out of here," Casey said shortly. There was no sign of welcome on his face. "Raine is on her way over."

"Way to greet somebody who dragged his ass out on a day like this just to help you out," replied Detweiler, rubbing the cold out of his hands. He glanced around in the way he had, checking blind corners and deep shadows, but his expression didn't change. "I've got bad news and I've got bad news. Which do you want first?"

Casey muttered, "Crap." Then, "You couldn't have called?"

Detweiler stuffed his hands into the pockets of his dark raincoat, hunching his shoulders. A few drops of rain rolled off the fabric and splashed on the floorboards. "I thought you'd want to hear it in person," he said. His face, never a portrait of a good time, looked particularly grim. Casey braced himself.

"I'm sorry, kid," Detweiler said. "They found Freddie's body yesterday, stuffed in the trunk of his car in a parking lot over in South Carolina. Shot through the head."

Casey closed his eyes slowly, letting it sink it, then opened them again. "Damn it," he said softly. He ran a hand over his mouth and repeated, in barely more than a whisper, "*Damn it.*"

"We always knew it was a possibility," Detweiler said, by way of slim comfort. "A strong possibility."

Casey breathed in, breathed out. Rain pinged on the metal roof, and though the porch was completely dry, he felt the chill dripping down his spine. He said in a moment, "I don't suppose…"

Detweiler shook his head before Casey could finish. "No phone, no laptop, no personal anything. They identified him by his fingerprints. Looks like he was killed two, three months ago, about the time he lost contact with you. Whatever he took with him—that's assuming he left here alive—disappeared the same way he did."

Casey nodded and swallowed hard. Freddie was smart. He wouldn't have left anything incriminating on his electronics, so even if they'd been stolen, nothing could be traced back to him. Not easily, anyway.

Casey said, "Any idea how they got to him?"

Detweiler shifted his gaze, glancing around as though gathering information from the clouds, the drizzle, the gray day itself. "My guess?" he offered eventually. "Smokey Beardsley. He's the only one around here who could've identified him. Deacon got the info from Smokey, tracked down Freddie, and when he was sure the trail was cold, he came back here and got rid of Smokey. You were just lucky he was already dead when you got here, or Smokey would've given you up too."

Casey said heavily, "Yeah. Lucky."

Detweiler gave him a moment, then said, "You ready for the rest?"

Casey didn't bother replying.

"Deacon is working a deal," Detweiler said. "They couldn't pin Smokey's murder on him and looks like he's going to plea for time served on everything else they had. He's getting out."

Casey said flatly, "Of course he is."

"Could be next week, could be next month, could be tomorrow. But here's the bad news. It was local cops that put him away—not directly, of course, but they're the ones who gave the Feds the evidence they needed for the raid. Word on the street is you're the one that tipped off the locals about Deacon. So, when he gets out, guess who he's going to come looking for? You don't want him to find you here, Casey. Seriously."

Casey drew in a sharp breath and made a decision. "Okay. Listen, Detweiler, there's something..." But at that moment they were both distracted by Raine's SUV pulling into the driveway. Casey smothered a groan. "And this day keeps getting better and better."

Detweiler glanced at the car. "I don't know what you've got going on," he said, "but that's another thing. If you've got any regard for that young lady at all, I'd suggest you tell her the truth—or anything else you can think of—and run for the hills. Otherwise, she's going to be in it as deep as you are, and you know I'm right."

He turned as Cisco galloped up the steps and stopped, grinning, to shake the dampness off his fur. Raine followed quickly behind him, pulling the hood of her jacket over her hair. "Sorry!" she called. "Cisco, sit!"

Cisco obediently sat and offered a muddy paw to Casey, who quickly knelt to pet him, trying to gather his thoughts. Detweiler turned smoothly and offered his hand to Raine.

"Ms. Stockton? I'm George Deveraux. You're the owner of this property, I understand?"

Raine nodded her head hesitantly, glancing at Casey. Casey didn't meet her eyes. "That's right," she said.

Detweiler went on easily, "I'm in investment real estate, and I heard this place might be going up for sale. Your handyman here doesn't know anything about it, so I hope I'm not mistaken."

"Actually," Raine said, "you are. I hadn't planned on selling."

"Well, that's disappointing. But a lot of people say that at first, until they see how much is involved in maintaining investment property. If you change your mind, I promise we'll give you a fair price." He reached into his coat pocket, then his pants pocket, then patted his other pockets, looking flustered. "Well, that's embarrassing. I don't seem to have any cards on me."

"That's okay," Raine assured him. "I'm really not interested in selling."

"Perhaps I could check back with you in a few weeks?" he suggested.

"No," she said firmly. "Even if I did want to sell, my fiancé is in real estate, so…"

"Oh," he said, feigning disappointment. "I guess that's that, then." He offered his hand again. "Well, it was nice to meet you, anyway." He slumped off toward his car, and Raine looked at Casey. "That was weird," she said.

Casey straightened up from petting Cisco. "Yeah," he said. "Dude just wandered up, looking to buy the place."

"My uncle said sometimes people like that scour the obituaries, looking for opportunities."

"I guess," Casey agreed. They both watched Detweiler drive away, and Casey reached to open the door. His mind was racing, but the words were easy and automatic. "Let's get in out of the cold. So, what's up? Did you have a good trip?"

Cisco scampered on ahead, toenails clicking on the floor,

sniffing every corner and floorboard for dropped crumbs. He found a roll of masking tape and picked it up, his tail swishing proudly as he brought it over to Casey. Casey took it from him, making a fuss over him and rubbing his ears, glad for the distraction. Cisco went in search of more treasures, and Raine pushed back her hood and dug into her purse. She withdrew a stiff envelope and handed it to him.

"This came," she said simply.

Casey opened it and withdrew the contents. He looked at the words on the paper in silence for a long time. "Okay then," he said at last. He folded the paper and replaced it in the envelope. "I guess that's it."

He returned the envelope to Raine and smiled a little uncertainly. "Looks like I have a sister."

Raine's smile was just as hesitant, and also a little wry. "Yeah," she said. "And I guess I have a brother."

And everything had just gotten way, way more complicated.

CHAPTER TWENTY-EIGHT

"I can't stay," I told Casey. I felt suddenly a little shy, and I stuffed my hands into the pockets of my coat as I perched on the edge of the futon. "Miles's mother is here and it's our first night back and she's making supper..." I trailed off awkwardly. A normal person would have added Why don't you join us? But I wasn't quite ready for that. And I was sure Miles wasn't either.

Cisco found one of Casey's work boots and happily brought it over to him. When Casey thanked him and rubbed his shoulders, Cisco scampered off in search of the other one. "That is one smart dog," Casey said and sat on the hearth across from me.

"You know if you keep making a fuss over him, he's going to keep doing it," I pointed out as Cisco dropped the second boot in front of Casey.

"Ah, that's okay," Casey said. "I think it's cute." He dug in his pocket and found a piece of beef jerky, which Cisco gulped down with a single delighted swipe of his tongue.

I rolled my eyes. "You won't think it's so cute when he piles up everything you own in front of you. He's a retriever, that's his job."

"Fortunately," Casey pointed out, "I don't own much."

Cisco trotted off in search of more things to steal, and I took a breath. "Listen, Casey, I wanted to... well, apologize for some of the things I said the other day. And for kicking you. I guess sometimes I act first and think later."

He shrugged. "That's okay. Not the kicking part," he added darkly. "But everything else—well, I don't guess I gave you much reason to trust me. I'm just a bum who lives in his van and lied about his name."

"The thing is..." I lowered my gaze, trying to formulate my thoughts into words. "All this time I've been more or less hoping that the report would come back negative, that my father had never had a child with another woman, that he hadn't brought that woman into our lives and our home and lied to my mother about their affair for all those years... that my entire family history wasn't being rewritten in front of my very eyes, you know? So maybe I was more mistrustful than I should have been."

He started shaking his head. "No, Raine, listen. There are some things we should talk about."

I held up a quick, staying hand. "Just let me finish, okay?" I drew a breath. "Because now that we have the report, I realize a part of me knew the truth all along." I looked up at him. "I look like my mother," I said. "I always have. The only thing I got from my father was his stubbornness and his big feet." I smiled faintly, then said seriously, "You have his laugh, Casey. The minute I heard it, I knew. And I just wanted to tell you— I'm not sorry about the way things turned out."

Something odd crossed Casey's face—like annoyance, or anger, or maybe just embarrassment. He looked away, his jaw stiff. "Listen, Raine..."

But I plowed on. "It's okay, I know what you're going to say. We're both grown people and we have separate lives and all, and you only agreed to stay until we got the DNA results back. That's fine, but I've been thinking about how Maude gave up her child and never said a word about it all those years to anyone, and I think she did it for us, my mother and me, to save our family. My family. It doesn't seem fair. So, what I wanted to say was that I'd like you to stay, if you want to, and finish the house." I managed a nervous smile. "I'll even make you a good deal on the rent if you want to hang around after its done. By rights this house should be yours anyway..."

"Raine, don't." His face was tight. "That's not—"

"Why not?" I insisted. "Okay, so you don't have to make some big commitment, I get that. But couldn't you stay for a little while longer? Give us a chance to get to know each other, give *you* a chance to get to know your family and the place your mother loved? There's still a lot of work to be done on this house, and come spring you'll have more work than you can handle with the contractors starting up again and the summer people fixing up their houses. You said yourself you don't have anywhere else to be, and isn't that why you came here? To find your family? Well..." I spread my arms open wide. "I'm it."

By this time Cisco had added a caulk gun, a screwdriver and a pair of pliers to the pile at Casey's feet, and he was now galloping around the room, nose to the ground, looking for more. Casey followed his movements absently, his expression troubled. I could tell he was wrestling with a decision, but I couldn't figure out why. Then, instead of answering me, he said, "What is he doing?"

I grinned. "It's a game we play. Part of his training, actually. Here, let me have your wallet. I'll show you."

He looked at me skeptically, and I returned dryly, "You can trust me with it."

He turned over his leather wallet and, while Cisco was sniffing the floorboards for more treasure, I slipped the wallet under the futon cushion and stepped back. "Watch this," I said, and called, "Hey, Cisco, go find."

Cisco whirled around and started excitedly sniffing the area around our feet, moving in wider and wider circles. In less than a minute he had located the hidden wallet and, tail swishing proudly, brought it over to Casey. "That was an easy one," I told Casey, rewarding Cisco with a liver treat. "Now you try. Go hide your keys in the kitchen somewhere. Make it hard."

Casey was grinning when he returned from the kitchen. "He'll never find them," he assured me.

It took Cisco even less time to find the keys hidden in a closed cabinet beneath an upside-down cardboard box.

"That is some amazing stuff," Casey said, delighted. "How does he do that?"

"It's part of his search-and rescue training," I explained as we walked back into the living room. "We work on it all the time, and he's been rewarded for it so much that he thinks it's a game. That's why he kept bringing you all that stuff. He wanted to play the game."

Cisco had stopped across the room from us and was digging at the wall with both paws, his nails leaving gouges in the already-scuffed paint. That was not part of the game. "Hey!" I clapped my hands sharply. "Stop that!"

Cisco looked around, grinning at me, and then immediately resumed pawing the wall. I got up and caught his collar, pulling him away, and saw that it was an electrical outlet cover he'd been scratching at, not the wall. The minute I released his collar, Cisco returned to the outlet, sniffing it vigorously.

"He smells something behind there," I said.

"I wouldn't be surprised," Casey said, coming over to me. "All these outlets need to be caulked. Cold air is coming through all of them."

"Miles said it could be rats," I said, watching thoughtfully as Cisco started scratching the wall again.

"Could be," Casey agreed. "You probably shouldn't let him do that, though. I wouldn't want him to get a shock."

"I read an article once about a golden retriever who kept doing that," I said. "Scratching at an outlet like that. Turns out there was some kind of electrical short or something that could have burned the house down. He could smell it or hear it; I can't remember which." I looked around for the screwdriver Cisco had found. "You should check it out."

Casey frowned as he watched Cisco bury his nose against the outlet, then start scratching again. "Yeah, maybe I will, later."

I spotted the screwdriver and picked it up. "Why not now?" I elbowed Cisco out of the way and knelt on the floor, unscrewing the single screw that held the cover in place.

"Hold on, Raine, you're not going to be able to tell anything that way. Let me get my voltage tester."

But I already had the cover off. Casey knelt beside me, and I held Cisco back with one arm as I turned on the flashlight app on my phone and shined it inside.

"What in the world?" I said.

Both Casey and I reached for the small object nestled beside the electrical apparatus inside the box, but I was closer, and my fingers were smaller. I reached it first and pulled it out. I looked at it in puzzlement.

"How in the hell," Casey demanded incredulously, "did he know this was there?"

I remembered Cisco, who was sitting and grinning and waiting for his treat. I pulled out a liver snap from my coat pocket for him. I never, and I mean never, go anywhere without them. "That's what I was trying to tell you," I answered Casey. "He's trained to search for human scent. Without a specific target, he'll look for anything with human scent on it that's hidden. He didn't know the game was over."

Casey looked skeptical for a moment, then held out his hand. "Let me see that. What is it?"

"It's a thumb drive," I said, holding it up for him to see. "Did you put this here?"

He shook his head, staring at it. "I don't even have a computer."

That seemed strange, since the scent would have to be fairly fresh for Cisco to alert to it like that. Unless, possibly, it bore the scent of someone else he knew and loved. "Maybe Maude did," I speculated.

He said carefully, "I can't think why she would do that. I

mean, pretty crazy place to put something like that."

"Maybe," I suggested, "it has something on it she didn't want anyone to find." I looked at him in cautiously growing excitement. "It could even have to do with you, Casey. It could be baby pictures, or a letter, or documents of some kind."

He shook his head, frowning. "That's pretty far-fetched," he said. "More likely it's just some random thing somebody misplaced. I've been in the construction business a long time and I've seen all kinds of things get forgotten and sealed up in walls. It's probably just the builder's invoices and payroll and stuff."

"They didn't even have personal computers when the house was built," I told him impatiently, standing. "Anyway, there's only one way to find out."

He stood too, and said quickly, "What are you going to do?"

"I'm going to take this home and plug it in to my computer," I informed him.

"No." He reached out as though to take the drive from me. I turned away protectively. "Are you crazy?" he insisted. "There's no telling what kind of malware is on that thing. And even if it's a perfectly harmless program it could conflict with something else on your system and cause a crash."

I frowned, remembering the lost e-mails and contacts from the last crash, and all the weeks of misery they had caused. "Yeah," I agreed, deflated. "You're right."

He opened his hand again. "Let me take it to the library tomorrow and use one of their computers to see if there's anything malicious on it. Public computers are always well protected against that kind of thing."

I brightened with relief. "So," I informed him, "is Miles. His system has the best security in the world running on it, and I don't want to wait until tomorrow. Come on," I urged, "aren't you curious? Don't you want to see what's on this thing?"

Once again, I could see a struggle in his eyes that I didn't understand. Then he smiled wryly. "Yeah, I guess. Now you've got me wondering. If you're going to check it out now, do you think it would be okay if I tagged along? Or," he added quickly, "would that get you in trouble with your fiancé?"

Maybe if he hadn't said that, I would have hesitated. I knew Miles was less than comfortable with Casey and that he was justifiably cautious about who he invited to his house. But there was something about the suggestion that I would be worried about "getting in trouble" with anyone that raised my natural ire.

I said, "Why don't you follow me over there? Come on, Cisco."

In the car I sent Miles a quick text: *DNA results positive. Bringing Casey home with me, we need a favor. OK?*

To which he responded, within seconds, *Bring it on.*

And that is only one of the reasons I love him.

Sometimes I like to keep a list.

CHAPTER
TWENTY-NINE

It was twilight when we arrived. The rain had stopped but the gray clouds remained, and the great glass A-framed monolith that was Miles's house glowed like a spaceship in the gloom. Casey got out of his van and walked up beside me, his expression awed as he took it all in.

"Holy..." He glanced at me and finished, "Sorry. I can't think of anything that isn't a swear word. Jeez, girl, is this what you're marrying into? Go for that."

He held out his hand, hip-high, for a low-five and I felt compelled to slap his palm lightly in response, although I accompanied it with an embarrassed shrug. "It's not all it's cracked up to be."

"Oh yeah?" He eyes swept his surroundings busily as we walked around the side of the house, Cisco racing ahead. "What's the downside?"

I had a quick flash of Miles pointing to himself and pronouncing dryly, *Babe. You won the lottery.* But I quickly pushed it aside and walked faster.

"Security guards with guns," I replied, and when he looked over his shoulder in some alarm, I explained, "Not so much now, but when Miles is out of the country, or when there's been some kind of threat, or he has important people staying here." I shrugged. "To tell the truth, he's been a lot better since I started complaining about it."

The garden lights came on as we rounded the corner of the building, painting pools of shadow and light which, even in the naked heart of winter, was a starkly beautiful picture. The swimming pool was covered this time of year, but Casey grinned when he saw it. "It's shaped like a dog bone," he observed.

"Melanie's idea."

"I like her already."

I put my hand on the handle of the side door and the lock clicked open. Miles was waiting in the hallway on the other side, having no doubt been alerted to our approach by his security cameras. Cisco proudly led the way inside, tail waving, taking full credit for bringing his new friend home. Miles greeted me with a quick kiss and shook Casey's hand which, all things considered, I thought was very gracious of him. Cisco sat patiently waiting until Miles tossed him a treat, and then my loyal dog—who was, after all, responsible for all of us being here—scampered off in search of Pepper.

Casey glanced around appreciatively and said, "Amazing house. Smart home?"

"It is," Miles agreed pleasantly. "Axis-6000 with integrated interior and perimeter cameras, AI processing, state-of-the-art independent transmitters."

"No lie." Casey looked at him with new respect. "I've read about those, but I've never seen them in action. Man, I'd love a chance to install one of those systems."

"He can order an espresso while he's in the shower," I replied, impatient to get on with it. "Don't know why he wants to, but he can. Miles, look, we just need to use your computer for a minute."

"Not the one that controls the house," Casey pointed out quickly. "We're trying to avoid uploading malware."

I explained about finding the thumb drive while we walked the few steps to his office, and Miles seemed amused as he remarked, "You two remind me of something out of a Hardy Boys mystery."

I asked, "Who are the Hardy Boys?"

Miles gave me a dry look and held out his hand for the thumb drive.

Miles's office is the color of an evergreen forest, accented with snow-white rugs and furniture and a collection of truly hideous modern art on the walls. Needless to say, the dogs are not allowed in here. The centerpiece is a huge L-shaped glass desk with waterfall edges that seems to float in space. There is a bank of computer monitors behind that desk that, as far as I have been able to determine, don't do much except display the time in Tokyo and monitor the world's various financial markets. There is also a cabinet behind the desk, from which Miles now took a compact laptop.

"This one's not connected to the internet," he said as he set it on the desk and booted it up. "And it's got a search-and-destroy malware program on it that should take out anything that we don't want to see."

Miles is in his element with this sort of thing. Like I said, he may not be a tech genius, but he's close enough for me, and what he doesn't know, he knows how to find out. Casey and I watched as he plugged in the thumb drive. The computer whirred away for a minute, then the screen filled with code.

"Well, that's helpful," I muttered.

"Hold on." Miles tapped some keys, and the screen cleared to a bright white background. A red circle with a slash through it—the universal sign for forbidden—was in the center.

"Encrypted," Casey murmured. He rubbed his jaw uneasily.

"Maybe not." Miles did some more stuff—I honestly can't tell you what except that it involved a lot of fast typing, some disappearing screens, some rebooting—and suddenly a neat column of numbers appeared on the screen. Miles sat back in his chair.

"Whoever encrypted the file," he said, "was either in a

hurry or didn't want the code to be too hard to break. This is pretty basic."

I looked at him suspiciously. "How do you know all this?"

He winked at me. "Just be glad I'm on your side, baby."

I turned my attention to the screen. Casey still had not said a word, but no wonder. I was as confused as he was. I'd expected baby pictures. "What is this?"

Miles spent a few moments working the keyboard and clicking the mouse, typing numbers, entering and exiting programs. After a time, he sat back, brought up the contents of the thumb drive again, and studied it in silence. "I don't know," he admitted at last. "These are files of some kind—could be account numbers, could be client numbers, could just be codes for something else—but I can't get into them. They're password protected, and each file has a different password."

I frowned. "I don't get it. Why would Maude have anything like this? And why would she hide it behind an outlet cover in her house?"

Miles said gently, "I doubt very much she did, hon. Remember the house was empty for a long time, and then rented after that. At any rate..." He removed the thumb drive and offered it back to me. "This is not something we're going to figure out. You could turn it over to the authorities, I guess, since it's found property. Or I could have my team take a look at it, see if they can break the code."

Casey said, "Why don't we—"

But I spoke over him eagerly, "Yes, do that. I want to know what's on it." I glanced at Casey. "Don't you?"

Casey shrugged, but his smile was weak. "Like I said, probably just invoices and stuff."

Miles got up and crossed the room. He slid back a panel that was disguised as a piece of abstract art—a particularly ugly piece, if I may say—to reveal a small wall safe. He typed in a code, opened the safe, and placed the thumb drive inside. "You may be right," he said. "But just in case it is something important, better safe than sorry."

"Of course," said Casey hesitantly, "there's no telling how old that file is, or who put it there. Even if it was important once, it might not mean anything now."

"True enough," Miles agreed. "But that's not a problem for civilians to solve."

"Oh, there you are!" exclaimed Rita from the door. "Raine, I'm glad you're back. Dinner is almost ready. Miles, are you going to make the salad? Oh." She noticed Casey for the first time and stepped into the room, her hand extended, her smile welcoming. "I didn't know you had company. Hello, I'm Rita Young, Miles's mother."

Miles said, "Mom, this is Casey Macintosh. Raine's brother."

"Half-brother," Casey corrected quickly and came forward to shake Rita's hand.

"Oh!" Her face lit up with delight and she closed both hands around Casey's. "Oh, I've heard so much about you! Well, not nearly as much as I'd like to, of course, but how wonderful that you're here! You're staying for dinner, right?"

"No, ma'am." Casey literally started to back away. "No, I thank you, but I can't."

I tried to help him out. "Maybe another time would be better. Casey just stopped by for a minute..."

"Nonsense, he's here now and I won't take no for an answer. You don't have plans for dinner, do you, Casey?"

"Well," Casey floundered, and just then Melanie skidded to a stop at the door.

"Casey?" she repeated. "Raine's brother?" She stepped forward, looked him up and down thoroughly, and then confided to me, "Wow, Raine, he's really cute."

I couldn't help grinning, and neither could Casey, though he fought it. Miles tugged at one of Melanie's curls and said, "Go set another place at the table and mind your manners. We have company."

So, it was settled.

There followed one of the weirdest evenings I have ever

spent. Between Melanie's relentless grilling ("Where did you go to high school?" "Did you play any sports?" "What was it like to be an orphan?" "Do you really live in your van?" "Can I see it some time?"), Rita's far more refined, but just as determined, attempts to draw him out and Miles's serene, almost Machiavellian enjoyment of the whole thing, it was hard not to feel sorry for Casey.

I've got to say, I wouldn't have been half as comfortable in his place, but Casey handled it like a pro. He made Melanie laugh, he charmed Rita, he was easy with Miles, and he even let himself be talked into staying for Melanie's Death by Chocolate dessert. I'm not sure who I was most impressed with—my soon-to-be family, for not probing too hard into Casey's past or his future plans, although I knew they were dying to do so—or Casey himself, who had to feel like a bug under a microscope in this ostentatious house with a bunch of strangers… at least one of whom, he had to suspect, did not trust him with the silverware.

Melanie proudly served her Death by Chocolate in the family room, and Casey made an elaborate display of appreciation as he tasted it. "Miss Melanie," he declared somberly, placing his hand over his heart, "never in the history of the world has chocolate ever died for so noble a cause. What a way to go."

Melanie giggled and scooched in on the sofa between her father and me with her own dish of the decadent confection. "You don't have to call me Miss," she said. "But I guess I should call you Uncle Casey, huh?"

Casey glanced quickly at me and then, almost imperceptibly, at Miles. He said, covering nicely, "Melanie, you can call me anything you want as long as you do it with a dish of this chocolate in your hand."

Personally, I thought he was laying it on a bit thick, but Melanie beamed her pleasure, and even Miles looked amused. Rita served coffee and Miles and Casey talked a little about the work on the house, as well as some of the other projects each of them had done. I thought it was a shame Miles had decided not to like Casey, because they really had a lot in common. Of course, none of us mentioned what had really brought Casey here tonight. All we needed was an eleven-year-old's active imagination fired up by a mysterious object hidden in the wall, particularly since none of us had any answers about what that mysterious object meant.

As soon as the dishes were returned to the serving tray and there was a conversational lull, Casey prepared to take his leave.

"Mrs. Young," he said. "Thank you for the delicious dinner and the hospitality. It's easy to see where your granddaughter gets her talent for cooking." And to Melanie he added, "I'll dream about that chocolate for weeks."

Rita made a polite objection as Casey started to get to his feet, but Melanie cried, "Wait! You can't leave yet!" She looked at me. "You've got to show him the tricks you and the dogs are doing for the first-graders tomorrow."

"Casey has already seen Cisco read," I told her, "and it was his idea to teach Rags to count."

"But he hasn't *seen* it." She wriggled off the sofa and raced toward the stairs. "Be right back!"

Casey grinned at me. "Did you really teach him to count?"

I shrugged modestly. "It wasn't that hard."

Rita said, "Is that tomorrow, Raine? Mart and I were hoping you'd join us for lunch."

"What time?" I asked and pretended to be disappointed when she told me they were scheduled to meet at 1:00. Of course, they wanted to get my input on flowers and food and bands for the wedding reception, but hadn't I done my part by picking the date? And the dress? And the daisies for Melanie's hair? "Sorry," I said. "I've got to leave for school by 1:30 and won't be out of there until 2:30, earliest. Probably closer to 3:00."

"Which is about the time I'll get back from Atlanta," Miles put in, deadpan. "Otherwise, I'd love to join you."

She made a slapping motion at the air from across the room. "This is a *ladies'* luncheon, mister. We'll let you know when you're invited."

I glanced at Miles. "You're in Atlanta tomorrow?"

"Just for a few hours. I thought I'd mentioned it."

The sound of thundering paws and galloping sneakers interrupted my reply, and the next few minutes were filled with the usual chaos that accompanies a golden retriever and a labradoodle puppy entering the room. I let them greet everyone, just as I would do tomorrow in the classroom, because even Cisco has a hard time concentrating when he thinks there might be someone out there who missed out on petting him. Melanie very officiously printed out the signs with the commands that Cisco could "read," and I proceeded with the program I had prepared about the importance of getting a good education and doing your homework. Melanie played the role Corny would take over tomorrow, holding Rags's leash and surreptitiously slipping him a treat every time he lifted a paw in response to my secret signal, a slight flexing of my pinky finger. With my back to the audience, no one could tell I was cuing him, but dogs are amazingly astute when it comes to body language, and we had practiced this a lot. When he had counted to six, which was the age of most of the children in the classroom, I announced that Rags was learning to do math, but he wasn't very good at it, so I really hoped he had done his homework. I then asked him to add two-plus-two and failed to give him the signal. Rags, of course, did not respond.

"Oh-oh," Melanie said, which would be Corny's line tomorrow. "Did somebody forget to do his homework?"

I shook my head sadly and said, "Rags, shame on you." I put my finger to my lips, and Rags, hesitating only a bit because he was, after all, just a puppy, put his paw over his muzzle and bowed his head in shame.

My audience of three burst into laughter, just as my audience of thirty would do tomorrow, and I demonstrated what a well-educated dog could do by turning to Cisco and asking the same question. Cisco, who had performed this trick enough that he barely needed the cue, barked four times in reply. I tossed him a treat, took my bow, and we all accepted the enthusiastic applause of the audience.

"Raine, that was amazing!" Rita exclaimed, stroking Cisco's ears. "How did you do that?"

Casey was still laughing. "You are really something," he told me. That laugh, those dancing eyes. "And so are your dogs." He stood to give each of them an enthusiastic ear rub.

"I was supposed to be the assistant tomorrow," Melanie pointed out, eager for her share of the praise, "but Dad wouldn't check me out of school. I could have gotten a public speaking credit for it, too," she informed her father resentfully.

Before an argument could ensue, Casey said, "Well, I'm glad I got to see this version, then. It wouldn't have been nearly as good without you."

He turned back to Rita. "Thanks again for dinner, Mrs. Young, and a wonderful evening." He winked at me. "Not to mention the show. Goodnight, everybody."

Miles stood to shake his hand, and Melanie called happily, "Goodnight, Uncle Casey."

I tried to read his expression at that but couldn't quite manage it.

I walked him to the door. The security lights flooded the circular drive where our vehicles were parked when I opened the door, and we stepped out into the chill front porch. Because I couldn't think of anything else, I said, "Well. I guess this day didn't turn out like we expected. Either of us."

Cisco wriggled through the half-closed door to join us, and we both laughed a little as Cisco did his "up" trick, offering both paws to Casey. Casey took Cisco's paws, rubbed noses with him, and then hugged him with both arms before letting him drop all four paws to the floor again.

Casey smiled and nodded back toward the light that spilled from the open door of the house. "You've got a good thing going here, kid. Don't mess it up, okay? Not for me, not for anyone."

Then, unexpectedly, he gave me a quick, awkward hug and hurried down the steps.

"I'll talk to you tomorrow!" I called after him.

He returned a backward wave but did not reply.

Miles was waiting in the foyer when Cisco and I returned. I draped my arms around his neck and kissed him, then stepped back to look at him. "I'm sorry," I said, "and thank you. Are you mad at me?"

He chuckled softly. "Sugar, being mad at you is like yelling at the wind for blowing."

"Still, I should have asked you before inviting Casey over here."

"You did ask me," he reminded me. "And if I'd been worried about it, I would have said something. Give me some credit."

"Does that mean you're not mad?"

"Nope." He gave my bottom an affectionate pat as we turned to go upstairs. "It means I yell at the wind a lot."

CHAPTER THIRTY

The man who would eventually change Buck's life was named Billy Aikens, and he was the top law enforcement officer in the pre-Civil War town of Mercy, Georgia. He was a robust, good-looking fellow in his late sixties with a head of thick, white hair and a neatly trimmed white beard who proudly admitted to playing Santa Clause every year at the town Christmas party. He took Buck on a tour of one of the prettiest little towns Buck had ever seen, settled on the banks of a wide, still blackwater river with white-columned mansions and flowers that bloomed like something out of a gardening magazine in the middle of February. But it wasn't until the two of them sat beside the fountain in the town square—in their shirtsleeves, in February—and started to talk about their philosophy of law enforcement that Buck started to think he might be able to see himself in that place, in that job.

Billy asked him an odd question that day. He asked whether or not Buck had ever crossed a legal line during the performance of his duties. It had seemed like one of those trick interview questions to Buck at the time, and he'd answered it honestly because he had nothing to lose. But over the next few months he would think about that day, that question, and his answer. A lot.

But on the cold, wet Tuesday morning following his return from four days at the beach, the last thing on Buck's mind was the ethics of law enforcement. All he was really thinking, as his truck wheels splashed through puddles and over cracked asphalt on his way to work, was how ugly his hometown was. The bare branches of trees tangled with utility wires. Brown, muddy lawns. Roofs covered with blue tarps from the last storm, awaiting good weather for repair. Children's toys abandoned in yards, swings hanging by one rusty chain. This was a place where people did the best they could, and it was never enough. He was not happy to be home.

His day started to go downhill when Marshall waylaid him as he entered the building and beckoned him into his office. "Running a little late, huh?" Marshall commented.

Buck glanced at his watch, and then at the clock on Marshall's wall, suppressing a groan. They'd been on Central Time in Panama City Beach, which was an hour earlier, and he'd forgotten to change his watch back. He was embarrassed to admit that to Marshall, though, so he said, "Sorry. Vacation brain."

Marshall closed the door and waved Buck into a chair. "So how did the job interview go?"

"Son of a gun offered me the job," Buck replied, taking his seat.

Marshall moved behind the desk. "And?"

"I've got 'til April to give him an answer," Buck said.

Marshall nodded, clearly distracted, and sat down behind his desk. "So," he said, "a couple of things. Bad news first. Dan Hammond had a stroke on Friday. They transferred him to Mission Hospital in Asheville, where he'll probably be for the next three to six months. He's expected to recover, but between you and me the chances aren't good that he'll ever return to the prosecutor's office."

"Jesus," Buck said, sinking back into his chair. "Holy Christ, I was only gone four days."

Marshall nodded sympathetically. "It's going to be a hard adjustment for all of us."

"I'll try to get by to see him this week," Buck said.

"I'm sure his wife will appreciate a call," replied Marshall.

"The office sent flowers. He's not allowed visitors just yet."

"Right," murmured Buck, remembering his own time in ICU. It seemed like yesterday.

"A fellow by the name of Joshua York is taking over from the DA's office. I don't know him, but I hear he's a real go-getter. Young, ambitious, you know the type. His daddy's in politics up in Raleigh, I think. Anyhow, he wants to go over your open cases with you this morning. Harrigan should be in on the meeting."

"Yes, sir."

"All things considered," Marshall went on, "I put Harrigan on full time. He needs to be shadowing you for the next month at least. I want him to be fully up to speed just in case you do decide to leave us."

That was the perfectly logical thing to do from a managerial standpoint, but Buck felt odd about it—almost as though Marshall had already made up his mind to let him go. Or maybe he thought Buck had already made up his mind to leave. And maybe he wouldn't be far wrong.

At Buck's hesitance, Marshall frowned. "You're okay with that, right? Is Harrigan working out for you?"

Buck said quickly, "Yes. I mean, he's got a little to learn about dealing with people in a rural community like this, but he seems like a good man. Solid cop. No problem here."

Marshall nodded and glanced down at his notepad. "One more thing. It's kind of strange. I had a call yesterday from the Charlotte field office of the FBI. They said you'd put in a request for a criminal background check on a..." He checked his notes again. "Kevin Christopher Kinsey, aka Casey Macintosh, aka Chris Kinsey, aka Kevin Macintosh..." He looked up. "And they politely requested that you back off."

Buck couldn't hide his surprise. "What?"

"The implication was that he's already under investigation by federal authorities and they don't want the locals scaring him off. At any rate, you're not going to be able to get anywhere with it. Who is this guy, anyway?"

It took Buck a moment to digest all this. "He was a person of interest in the Smokey Beardsley case. I thought he was connected to the identity theft part of it but haven't been able to connect the dots yet."

Marshall nodded. "Well, that probably explains it, then. The Petrova case is in the hands of the FBI now, and if this Kinsey person is involved, they'll know it. So let it go."

"Yes, sir," Buck said, but he couldn't entirely hide his uneasiness. He started to rise. "Will do. Anything else?'

"See York first," Marshall said. "And Buck..."

Buck paused at the door. "Don't make me wait until April to know what you decide."

Buck nodded and left, hoping he didn't have to wait until April to know as well.

CHAPTER THIRTY-ONE

We were a big hit at William Bartram Elementary School, as of course I knew we would be. Corny wore red bib overalls with a multi-color striped shirt and bright yellow sneakers; with his fuzzy orange hair peeking out from beneath his new ski hat—which he declared "matched perfectly"—he was every bit the clown. Rags completed the look with his naturally goofy appearance and a brightly colored ruffled collar. Cisco and I wore our therapy dog team vests, which I suppose made us the straight men, but that was fine with me.

Just as I was setting up and the teacher was introducing us to the class, I got a text from Casey: *Left my jacket at your mansion (smiley face). Okay if I come by and get it?*

I replied, *No one is home but the housekeeper will let you in. I'll text her.*

He replied, *Thnx* even as I was texting Mrs. Banks. *My brother is coming by to get his jacket. It's ok to let him in.*

I had absolutely no excuse for the silly little thrill I felt when I typed the words "my brother."

In retrospect, I should have known. Of course I should have. There were a hundred things that, looking back, I should have clearly seen or done differently or at least thought about for a minute, starting with the first day I met Casey. But, hey. I didn't. I think I've been punished enough for that.

We finished our program, the kids were crazy about it, and because I know the teachers depend on us to take up the last hour of class time, I let all the little monsters ask their questions and I answered each and every one. "Questions" of course is a loose term, since the hands that shot up were mostly followed by things like, "I had a poodle once. He pooped on the rug." And "My Grandma has a chihuahua. She says it's from Mexico, but it doesn't speak Spanish." Uh-huh. It's all part of the gig.

When Jolene's little boy raised his hand, I was eager to call on him. I figured if he had something to say about dogs, it would at least be interesting, and I was right.

"My mom is a dog trainer, too," he said. "We used to have dog named Nike. She was a police dog. She doesn't live with us anymore."

"I knew Nike," I told him. "She was an amazing dog. I worked with her and your mom a lot. They're both real heroes."

And while he beamed under the praise, I had a chance to educate the class about the role of police dogs and how they are so brave that they sometimes have to leave their families to go live with other people who need them more. This took up the last ten minutes of class. I handed out brochures for the humane society and for Dog Daze, reminded all the kids that Rags was up for adoption, and then, blessedly, the bell rang.

Most of the children surged for the door, but a few came up to pet the dogs. Jolene's boy, Willis, was among them. "Wow, Ms. Stockton," he said, pushing his way forward to me. "That's the best dog I've ever seen in my whole life."

I smiled at him. "Thanks," I said, stroking Cisco's ears. "He's pretty smart, all right."

Willis glanced at Cisco briefly. "Oh," he said. "Yeah, he's nice, too, but I meant this one." He gestured to Rags, his eyes shining. "Is it okay if I pet him?"

I assured him that it was, and my eyes met Corny's meaningfully over the tangle of little boy and dog, the one hugging and the other licking and wiggling in pure delight. I made a mental note to call Jolene about the possibility of adding a new member to her family. But of course, in light of ensuing events, I never did.

Corny and I were back at Dog Daze, unpacking the car and congratulating ourselves on a job well done, when the text came from Miles. It said, *Didn't want to call in case you were still in class. I'm going to have to call the sheriff. I'm sorry.* There was a fourteen-second video attached.

Of course, my heart slammed into my throat when I read the part about the sheriff, and it stayed there as I opened the video. I stood on the stoop of Dog Daze with Rags's portable crate leaning against my leg and rain dripping from the eaves and watched the black-and-white footage slowly unravel my day, and my heart.

At first, I didn't understand what I was seeing, and I had to start it over midway through. But there was no mistake. Casey walked into Miles's office and crossed the room to the ugly piece of art that hid the safe. He swung the artwork aside, tapped a code into the keypad, removed something from the safe, and returned everything to the way it was before. He left the room, pausing on his way out to retrieve the windbreaker he had apparently dropped behind a chair the night before. Fourteen seconds.

My fingers shook as I typed, *What did he take?*

The thumb drive.

That's all?

Yes, he answered. *Are you on your way home?*

I typed, *Not quite.*

He replied, *Do you want me to wait until you get here?*

I turned off my phone without replying.

There was a red haze clouding the edges of my vision as I opened the door and called out to Corny to please finish putting things away for me. Cisco wiggled through the door and raced ahead of my angry strides toward the car. He leapt past me and into his place in the backseat as soon as I opened the door, and I was so mad that I didn't even stop to put on his seat belt.

I slammed out of the parking lot at a furious pace, and I'm sure I exceeded the speed limit by at least twenty miles per hour on my way to Maude's house. I vaguely remember seeing a black SUV parked in the weeds on the side of the road near the row of mailboxes just before I got to Maude's driveway, but fortunately I didn't see another vehicle on the way over. My driving was so reckless I even scared myself. The rain had stopped but the roads were shiny and wet, and muddy water sprayed my SUV as it bounced recklessly down Maude's rutted drive.

Part of me was surprised to find Casey's van was still there. I pulled up behind it, blocking him in, and threw open the door. I came around the passenger side of his van as he came from the driver's side, a welcoming smile on his face. "Hey, Raine. How did the show go?"

"You lying son of a bitch!" I screamed at him. I approached him with my fists balled up, the heat in my chest exploding into my face and through my voice. Cisco galloped beside me but slowed down, his tail wagging low, and looked at me in confusion when I started yelling.

Casey said, "What the—"

"You broke into Miles's house! You opened his safe and you stole the thumb drive! You sat there, you *sat there* and ate his food and made jokes with his little girl and flirted with his mother and all the while you were planning to come back and rob him!"

With every word I yelled at him his face lost animation, and now he stood, expressionless, just watching me.

I was shaking with rage, but nothing could stop me now. I dragged in a choked, gasping breath. "I trusted you! I made Miles trust you! After everything I told you, everything we'd been through, Melanie and me and Miles, everything you promised—it meant nothing to you! Miles was right all along, you were just conning us, waiting for your chance. Damn you, Casey! Damn you!" I stopped, my shoulders heaving, my throat burning, afraid if I spoke one more word I'd burst into tears. I didn't want to cry. I wanted to scream.

"You're the one who hid the drive in the outlet," I said in a low, tight voice. "I knew it had to be you, or Cisco never would have alerted to it. But you made me doubt my own dog. What's on the drive, Casey? What could possibly be so important that you would do this to me, to *us*?"

Casey's expression was smugly amused. "My future," he responded simply. "Something you can't relate to, can you, Raine Stockton? Your daddy was a judge, your mama a socialite, your uncle the local sheriff. And look who you're getting ready to marry. One of the richest men in the country. Oh, yeah, your future was written on gold leaf the minute you were born. Not so much for me. Some of us had to work a little harder to get there and, hey, if I hurt your feelings along the way, sorry about that. But I've got other priorities."

Every word he spoke was like a knife wound to my heart. I could actually feel the blood draining from my core, pooling in my fingertips and my toes. I said hoarsely, "I believed you. And you lied to me."

Casey's lips turned upward in a small, contemptuous smile, and he lifted one shoulder carelessly. "What can I say, sis? You knew I was a snake when you picked me up."

I just stared at him.

"At least I come by it honestly," he went on easily. "The son of a crooked judge and a woman who spent thirty years living a double life. What did you expect? And before you go all self-righteous and judge-y on me, you need to remember we come from the same bad seed. Maybe we're not as different as you think, huh?"

I felt cold. "I'm nothing like you. I would never betray a friend."

He laughed softly. "Friend? Really? You people were the

easiest marks I've ever met. All I had to do was pretend to be the kind of guy you wouldn't mind being related to for a few weeks while I looked for the drive. And you didn't even mind me tearing up the house in the process." He laughed again and shook his head. "Believe me, I've done a lot worse for a lot less."

"Where is it?" I demanded in a low, shaking voice. "Give it to me."

"Not going to happen, I'm afraid. Besides, you wouldn't know what to do with it if you had it."

"Miles has already called the police."

He nodded. "I figured. Which is why, if you'll excuse me, I really have to get going. It's been nice meeting you, Raine." He winked at Cisco. "You too, buddy. Now..." he gestured toward my car, which was blocking him in. "Do you mind?"

That was the moment when something inside me snapped. The way he winked at Cisco, the way he called him buddy. I lunged at Casey with a roar, my fist drawn back, and swung at him as hard as I could. I felt bone crunch and blood spatter as my fist hit his face. He cried out and staggered back. Cisco rushed forward, barking. Casey lost his balance and fell backward, and my forward momentum sent me to the ground on one knee, gasping for breath.

Cisco rushed to Casey as I staggered to my feet. Blood was gushing from Casey's nose, and he tried to staunch it with his fingers. He turned on his side, trying to stand up, and grasped Cisco for assistance, leaving a bloody smear across Cisco's vest. He said in a hoarse, muffled voice, "Get out of here, Raine. You have no idea what you're up against."

"Neither," I replied, breathing hard, "do you."

"Go!" he shouted hoarsely. He was coughing and choking on blood. "Damn it Raine, I don't want to hurt you!"

And just like that, all the fight went out of me. I said dully, "You already have." Then, "Cisco, here."

I'll never forget the look in Cisco's eyes as he looked from Casey, bleeding on the ground, to me. But my good dog made the right decision, as he always did. We got in the car, and I drove away from there without looking back.

CHAPTER THIRTY-TWO

As soon as Raine's SUV left the driveway, spewing an angry cloud of mud and gravel in its wake, a light-haired man in a dark windbreaker exited the van, holding a gun leveled at Casey. From inside the house another man, less intimidating only by virtue of the fact that his hands were in his pockets, approached at a measured pace.

Casey struggled to his feet, wiping blood from his face with the back of his hand. He looked from one to the other of them. "Okay," he said, struggling to breathe through his shattered nose. "I told you, didn't I? She has nothing to do with this. She doesn't have the drive. She didn't even know what was on it."

"The question remains," replied Deacon, "why you stole it in the first place."

"I can explain."

"You always could. You were the brightest of my boys, Kevin. What a pity I must do what I have to now. Give me the drive."

Casey raised his hands, palms up, cautiously. "Listen, Deacon, take it easy. Yeah, Freddie stole the bank account numbers from the old man, and I stole them from him. But I always meant to get them back to you. I would have done it last night if it hadn't been for the girl interfering, locking up the drive in her boyfriend's safe. You know me. I'd never screw you."

"Maybe not," said the dark-haired man who came from the house. "But you sure managed to screw me, didn't you, son?" He smiled, stopping a few feet behind Deacon, who held the gun leveled at Casey's chest. "Why do you look so confused? Is it because I'm not as old as you thought I was?"

Casey felt everything inside him dry up—his saliva, his blood, his guts. He did not know the name of the newcomer. But he did know no one had ever seen the face of the old man and lived.

"I've been loyal to you," Casey managed hoarsely. His tongue felt like cardboard. "You know I have."

"Give me the drive," said Deacon.

Casey lowered one hand cautiously, his eyes on the person everyone knew only as the old man. "It's... it's in my pocket," he said. "I didn't lie. I told you I'd get it back and I did. Doesn't that prove something?"

The old man, who was actually on the near side of forty, inclined his head graciously. "It does," he said. "It proves you valued the young lady's life more than your own. Some might call that an admirable quality. I, myself"—he shrugged—"am indifferent. The drive, please."

Casey reached into his jacket pocket and produced the thumb drive, which Deacon quickly snatched from his fingers and handed over to the old man.

Casey's eyes shifted rapidly from one man to the other. "So," he said, "we're good, right? You got what you wanted. We're all square."

The old man held up the thumb drive, examining it in the sunlight as though he could verify its contents by mere visual examination.

"Naturally," he said, "I'll have to authenticate the contents. I can check it from my car. It should only take a minute. Meantime," he glanced at Deacon, "shoot him."

CHAPTER THIRTY-THREE

Buck's day didn't get any better. He couldn't find anything in particular to dislike about the new prosecutor. He was young, energetic, determined and aggressive. He was on a mission to wipe out crime in Hanover County, and he apparently intended to do that by putting every deadbeat dad, first-time drug offender, DUI and shoplifter in state prison. In order to do that, of course, he first had to bring each and every case to court and argue for maximum penalties. In order to do that, Buck and Harrigan had to review every case and make sure it was bulletproof. That was the job, of course, and Buck took it in stride. Nonetheless, he gave Joshua York about six weeks before the county judges took a look at their already overcrowded dockets and had a come-to-Jesus meeting with their over-vigilant prosecutor. Until then, though, it looked like Buck would be putting in some overtime.

The meeting with York went past lunch, and then an hour and a half beyond that while he cleaned up the case files that York wanted to see on his desk before the end of the day. Buck was just about to walk across the building to Jolene's office and see if she was up for a late lunch when he got the call from Miles Young.

Miles had never called him on his personal line before. He

could think of only one reason he would do so now.

"Lawson," he said sharply. And without waiting for a reply he demanded, "Is Raine okay?"

"She's fine," the other man said, and Buck's heartbeat slowed a little. "Physically, at least. Otherwise, probably not. Listen, we had an incident here today that I thought you'd want to handle personally. If you'd rather I report it through the system I will. Otherwise, could you meet us here at my house?"

Buck didn't waste time with questions. He said simply, "On my way."

Harrigan was coming into the office as Buck was going out, and he remembered Marshall's order to have the detective shadow him. He said, "We've got a call. It doesn't sound like an emergency, but we need to check it out."

"Thank God," said the other man fervently. "I could stand a minute out of this office."

"Yeah, me too." He hesitated. "Listen, why don't I meet you at the car? I was thinking about asking Deputy Smith to join us in case we need backup."

Harrigan's grin suggested he saw through the ruse. "Yes sir, no problem."

He moved off, chuckling and murmuring something about youth being wasted on the young. Apparently, there were no secrets in the Hanover County Sheriff's Office, even from the new guy.

CHAPTER THIRTY-FOUR

I did not go straight home. I drove west on the loop of Deer Run Trail and took the first right off the highway, an unmarked dirt road that led into a deserted wildlife preserve. I parked my car in the shadowed woods on the side of the road and got out, breathing hard, holding my knees and trying not to throw up. I don't know how long I stayed there. I walked across the road and gazed at the sky through the gaps in the bony trees. I tossed rocks, hard, at nothing at all. I let my mind race. I tried not to scream out loud. I tried not to think about what a fool I'd been, how easily I'd been had, how much Casey's words had hurt me and how much, I now realized, I'd been living the life of an imposter my whole life. I cried, and I was furious with myself for crying.

All the while, Cisco watched through the window of my car, shifting restlessly, licking his lips, wanting to help. But this one even Cisco couldn't fix.

When I finally returned to the car and turned on my phone, there were five texts from Miles.

Where are you?

ETA?

What are you doing in Cullowhee Gap?

Here I realized he must have been worried enough about

me to turn on the tracker on his phone. He probably knew I'd been to Casey's, too, but he should have been able to figure that one out on his own.

The next two messages were: *Do I need to come looking for you?* And *Police are here. Waiting for you.*

That last one had been sent twenty minutes ago. I sniffed, swiped a hand across my face, and squared my shoulders. I typed back, *On my way.* I fastened my seat belt and started the engine.

Two sheriff's deputy cars were already there when I reached Miles's house, and I parked behind them. I was tired, wrung out, emotionally and mentally spent. I couldn't even cry anymore. I had no more anger to feel. When I noticed Cisco's vest, and mine, were splattered with Casey's blood, I felt nothing but a mild revulsion. I stripped both of them off and stuffed them in a tote bag in the back of my SUV and didn't think about them again. Then I walked into the house, did my best to wash off the muck and melted mascara from my face, and went to face the music.

Cisco had raced ahead of me and was already making a complete fool of himself over Buck when I reached Miles's office. Buck was there with another man I did not know, both of them sitting on the white sofa across from Miles. Jolene was there too, wearing her usual charming expression of stern disapproval as Cisco wiggled and spun and tried to climb into Buck's lap while Buck, of course, did nothing to discourage him. There were also faint muddy paw prints on Miles's white rugs. Terrific. Mrs. Banks would have a fit.

Miles got to his feet when I came in, looking concerned. "Baby, are you okay?"

I realized then that my halfhearted effort to clean up in the hall bathroom had fallen short. My jeans were torn and muddy where I'd hit the ground, my hair was wet and tangled, my eyes were red with crying.

Buck, giving Cisco's ears a final enthusiastic rub, stood too. "What happened to your hand?"

And oh, yeah. My knuckles were scraped and bruised, and my hand was already starting to swell. I said, "I punched Casey in the nose."

Miles put his arm around my shoulders. "Let's get some ice."

I shook my head and pulled away. "No, I just want to get this over with. Cisco. Here."

Sometimes even a dog as intractable as Cisco can tell when you're in no mood to be trifled with. I sank wearily to one of the designer chairs and Cisco came—albeit reluctantly--to lie on the floor at my feet. He did not, however, take his hopeful eyes off Buck.

Buck said, "Raine, this is Detective Brett Harrigan. He's working with me in the investigator's office."

Brett Harrigan got to his feet as though to shake my hand, noticed my injury, and changed his mind. He said simply, "Pleasure, Miss Stockton." He sat back down again.

Miles said, looking worried, "Have you been with Casey this whole time?"

I shook my head. "I took a drive. I needed... some time."

I saw a quick look pass between the officers, but Jolene got right down to business. She said, "I spoke to the housekeeper before she left. She said you texted her to let Mr. Macintosh in. That was at 2:07, correct?"

"I guess. About that."

"He arrived five or ten minutes later, said he didn't need her to show him the way, and left with his jacket less than two minutes later."

"He said he left it here last night," I said.

"So, he gained entry to the house with your permission," Harrigan clarified.

I shot him a sharp look. "Nobody gave him permission to break into Miles's safe," I returned.

Buck said, "We've pretty much got the whole story from Mr. Young, and we've seen the security footage. I don't suppose you have any idea how he knew the combination to the safe."

I shook my head. "I don't even know it."

Miles said, "He might have memorized it while I was opening it last night. More likely he recorded me on his phone inputting the code."

Buck made a note. To me, he said, "Why did you go to see Casey?"

I gave him an aggravated, impatient look. "Why do you think?" Then, because this was a police interview, after all, I added, "To ask why he did it. To get my stolen property back."

"And did you?"

I scowled. "No."

"Did he tell you what was on the drive that was important enough to break into a safe for?"

I shook my head tiredly. "His future, he said. He just laughed at me when I told him to give it back. Then I punched him and told him to get off my property and he said gladly, and I left." I hesitated. "Maybe he didn't say gladly. But he was packed and ready to leave when I got there. He was just waiting for me to get my car out of his way."

I added, "He's the one who put the drive behind the outlet cover, though, I'm sure of it. And he had to know he was being recorded when he broke into the safe. Miles practically gave him a tour of his security system."

Buck looked at Miles. "You said there was nothing but a list of numbered files on the drive. I don't suppose you made a copy."

Miles said, "I tried, but there was another layer of encryption that prevented it." He glanced at me and seemed to make a decision. He said, "There's something else. I wanted to wait until Raine got here to show it to you."

He went to his desk, picked up a legal-size report folder and handed it to Buck. "I got this from my investigator while I was in Atlanta today," he said. "It's the updated results of his background check on Casey Kinsey Macintosh."

I stared at him. "You said he didn't find anything!"

"But I didn't say he would stop looking," Miles said.

He pulled up one of the curvy, white, art-deco footstools that dotted the room and sat close to me, taking my hand. "According to this, Casey Macintosh—only one of his aliases, by the way—went to prison six years ago for passing bad checks. He served three months of an eighteen-month sentence. During that time, he appears to have hooked up with something called The Chain Gang, which is a kind of white-collar crime ring run by a man named Dimitri Petrova, street name Deacon."

At this Buck looked up sharply from his study of the folder, and he and Harrigan exchanged a look.

Miles went on, "A year later he was arrested for passing counterfeit bills, but charges were dismissed. Two years after that Casey was sentenced to three years for breaking and entering and served two months. Eight months ago, he went back to prison for a parole violation and served three weeks of a two-year sentence. All these arrests were in South Carolina, by the way, not"—he looked at me with sympathy in his eyes —"Colorado."

"So, my brother is a professional criminal," I said dully. "Somehow I'm not surprised."

Buck's lips were tight as he closed the folder. "May I keep this?" he asked.

"No." Miles got up and took the folder from him, returning it to his desk.

I could understand his attitude. If the police had done their job in the first place, none of us might be here now. But Buck was mad, and I could understand that too.

Buck turned to me. "So, he refused to return the stolen property, and you punched him. Did he hit you back?"

I shook my head.

A silent message seemed to pass between Jolene and Buck. He looked down at his notebook, and then at me. "The problem," he said carefully, "is that without the evidence we don't know the value of what was stolen. Could be millions of dollars, could be $5.00, which is what one of those portable drives cost in the drugstore. Technically, you own the property where the drive was located. But you hired Casey to work for you in exchange for rent, which means he was a legal tenant, so he might easily claim the drive was his and *you* stole it."

Buck turned to Miles. "The suspect didn't break into your house; he was allowed in by your housekeeper, who had permission from your fiancé. Obviously, he didn't have permission to enter your safe. But he only took what he might later claim belonged to him, and we're not entirely sure how he gained access to the safe. He might claim in court that it was the same way he gained entry to the house."

I stared at him.

Buck went on, "What I'm saying is that, without any physical evidence of what was on the drive, and given all the extenuating circumstances, it's up to you to press criminal charges. I'm happy to pursue an investigation if you do."

"Which," Miles clarified, "might only result in a misdemeanor charge."

Now I stared at Miles.

Buck said, "Listen, it's up to you. I just need to know what to say in my report."

Miles looked at me, waiting for my decision. I didn't have to think hard. "He's not going to court," I said dully. "He's a professional scam artist. You're not going to catch him. Whatever he wanted on that drive, he's already gotten, and he's long gone. I'm over it. I never want to see him again."

Miles turned to Buck with a slight raise of his eyebrow. "You heard the lady," he said. "No charges."

Buck pressed, "Are you sure? Because..."

I stood abruptly. "Are we done? I want to take a shower, and my hand really hurts."

Buck stood too. "Raine, listen, this may be more complicated than you realize. If you change your mind..."

"I won't," I said.

Miles and I walked with them to the door, and when they were gone, we stood together in silence for a long, sad moment. Then Miles said, "I'm sorry, sugar."

I shook my head slowly. "The worst part is not losing a brother. It's not even that he used me or lied or stole from me. It's that I let him. Even after he admitted lying about his background. Even after he lied about his name. I kept giving him chance after chance. It was like I *wanted* him to play me for a fool. I wanted to trust him. I was a complete idiot. And now... I can't even trust myself anymore. That's the worst part."

Miles massaged my shoulder gently. "Raine," he said, "I hope that's not true. You're not an idiot. And you never trusted him either, any more than I did. You know that."

I turned my head to look at him.

"You never once offered him Rags," Miles reminded me. "He was the perfect candidate, you asked everyone else who crossed your path, but never Casey. Because you didn't trust him."

I had no argument for that, mostly because I had no defense. I had let someone into Miles's home, into his daughter's life, but I didn't trust him with a dog. Guilty as charged.

"You were hoping he'd prove you wrong," Miles went on. "You gave him every chance to do so. But in the end, he made a different decision. I feel sorry for him, not you. He'll never know what he missed out on."

And that was it. I thought I was all cried out, but I wasn't. I turned my face into Miles's shoulder, and he held me while the tears spilled out. Because I would never know what I'd missed out on either.

That was the worst part.

CHAPTER
THIRTY-FIVE

Jolene frowned as the three of them walked back to their vehicles. "How the hell do you serve three weeks for a parole violation? Or two months of a three-year sentence, for that matter."

"You've got somebody with a lot of power looking out for you," Harrigan said. "And I understand that Deacon takes good care of his gang. He can't afford not to," he added, "given the amount of revenue they bring in."

"Damn it," Buck muttered. "We almost had him." He told the other two about Marshall's conversation with the FBI, and his instructions to back off. "So, law enforcement can't get the tools we need to make an arrest, but a guy with a few million to toss around just has to snap his fingers."

Harrigan pointed out, "This could mean the FBI is closing in on an arrest. In fact, it probably does."

"Maybe," Buck was forced to agree. His tone was disgruntled. "But he committed a crime in my county."

"So, wait," Jolene said. "This dude *is* Stockton's half-brother, and he *is* an apparent suspect in a high-level criminal investigation, and he *did* break into a safe to rip her off, which is why you can't file charges against him."

"That's pretty much the size of it," admitted Buck

unhappily.

Harrigan said, "I'll write up the report. But if they're not going to press charges, there's not much we can do."

Buck frowned fiercely. "I know you're right, but I'd give a lot to talk to the guy. Give me five minutes, and I'll find something to bring him in on."

Harrigan said, "Let me know if you think of anything." He walked to his car.

"You know," Jolene said thoughtfully, watching Harrigan drive away, "if you think about it, there really is only one prosecutable crime here." She looked at Buck. "Assault."

Buck gave an unamused grunt of laughter. "Oh, right. Let's go in and arrest the victim. That's going to go over real well with Mr. Moneybags."

"Not what I had in mind at all," she replied mildly, taking out her phone. "But we would be derelict in our duty if we didn't dispatch a unit to Casey Macintosh's home for a welfare check."

A small smile twitched at Buck's lips. "He's probably gone by now. But if he's not, charge him with anything from trespassing to holding his mouth crooked. I want him in my office."

"Are you going to send a copy of the report to the FBI?"

"Not unless we can make an arrest. Without one, we've got nothing to report." He glanced at her. "Want to grab a late lunch?"

She finished making her phone call, then gave him a slightly incredulous look. "It's almost time for supper," she said.

He glanced at his watch. "Damn," he muttered. "Central time."

She grinned as she placed her hand on the door handle. "How I ever hooked up with a man who can't even tell time is beyond me. But, yeah, I could use a burger. And Buck," she added just before she got into the car, "I'm sorry to say it but I think Stockton is right. This Macintosh is a professional. We're never going to catch him."

It turned out she was right, and so was Buck. There was no sign of Casey Macintosh when sheriff's deputies visited his last known location twenty minutes later. Upon entering the premises through an unlocked door to make a wellfare check, the only signs of previous habitation were a dusty futon and, in the bottom of a cabinet next to the sink, a box of dog biscuits.

PART THREE

CHAPTER THIRTY-SIX

Casey's body was found three weeks later.

We'd had a spate of really bizarre weather since Valentine's Day: six inches of snow followed by three inches of ice followed by ten straight days of rain followed by a week of temperatures in the seventies. Floodwaters rose and receded. Everything smelled like rot. Insects and animal life ran amuck. Blooms died on the vine. And tourists, mistaking the clear signs of Armageddon for an early spring, flocked to the mountains again.

One of those tourists decided to wander away from his campsite in search of the perfect photo op. When he didn't return after three hours, his wife became worried and called the ranger station. The ranger station called in the Carolina Wilderness Search and Rescue Team, of which Cisco and I are members. Later there might be helicopters and search drones, but canine search and rescue teams are almost always the most efficient first responders, and 85 percent of the time we find our man. That other 15 percent is what keeps us up at night.

The Cullowhee Gap Wildlife Preserve is a state-maintained wilderness area on the northeast side of the county. There are some beautiful hiking trails and about a half-dozen primitive camping sites. In the spring and summer, it's lush with bright pink mountain laurel and rhododendron, wild blackberries and Cherokee roses. Roaring waterfalls and spectacular gorge views are always around the next bend. Black bear, deer, bobcats and coyote roam freely. Foxes will come right up to your campsite to steal food. Wild boar have also been known to ram cars, and rattlesnakes are prevalent. For this reason, the wilderness experience is recommended for experienced hikers and campers only. But of course, very few people ever heed this warning.

Generally, on a search such as this, Cisco and I would be the only responders, since the members of our tracking club all cover different territories in their own counties. But this early in the season, everyone was anxious to get their dogs out and back in search mode, so we had eight teams show up that day, a team consisting of one human and one dog. Our team leader, Hank, assigned us in teams of two: northeast, northwest, southeast and southwest. Cisco and I, with a sharp German Shepherd handled by twenty-something Tony Farlow from the neighboring county, were to work our way north along the edge of the Cullowhee Gorge while the other teams worked south. I objected to that, pointing out that there was nothing northward except brush and bare forest, and a person looking for photographs would have been far more likely to go toward the waterfalls. Hank and I argued about that while the others stood around looking impatient. However, I do know when to quit an argument and obey orders, and somebody had to take the north trails. At least it was good exercise.

The day was sunny, and the temperature was in the low fifties, a good day for a hike. I stuffed my jacket in my pack after the first half hour and didn't even bother pulling on gloves. The woods were still barren in March, trees skeletal, grasses dead, blackberry bushes nothing but thorns and winter-broken branches. Cisco kept his nose to the ground and his pace meandering as he happily sniffed out wildlife, but I could tell by his demeanor he had picked up no sign of our missing tourist.

I was not surprised to be proven right when, an hour and a half later, Hank recalled all teams. The missing man had been found three miles south of the campsite, limping his way back with a turned ankle and a camera phone filled with pictures of waterfalls. I radioed back with a "Roger, copy that" and turned Cisco back toward our rendezvous point. Not five minutes later, Tony radioed. "Team Two, what is your location?"

I was Team Two. I checked my compass and read off the coordinates. He replied, "I'm just across the gorge from you. Look three degrees west halfway down the gorge. What do you see?"

I stopped and took out my binoculars, searching the area he'd described. I caught a glint of light midway down the rocky gorge and focused in on it. Sunlight glinting off metal. I put down my binoculars and picked up the radio. "This is Team Two. Tony, is that a car?"

"That's what I'm making out," he replied. "From here, it looks like a pretty bad wreck. I'm going to call it in."

I called Cisco over to me and surveyed my surroundings. Access to the gorge from this side was more of a gentle slope than a vertical drop, and with the undergrowth as sparse as it was this time of year, I thought I could make out a deer trail not too far away. I said, "Tony, I think I can make it down there. Go ahead and call it in. I'll let you know what I find."

"Copy," he said. "I can tie off and rappel down to the ledge about fifty feet above the site and hike the rest of the way. I'll meet you there. Team Three out."

Sometimes Tony could be a bit of a show-off.

As soon as I started down the deer trail, Cisco scented the air and started to pull ahead with such enthusiasm that I had a hard time keeping up. The incline was not as gentle as it looked from the top and I slipped and slid on the pine-straw-covered surface. I didn't dare call Cisco off, however. It was likely, of course, that the only thing he was tracking was the deer that had made the trail. But it was equally possible that someone had survived the wreck that had landed the car at the bottom of the gorge, and if so, Cisco was doing nothing more than his job.

Only it wasn't a car. It was a silver-gray van.

I arrived sweaty and gasping to see the vehicle had landed on its roof, leaving a swath of broken trees on its way down. The side panels were caved in and the windows broken. The back doors looked as though they had been wrenched open during the fall; one of them was hanging loosely by its hinges. But there was enough left of the back bumper for me to see the tag. A Colorado tag.

Cisco pulled the leash from my suddenly slack fingers and galloped toward the van. I opened my mouth to call him back, but all that escaped my lips was a hoarse whisper. "Casey!"

I ran toward the van and didn't try to stop Cisco as he wriggled through the open back door and into the rubble inside. I flung myself on the ground beside the cab of the upside-down vehicle, peering through the shattered window. I called in a slightly stronger voice, "Casey! Are you in here? Casey!"

I reached inside and grasped the steering wheel to pull myself forward, but I could only make it partway through the opening. Cisco hadn't gotten very far either; I could hear him panting and moving around just outside the vehicle. I called out again and shone my flashlight inside. The upside-down driver's seat was empty, as was the passenger seat, although I thought I saw a smear of something dark that could have been dried blood. Neither seat belt was fastened. I swept the back with my light as best I could, but it was a jumble of broken furnishings and dislodged containers, their contents scattered everywhere. I called Casey's name; I listened hard for signs of life. I heard nothing. I wriggled back out of the window and fumbled for the radio.

"Team leader, this is Team Two," I gasped. "I'm at the site of the wrecked vehicle." I gave my coordinates. "I don't see anyone inside but I'm unable to gain entry. There may be blood on one of the seats and the dashboard. No seat belts. Cisco and I are beginning a perimeter search for survivors now."

Hank replied, "All teams, rendezvous at these coordinates. Law enforcement and Fire and Rescue are on their way. Team two, search a one-hundred-yard grid in all directions and report back."

"Copy that."

I was about to sign off when Tony reported in, "Team Two, this is Team Three. I have reached the ledge. I can see the wreck. Rocket and I will be making our way toward you."

"Copy, Team Three. Team Two Out."

I hurried to the back of the van and stretched inside until my groping fingers closed on a sweatshirt that had spilled from the drawer. I tugged it free, and my heart caught in my chest as I looked at it. It had the logo "Rocky Mountain High" on it and a sketch of rugged mountains in the background. Casey had been wearing it the day we'd sat on the floor and heated fried chicken in the fireplace.

I bundled it up quickly and showed it to Cisco. He sniffed the garment happily, remembering his friend. When I commanded him to track, he gladly obeyed.

But I could tell immediately he was not picking up a scent. He circled the van twice, three times, growing increasingly frustrated each time. Once I thought he had something. He took off into the woods about fifty yards then abruptly stopped and backtracked. I felt despair growing. If the accident had happened before the snow, ice and subsequent rain, even the most talented tracking dog would be hard put to find a scent. Not that it would have mattered. The bad weather had started three weeks ago, and the chances of anyone surviving both an accident like this and three weeks in the winter wilderness were slim indeed. What had Casey been *doing* out here anyway? There were no paved roads in the preserve, no access to the gorge except through hiking trails and logging roads. How had he even found the place?

We had been searching in futile circles about half an hour when the radio crackled again. It was Tony, and his voice sounded weak and shaky. "Um, all teams. Rocket has alerted to human remains." He gave the coordinates. "We're about five hundred yards above the site of the wreck. We're going to need chopper extraction. And…" A pause. I thought I could hear his choppy breathing. "Law enforcement."

Hank started giving orders over the radio, but I heard nothing else. I stuffed my radio into my backpack and called Cisco to me. We half-ran, half-crawled up the rugged incline to where Tony and Rocket were waiting four hundred yards away. I broke through the brush and saw Tony had set out flags around the perimeter of a mylar blanket that he had spread on the ground. Beneath the blanket was an uncertain shape. I could smell vomit and realized it must be Tony's.

I stopped short, breathing hard, a dozen yards from the site. When Cisco plunged forward, I called him back sharply. Rocket was on the other side of the body, her head on her paws, and Tony squatted beside her, stroking her fur. He looked pale and shaken, and when he saw me, he stood.

"Don't look, Raine," he said. His voice was a little choked. "It's bad. I figure he was ejected from the vehicle on the way down, but there's been…" He swallowed hard. "Animal activity and… it's bad."

I dropped Cisco's leash and gave him the hand signal to stay. I couldn't speak, I couldn't breathe. But I also couldn't stop my feet from moving. I took one step, and another, and yet another, until I was close enough to peel back the edge of the blanket from the corpse. But I didn't have to. I had already seen what I needed to know.

One lifeless arm remained uncovered by the blanket. It was torn and spattered with mud, but around the wrist, clearly visible, was the tattoo of a chain.

It was Casey.

CHAPTER THIRTY-SEVEN

I sat shivering on a camp chair at the top of the gorge while the landscape filled up with emergency vehicles. Somebody brought me a paper cup of coffee, which I used to warm my hands. Cisco pressed his furry body against my legs, but even his warmth couldn't penetrate the core of ice in my soul.

I overheard one of the first responders report, "Blond male, six feet tall, approximately 175, age indeterminate. Partially clothed in jeans and navy nylon jacket. Significant predator and insect activity make further identification difficult."

Tony and I waited at the scene to give our statements to the police while the rest of the team continued to search for possible survivors. I could have told them not to bother. Casey didn't know anyone in town but me. He had been alone in the van.

A deputy took my initial report, then told me to wait in case there were further questions. Eventually Jolene came over, along with that detective I had met at Miles's house —Hammond, Harrington, somebody. "Where's Buck?" I asked Jolene, looking around for him. Every cop and emergency responder in two counties was there by this time, but there was no sign of Buck.

"In a training class," Jolene said. "He will be for the rest of the week. You remember Sergeant Harrigan?"

Harrigan, that was it. I nodded, and he responded, "Miss Stockton."

Both Jolene and Harrigan had their notebooks out. Jolene said, "I understand you identified the deceased as Casey Macintosh, your half-brother."

I nodded and swallowed hard. "Tony said his face was…" I swallowed again. "That there wasn't much left. But I recognized the van, and the tattoo on his wrist. There used to be a pinkish butterfly design in the center of the chain that I thought was a birthmark, but it was probably a stamp of some kind. It looks like it washed away."

"Can you give us any other identifying marks or characteristics?" Harrigan asked when he had finished writing in his notebook.

I started to shake my head, then remembered. "He said he had a dragon tattooed on the other arm, but I never saw it."

Harrigan and Jolene exchanged a look.

I said hesitantly, "What?"

It was Jolene who replied. There wasn't much that rattled her. "The remains aren't completely intact," she said. "So that information isn't helpful."

I tried not to let that sink in. My fingers tightened in Cisco's fur.

Harrigan said, "We didn't find any ID on the body, but we did find a wallet with a driver's license and other identification belonging to Casey Macintosh in the van. Also, a phone. Smashed, I'm afraid."

I nodded. "He lived in the van. That is, until he moved into Maude's house. And then, the last time I saw him, he was on his way out of town. So, everything he owned would've been in the van."

Harrigan said, "When was the last time you saw him?"

"The day—the day Miles called you about the break-in. I told you about that."

Harrigan said, "That was the day you confronted Macintosh about breaking into your fiancé's safe, is that right?"

I nodded.

"And there was a physical encounter of some sort, if I recall."

I said dully, "I punched him in the nose."

"Is that all?"

I stared at him. "What do you mean?"

"I mean," replied Harrigan, "how did you leave him?"

I could hardly bear to remember that. Casey, angry and defiant, his face smeared with blood. And now... his face was unrecognizable. I managed only one word. "Bleeding," I said.

Jolene said, "You said he was leaving. Any idea where he was going?"

I shook my head. "I just told him to get out. He said that was exactly what he planned to do. I got in my car and drove away. That's the last time I saw him."

"And you haven't heard from him since?"

"No."

Jolene said, "Any idea what he was doing out here? It's pretty far from civilization."

I frowned, my fingers once again tightening in Cisco's fur. He looked up at me curiously. "I can't figure that out. Maybe he was lost? But the only way to get here from Casey's place— I mean, Maude's place—would be to take Old Highway 12 and then turn onto Dolittle Road, and then you'd have to know exactly which turnoff to take to get to the gorge. It's not even marked. In other words, this is not a place you find on your way to someplace else."

Harrigan said, a little dryly, "We know. We had a little trouble finding it ourselves. But you seem familiar with the area."

I nodded. "It's my job. Besides, I grew up around here. I know most of the out-of-the-way spots." I looked at Jolene. "Do you have any idea when..." Again, I swallowed back bile. "You know, when it happened?"

She said, "We'll know more after we finish our investigation, and the medical examiner will have the final word. My guess? It wasn't recent."

I really couldn't let my mind go there. That my last words to Casey had driven him to this place and off the edge of a cliff... that he had lain here, prey to the forest wildlife, for three weeks... No. I couldn't.

Jolene, accustomed to being in charge, said brusquely, "Okay, Stockton, I'll get a deputy to drive you back to your car. We might have more questions for you when we finish the investigation."

Before I could reply, Harrigan said, "About that thumb drive you said Macintosh stole... any idea what happened to it?"

I was confused. "I told you before, Casey took it. I told him to give it back, but he wouldn't. So, I left."

There was an odd look in the detective's eyes. Was it skepticism? "We didn't find a thumb drive on the body. And so far, no sign of it in the van."

I didn't know how I was supposed to respond to that.

Harrigan said, "The other fellow..." He flipped a page in his book. "Tony, he said that some of you carry weapons for personal protection when you're on a search. Do you?"

I didn't see what that had to do with anything, but I replied, "Yes. My husband—my ex-husband—insisted on it. Not for personal protection so much as for rattlesnakes and copperheads."

He said, "May I see it?"

So, I took my gun out of my backpack, ejected the magazine, and handed it to him. He looked it over casually. "This is some serious firepower," he observed.

"I spend a lot of time in the woods," I answered. "Bears, wild boar... aggressive wildlife is rare, but it happens. My uncle and my ex are both law enforcement. They wanted me to have a gun that would do the job if I ever needed it to."

"You take good care of it. Ever had to use it?"

"A couple of times. I scared off a coyote once. And shot a

rattlesnake."

He returned the gun to me. "How often do you clean it?"

"My father cleaned his guns once a week. I try to keep it up when I remember." I returned the gun to my pack and turned back to Jolene. "Listen," I said with difficulty. "I guess I'm—well, it looks like I'm Casey's only relative. I should make arrangements for, you know, final arrangements. Should I wait here until they bring the body up? Who should I talk to?"

Jolene said, "We'll notify you when the medical examiner releases the remains. It could be a week or so. But there's no point in you staying here any longer. This will probably go on into the night. The crime scene van is coming from Asheville, and last I heard it was a good hour out. We can't do anything with the body until they finish their investigation."

I stood slowly. "What are you talking about? What do you need with the crime scene van?"

It was Harrigan who answered. "From what we can tell," he said, "Mr. Macintosh didn't die from injuries sustained in the fall. He appears to have been shot in the face at close range with a high-caliber weapon."

CHAPTER THIRTY-EIGHT

The days that followed were strange indeed. I walked around with a gut-punched feeling, wishing the nightmare would just go away. I'd wake up in the morning and for a brief moment feel like myself again, unable to recall what that nagging uneasiness in the back of my mind was about. Then it would come back to me, and darkness would descend again. I had a half-brother. I had a half-brother I barely knew but really liked, a brother who'd turned out to be a liar and a thief, a brother who now was dead. Not just dead but murdered.

The medical examiner confirmed the cause of death to be a gunshot wound to the face, likely caused by a high-caliber weapon like a .44 Magnum. Manner of death: homicide. The forensic estimate of the time of death was around three weeks previously. Oddly, the fingerprints had been chemically altered to the extent that it was impossible to get a clear print, or even a partial. Or perhaps it wasn't odd at all. Who knew what Casey's background really was, or who he had been before he crossed my path?

"I think he was killed for whatever was on that thumb drive," I told Miles. I couldn't stop obsessing over it, and Miles, as patient as ever, understood. "He hid it in that outlet before we got there that day; he had to have. I don't know why he did it, but his scent had to be fairly fresh, or Cisco wouldn't have gone straight to it like that. He wasn't hiding it from me. What did I care about some random electronic device? I probably wouldn't have even noticed it. And why wouldn't he just put it in his pocket if he didn't want me to see it? No, he was hiding it from somebody else, and it was important enough for him to come up with a really clever hiding place. One that nobody but Cisco would have probably ever found."

"Important enough," Miles agreed, "for him to break into the safe and steal it the next day."

"What *were* those numbers?" I fretted.

Miles shook his head. "We'll never know unless they find the drive and break the encryption."

I shared my theory with Buck when he came by to offer his sympathy on Casey's death, and to bring me up to date on the case. "We're holding the body until we complete the investigation," he told me. "It might be some time yet. I'm sorry, we try not to do that, but the advanced state of deterioration makes this an unusual case. The last I heard they weren't even able to get a reliable DNA sample."

Buck and I were sitting on my front steps in a bright splash of March sunshine. The air still had that cold winter tang, but where the sunshine fell across my arms, I was warm. Cisco, who had outdone himself with his enthusiastic greeting of Buck, now lay with his head on Buck's knee and his eyes half-closed in drowsy contentment while Buck stroked his ears.

I nodded dully. "It's okay. It's not like there'll be a service or anything. He didn't know anybody but me." *And the person who killed him,* I added silently to myself.

"Same deal with his belongings, I'm afraid," Buck added. "We'll turn them over to you when the case is closed, but this new prosecutor, York, is being pretty anal about holding on to evidence."

Again, I shook my head. The last thing I wanted was to have to go through Casey's belongings in the same way I'd had to go through Maude's. "He was killed for whatever was on that thumb drive, Buck," I said. "You find that drive, and you'll find his killer."

He gave me a quick, uncertain look. "To tell you the truth, Raine—and you probably don't want to hear this—it's starting to look like Casey was involved in some pretty serious mob activity. His fingerprints had been burned off. That's not something a small-time criminal does for kicks. That tattoo of his is the mark of that prison gang, The Chain Gang, that was mentioned in Young's investigative report. We know Casey had help beating the charges all those times he was sent up, and that's more or less the mark of a mob operative. And the way he was killed... that was an execution."

I said forcefully, "Then why isn't that guy—what did you call him?—that Deacon, why isn't he a suspect? He has to be! The code that was on that thumb drive—whatever it was —it's got to be something the mob wanted. There's no other explanation, Buck!"

But Buck was already shaking his head. "For one thing, no one can find Deacon for questioning. He has gone completely underground. We don't have a bullet, so we can't do a ballistics match, we can't find the thumb drive... we basically have no evidence. For another, York doesn't want us to look at that angle. He's determined to keep it within his jurisdiction, and if we go much broader, he's afraid the FBI will take over. He's right," Buck added, somewhat bitterly. "And they should." He turned a resolute gaze on me. "Which brings me," he said, "to the other thing I wanted to tell you."

He took a breath. "Harrigan will be taking over this case. In fact, he's mostly been in charge from the beginning, since I was out of town when it happened, and this just makes it official. You see..." He paused just long enough to cause me to look at him curiously. "I've decided to take that job in Georgia."

My eyes widened with surprise. Beyond that—and on top of everything else that had happened—I didn't know what to feel. Or say.

"And," he went on steadily, holding my gaze, "Jolene is going with me. We're getting married as soon as we can arrange it."

"Oh." I sank back weakly. "Oh," I said again after a moment, and managed to add, "Um, congratulations."

He said, "I'm not scheduled to start until July, but they want me down there in June. Jolene and Willis and her mom will probably stay here the rest of the summer to close out our houses, and Jo has to work her notice... but it's going to be a good move for us, Raine. For me."

And the thing was, I didn't disagree. Jolene and Buck were such an unlikely match that they almost *had* to be destined for each other, and I thought they would be good together. It was just that, on top of everything else, it was hard to absorb. I really didn't know how to react.

Except that I felt like I'd had the rug pulled out from under me. Another punch to the gut.

I managed a strained smile. "I think so too, Buck," I said. "It's a good thing. Really." I reached across Cisco, who lay between us, to give him an awkward one-armed hug. "I'm happy for you."

He patted my back in return. "You know you'll always mean something to me," he said in that inarticulate way men have. "A lot. It's just... it's time."

I nodded, swallowing a lump in my throat, and we separated. "I know," I said a little hoarsely.

He glanced away. "Anyhow, I don't mean to get all sentimental. Plenty of time for that at my going-away party, right?"

This time all I could do was smile and nod. If I spoke, I would be the one getting all sentimental and it would not be pretty. First Maude, then Casey, now this. I didn't know how much more I could stand to lose. I dropped my hand to Cisco's fur, and my fingers brushed against Buck's. I quickly moved them away.

Buck went on, "So, like I said, I'll be here a few more months, but I've got another five days of classes in Georgia coming up next week, and I promised to take Willis wilderness camping for a couple of weeks during spring break, so the only fair thing to do is start easing Harrigan into my job now. I'm planning to work part time during May until I have to leave, but essentially he'll be in charge of investigations. He's a good man, Raine. You can trust him."

I nodded tightly, then said, "He needs to investigate Petrova."

He patted my knee and smiled. "I'll tell him."

He gave Cisco's ears one last brisk rub and stood. "Well," he said, "I'd better get going. I just wanted to fill you in."

Cisco leapt to his feet, tail waving happily in anticipation of some new adventure, and I caught his collar to keep him from following as Buck went down the stairs. "Buck," I burst out, unable to stop myself, "but if I need anything, I can call you, right?"

He looked back with a wink. "You bet," he said. "Anytime."

But it turned out he was wrong. Because when I called, he didn't answer.

CHAPTER THIRTY-NINE

Around the second week of April, I got a group text with a photo of Buck and Jolene at a wedding chapel. She looked absolutely stunning in a form-fitting, floor-length rose gown, holding a bouquet of pink and white flowers. He looked as handsome as ever. They were turned toward each other, and the expression on Jolene's face was so tender it made her look like someone I didn't even know. Buck looked at her in a way he had never looked at me. The caption was, "The first day of the rest of our lives."

I felt a little stab of pathos, but not much more. I passed the phone to Miles, who, without me even asking him to, tapped out a "Congratulations! Much happiness." reply. All Melanie said, when she saw the photo, was a disappointed, "No dogs."

I had lost what little enthusiasm I had ever had for planning my own wedding, despite encouraging texts from Rita, who had returned to Myrtle Beach to prepare for her move to the mountains this summer, and phone calls from Aunt Mart. I tried to distract myself with a new season of puppy classes at Dog Daze, but my heart wasn't in it. Corny took over the campaign to find Rags a new home, and as spring unfolded and more and more people returned to the mountains, we actually had a few good applicants. I found a reason to reject each one. Rags was all I had left of Maude, and thus of her son, Casey. Somehow letting go of him would be like saying a final goodbye to both of them, and I wasn't ready to do that yet. The truth was, I couldn't focus on anything except the unsolved case of my half-brother's murder.

It had been almost two months, and even Miles was able to get only the sketchiest information. That detective, Harrigan, came by to interview me a couple of more times, but he was not nearly as interested in providing information to the victim's family as he was in asking irrelevant questions. He wanted to know why I had argued with Hank about which direction to send the search teams on the day Casey's body was found. He wanted to know why my car was captured on a neighbor's doorbell camera approaching Casey's house, but not leaving it. I explained how Deer Run Trail formed a loop with access to the main road from the east and west, and how I hardly ever left the same way I arrived. He wanted to know if I had passed any other cars coming or going, and I told him about the black SUV I'd seen parked off the road. He made me go over and over the details of finding the thumb drive, and then arguing with Casey. I got the feeling, from the direction of his questions, that he thought whoever had killed Casey might have confronted him at the house, sometime after I left. Of course, I gave them complete access to Maude's house, but as far as I knew, they didn't find anything useful.

They interviewed Corny, briefly, about our day at the school, and what time we had departed and arrived home. They interviewed Miles, several times, about the evening Casey had spent at his house and the subsequent robbery. Miles had long since given them a copy of the security footage from the break-in, so what more they expected to learn, I couldn't imagine.

I had been around law enforcement long enough to understand that criminal investigations in small communities were rarely concluded quickly. But even Uncle Ro agreed that this one was taking longer than necessary and that, had it been up to him, the case would have been turned over to state investigators–or, as Buck suggested, the FBI–as soon as the autopsy results had confirmed the cause of death. He hinted that Marshall was inclined to do just that, but had been thwarted by the prosecutor, the estimable Mr. York, who seemed determined to name a suspect before involving any outside agency. All of us—Miles, Uncle Ro, Buck, Marshall—expected that, when an arrest was finally made, it would be from within the organized crime community.

We were wrong.

Corny and I had just finished exercising our boarders and cleaning their kennels early one Tuesday morning—the week after I got Buck's wedding announcement—when six sheriff's patrol vehicles pulled up my driveway, taking up all the space between my house and Dog Daze. Of course, the kennel dogs went crazy, not to mention my own crew. Cisco, Rags, Mischief and Magic, who had been playing in their own fenced yard in back of the house, charged the fence in a frenzy of excited barking. Corny and I scrambled to get the kennel dogs--some of whom were running in the Dog Daze play yard and others who had, only moment ago, been calmly minding their own business in the private enclosures outside their own kennels— safely back inside. There was a lot of noise and a lot of activity, and a couple of the deputies had even thought it was a good idea to turn on their flashers, and that kind of thing can work a pack of dogs up to the extent that they start turning on each other. The safety of the dogs was our first priority, and by the time I made it to the front office, gasping and sweaty, there were four or five officers already waiting there. Standing at the front of them was Detective Harrigan.

"What the hell?" I demanded.

He had a folded legal-sized paper in his hand, which he offered to me. "Miss Stockton," he said. "I have a search warrant for your house, place of business, vehicles and outbuildings. We are authorized to seize computers and other electronic devices, weapons, personal papers..." His voice faded into a droning buzz in my ears as I stared, unseeing, at the paper.

I felt, rather than heard, Corny come up behind me and stand there timidly, clearly as shocked as I was. When Harrigan gave an order and the officers started to move around the office and toward the back of the building, he whispered, "Miss Stockton, should I call someone?"

I managed, "No. No, protect the dogs. Do what the officers say. Don't let anyone get hurt." By that last, of course, I meant *Don't let any dogs get hurt,* but I was confident Corny understood that. He hurried off to comply, and I looked at Harrigan.

"What *is* this?" I had to raise my voice to be heard over the sound of barking. "What is this about?" The hand that held the search warrant was shaking, and he probably noticed, but at that moment I didn't care. I was more outraged than scared.

I'll give him this: Detective Harrigan has a great poker face. He replied, politely but firmly, "We'll probably be here for a while, Miss Stockton, so you might want to find a place to make yourself comfortable. And please put your dogs away."

I screeched at him, "I own a *kennel*! Where do you suggest I put them?"

Out of the corner of my eye I saw two of the gloved officers unplugging my computer, and I whirled on them. "Stop that! You can't take that! That's my business! My client list, my invoices…"

Now my hands were really shaking, and I almost dropped my phone as I fumbled it out of my pocket. "Where's Buck?" I demanded.

"I believe Major Lawson is on his honeymoon," replied Harrigan, but I punched Buck's number anyway.

It rang and rang, and finally went to an automated message. *This number is out of our service area…* I remembered then, very vaguely, something about wilderness camping. And just to demonstrate how upset I was, I almost dialed Jolene before I remembered who Buck was honeymooning with. I wondered if Harrigan and crew had deliberately waited until Buck was out of town before doing this, but that was crazy. Why would he intentionally piss off his boss?

Except Buck wasn't his boss anymore. And what could he possibly be looking for?

I called Miles, which was what I should have done in the first place. He was on his way to Atlanta for a meeting, but he somehow managed to decipher my mostly hysterical account of what was going on. The mere sound of his voice, calm and in control, lowered my blood pressure at least ten points.

"Okay, sugar," he said, "as soon as you hang up with me, call Sonny and don't say or do another thing until she gets there. Go to the kitchen, have a cup of coffee, stay out of the way. Can you do that? Say it."

"Okay. Yes," I managed, but it was difficult because what I wanted to do was wring Harrigan's neck, and I had plenty more to say to him. "I can do that."

"I'm turning around now. I'll be there in two hours."

I called Sonny and got the same instructions: "Do as you're told. Stay out of the way. Don't say anything. I'll be there in an hour."

The proudest thing I have ever done was to take my dogs to the house and sit quietly in the kitchen with a cooling cup of coffee on the table before me, listening to sheriff's deputies tramping around overhead, pulling out drawers and slamming closet doors while shushing my dogs and doing exactly as I had been told. That hardly ever happens.

Sonny arrived barely an hour later, listened to my brief account of the morning's goings-on, and asked, "What are they looking for, Raine?" Even as she said it, she was scanning the search warrant.

"I don't know," I answered. "The only thing I can think of is the thumb drive that Casey stole, but why would they think it was here?"

I had barely finished speaking when there was a light tap on the back door, and Detective Harrigan entered without waiting for an invitation. My four dogs, who had just settled down after Sonny's arrival, leapt to their feet again, barking and wagging their tails in greeting. All except Rags, whose leash I held, rushed the door to greet the intruder, who was accompanied by another uniformed officer. I called the dogs back sharply. Mischief and Magic, who really aren't very good guard dogs, looked abashed and returned to their place beneath the kitchen table, flopping down on their bellies. Cisco, who also isn't a very good guard dog, sniffed both men's shoes before returning to me and pressing himself uneasily against my knees. Dogs don't like their routines disrupted, and the fact that this debacle had upset my dogs was probably the thing for which I resented Harrigan most.

He had something in his hand, and he said, "Miss Stockton, do you recognize these?"

Sonny stepped forward. "I'm Sonny Brightwell, Miss Stockton's lawyer. She won't be answering any of your questions until we have a chance to talk."

But I said, "It's okay, Sonny." I looked in puzzlement at the two pieces of fabric Harrigan held in his hand. "That's Cisco's therapy dog vest," I told him, "and mine." Both were stained with dark smears, and I felt a sickening in my stomach as I remembered how the stains had gotten there. "We wore them the day we did the school program." And afterwards, when I had gone to confront Casey. I'd stuffed them in a tote bag because they were ruined with Casey's blood, intending to launder them later. But I had forgotten.

Harrigan held out an evidence bag with a small dark object in it. "What about this?"

"Raine," Sonny warned sharply, but too late.

"The thumb drive!" I gasped and took a step forward. "That's it! Where did you find it?"

Harrigan held up Cisco's vest. "In the pocket of this vest. Any idea how it got there?"

I shook my head. "That's crazy. I would have noticed when I put it on him, or while we were at the school. I put brochures from the humane society in his pockets and let him walk around and give them to the kids."

"Are you saying you didn't put the drive there?"

"No, of course not."

"Raine," said Sonny, "you need to…"

Harrigan persisted, "But this is the thumb drive you took from the outlet at your rental house, and that your fiancé later put in his safe."

I frowned. "I guess. I mean, it looks like it. I remember it had a red cap, just like this one. But you won't know until you plug it in to a computer."

Harrigan said, "We did."

He inclined his head to the other officer, and he moved forward. Before I knew it, he had twisted my hands behind my back and snapped on a pair of cuffs.

"Hey!" I cried. "What the—"

"Raine Stockton," he said, "you are under arrest for the murder of Casey Macintosh. You have the right to remain silent…"

CHAPTER FORTY

My father used to say the biggest mistake suspects made was refusing to exercise their right to remain silent. "The law allows these rights for a reason," he used to say, frustrated. "Why do people insist on ignoring them?"

I was determined not to make that mistake.

So, when Harrigan came into the interview room with an easy smile and a file folder in his hand, I said stiffly, "I prefer to wait for my attorney."

He turned on the video recorder in a high corner of the room, and then sat down across from me, putting the file on the table. "Raine," he said. He tilted his head toward me slightly. "May I call you Raine?"

I said, "No."

They had removed the handcuffs for the interview portion of my arrest, which I suppose was decent of them. Still, I rubbed my wrists beneath the table, where I imagined I could still feel the bite of steel.

He did not appear to take offense. "I want you to know I'm sorry about this," he said, making every effort to look sincere. "But you're from a law enforcement family. You know we have to go where the evidence leads. But we all also know the evidence only tells part of the story. I'm hoping you and I can work out the rest and put this thing to bed."

I had so many pithy replies loaded up. I verbalized none of

them.

He folded his hands atop the file folder, whose thickness was apparently supposed to suggest an excess of evidence. He leaned forward slightly. "No one thinks you're a cold-blooded murderer," he said quietly. "Let's get that straight. Buck couldn't speak more highly of you, even though you did divorce him. Your uncle was one of the most respected sheriffs this county has ever known. Even Marshall tells me you've assisted the sheriff's office on more than one occasion, and everyone who's worked with you admires you. But things happen, even to law enforcement officers. You see it all the time. We're all just humans when you get right down to it, and we make mistakes."

I exercised my right to remain silent.

He opened the file folder and pretended to glance over the first page. "Here's the problem," he said. "We know you argued with Casey Macintosh over the stolen thumb drive at or around the time he was killed. You told us Casey refused to return the thumb drive to you, and yet we found it in your possession. Hidden," he added meaningfully, "inside a bloody garment at the bottom of a tote bag in the back of your car. What's on the thumb drive, Raine? Why was it so important to you?"

I clamped my jaw down tight.

He nodded and went on, "As far as we can tell you were the last person to see Casey alive. The blood on the garments we took from your vehicle matches the blood from inside Casey's van, and both are a match for Casey's blood type. He was killed with the same kind of weapon you carry for personal protection. Your fingerprints were found on the steering wheel of Casey's van. We have a text message from Miles Young asking what you were doing at Cullowhee Gap, and since we know he has a tracking app on your phone, that places you at the scene."

I sucked in a breath, wanting to point out that there was a huge difference between Cullowhee Gap and Cullowhee Gorge and the road I had been on that afternoon didn't even lead to the gorge. But I was a judge's daughter. I kept my mouth shut.

Harrigan watched me carefully, clearly reading how hard it was for me to keep quiet. When I refused to give in to my own instincts for self-defense, he took an eight-by-ten photograph from the folder and pushed it across the table to me. "We have video camera footage of you driving Casey's van away from his house within an hour of the time you admit to confronting him over the thumb drive. This is a still shot from that footage."

"What?" I burst out. "That's crazy!" I looked at the blurry, greatly pixelated photograph of Casey's van which was clearly taken from some distance. All that could be seen of the driver was a dark head of hair and part of a cheekbone. How could anyone possibly think that was me?

I pushed the photograph back to him. "That's not me."

"It's clearly not Casey," he pointed out, and I started to realize that the photograph might have been nothing more than a ploy to get me to talk. "What we do know is that the driver is about your size, has dark hair like you, and knew how to get to the Cullowhee Gorge, which you admitted yourself is not something a lot of people know how to do. But you do. You also have enough wilderness experience to get back on foot and return to your car—with or without help."

"That's crazy," I repeated. My hands were so tight in my lap that my nails bit into my flesh.

He tucked the photograph back into the folder, unperturbed. "How did your fingerprints get on the steering wheel of Casey's van, Raine?"

For a moment I couldn't think. My heart was thumping in my chest, and I couldn't make myself focus over the sound of it.

I said hoarsely, "I'm waiting for my lawyer."

"On the day Casey's body was found, you argued against sending teams to the north ridge of the gap. Was that because you knew what they would find?"

The right to remain silent, the right to remain silent... I ground my teeth together and said nothing.

He looked at me gravely. "We're going to find out what's on that thumb drive we found in the vest," he said. "We have a cryptanalysis team going over it now. When we do, the story might change. But let me tell you what I think happened that day. Your boyfriend told you Casey had broken into his safe and stolen the thumb drive. You were hurt and furious. He was your brother and you trusted him. You let him live in your house for free, you introduced him to the people you loved, and he betrayed you. You drove over there to confront him. You demanded that he return the stolen property and get out. He refused. You pulled out your gun to show him you were serious. You never meant to fire it. You didn't want to hurt him, just to threaten him. But something happened. Maybe you tried to fire over his shoulder to scare him, maybe he tried to wrestle the gun from you, and it went off. You were horrified. You didn't know what to do. So, you dragged the body into the van, drove it to the gorge, put the van in neutral and let it roll over. But before you did, you searched the van— or even Casey's body—for the thumb drive. When you found it, you hiked back. There is over an hour you can't account for between the time you left your place of business to confront Casey, and the time you returned to Mr. Young's house for the police interview. For someone with your knowledge of the backwoods, that's plenty of time. I can make a case for second-degree murder right now. You never intended to kill your brother. The only premeditation involved at this point was your efforts to conceal the evidence when you realized we were looking at you as a possible suspect."

"I never..." I croaked but broke off. What I'd started to say was that I never imagined they suspected me. Not ever. Because I was innocent.

He waited a polite moment then went on. "But, like I said, the story will likely change when we find out what's on the drive. The charges could easily go from second- to first-degree and might even involve your boyfriend as a coconspirator."

I cried, outraged, "He didn't—" I caught myself again. I drew in a breath. I lifted my chin. "He's my fiancé," I said.

He nodded. "I beg your pardon, of course. My point is, you want to take advantage of circumstances while they're in your favor. And right now, the circumstances are about as good as they're going to get for you."

That's when I started to get scared.

They took me to my cell where I sat on the bed and waited for the deputy to escort me back to the conference room, where I held on to Cisco and told Sonny everything that had happened since Casey Macintosh had come into my life. She fumed over Harrigan trying to interview me without her present and promised retribution. She took copious notes, assured me the case against me was nonsense, and told me to get some rest. I would be out of there by this time tomorrow.

I got no rest. I lay stiffly on my cot listening to the shouts and screams and drunken profanities that echoed up and down the corridor until the deputy came to take me across the street to the courthouse the next morning. I was shuffled into a courtroom where I waited on a bench with a couple of drug dealers, a DUI and a spousal abuser for the judge to come in. Miles was in the front row of the gallery, right behind the lawyer's tables, talking to Sonny and two sharply dressed men I didn't know. When they brought me in I looked away. My hands were in cuffs. I couldn't meet his eyes.

One of the men with Miles came over to me and introduced himself. "Miss Stockton, I'm Virgil Breyer," he said briskly. "Mr. Young has retained me to represent you in this matter. Today's proceeding is fairly simple. The judge will ask you how you plea, you'll reply 'not guilty.' We'll argue bond, the judge will set a pretrial hearing date, and you'll be home this afternoon. All right?"

I murmured a humble thank you, he instructed me where to sit, and the waiting began.

I didn't know the judge. I didn't know the handsome young

prosecutor, who did his best to argue, in the most forceful of terms, that I was a threat to society and couldn't be trusted outside the confines of that eight-by-eight cell.

Me. A threat to society.

Bond was set at $150,000, which was outrageous for a rural county like ours, even on a murder charge. But the alternative was no bond at all. That was more than I could have raised if I had mortgaged everything I owned, but Miles didn't even blink. The judge set a hearing date for two weeks hence. An hour later my belongings were returned to me, and I was buzzed through the door into the vestibule, where Miles was waiting for me. He hugged me so hard I thought he'd crack my ribs. He held my face; he searched my eyes. All I could do was try not to cry. Understanding, he said simply, "Let's go home."

Melanie's school was on spring break, and she was waiting for us in the kitchen with chocolate smeared on one cheek, wearing a frilly apron. She had dressed Cisco up in a red bow tie and put a pink polka-dot bow on Pepper's collar. I laughed and hugged them and scrunched up my face against doggie kisses even as I wiped tears from the corners of my eyes. When I straightened up, Melanie threw her arms around my waist and said solemnly, "I'm sorry you had to go to jail, Raine." Then she stepped back and added, "I made Death by Chocolate to cheer you up."

Everything inside me twisted and I had to quickly bend to hug her again so she wouldn't see the expression on my face. She could not know how much the memory of that last night with Casey hurt. I didn't even know how much it hurt until this moment.

"That's the sweetest thing ever," I managed huskily. "But I'm really grungy and need to change first. Back in a sec, okay?"

I rushed from the room before my voice—and everything else about me—broke.

I filled the giant tub in Miles's master suite to overflowing with hot water and bubbles and buried myself in it up to my chin. I washed my hair three times. I scrubbed my skin until it started to bruise. I added more hot water, more bubbles. And I could not stop weeping.

Miles found me that way an indeterminate time later, covered in bubbles, muffling my sobs in my wet, updrawn knees. He sat down on the floor beside the tub and rested a comforting hand on the back of my neck. He didn't say anything. He just let me cry.

After a long time, I managed brokenly, "He... would be so ashamed of me!"

Miles asked gently, "Who would, sugar?"

"M-my... my father," I whispered.

Miles wrapped both arms around me and pulled me into his chest, soaking wet as I was, and just held me until I couldn't cry anymore.

CHAPTER FORTY-ONE

I remember the two weeks between my release and my hearing as flashes of a nightmare. Some moments are starkly clear, others a dark blur, like a landscape obscured by a thunderstorm. I had to cancel my training classes and close Dog Daze to boarders. The few people who kept their grooming appointments with Corny couldn't stop pestering him for information about me, the jailbird. The accused murderer. I couldn't leave the house for fear of the looks that followed me, the whispers when I crossed a threshold. I couldn't work, I couldn't sleep, I couldn't eat. I couldn't even help in my own defense. I have never felt so helpless, so completely out of control over my own fate. The lawyers were in charge. I could do nothing.

The purpose of a pretrial hearing, they explained to me, was to give the prosecution a chance to lay out its case before the judge and allow him to determine whether their case was even strong enough to take to trial. We, the defense, would not be allowed to present evidence or call witnesses, but we could ask questions. This was good for us, I was assured, since the prosecution basically had to show its hand and we did not. Since their case was almost entirely circumstantial, it was possible the judge would dismiss the whole thing out of hand.

But you know what they say: Hope for the best and prepare for the worst. That was exactly what my legal team—or I should say, Miles's legal team—was working day and night to do.

I told the lawyers about Casey's involvement with the man called Deacon and his apparent connection to the mob, but of course they were already exploring that angle. "But remember," the lead attorney, Mr. Breyer, told me via video conference, "we won't be presenting evidence at the hearing. We're just in the information-gathering stage at this point, in the unlikely event we do go to trial. To that end, what can you tell me about a man named Frederick Thomas, who rented the house on Deer Run Trail from October to December of last year?"

I shook my head. "I didn't even own the property then. You'd have to talk to the rental agent, Mr. Comstock."

He made a note. "According to my investigator, he was a contemporary of Mr. Macintosh. They seem to have met in prison while Thomas was doing time for internet fraud. They were both members of The Chain Gang you spoke of. Mr. Thomas was found murdered several weeks ago, in a manner not dissimilar to Mr. Macintosh."

"That's it!" I exclaimed. "It has to be. Casey must have been working with him—that's what he was doing here! And whatever they were working on was on that thumb drive. That's what got them both killed."

"That's the theory," agreed my attorney. He did not look happy about it.

"But," I insisted, "this is good news! If you can prove both murders were connected to this Chain Gang thing, you can find who did it."

"Theoretically, yes," he agreed. "But if this is embedded in organized crime, it may be easier said than done. After all, the FBI hasn't been able to break this gang after five years of trying. I'm not sure we'll be able to do so in the time we have to prepare for trial. However," he concluded briskly, "I'm confident it won't come to that."

His confidence, however, was not enough to help me sleep at night.

I had turned my own property over to Corny to take care of while I stayed with Miles in the big house. This time he didn't even have to convince me that his security system was a necessary advantage. Aunt Mart and Uncle Ro came by every day, Aunt Mart always with a casserole and an apologetic, "I know this is the last thing you need…" while she unpacked enough food to feed an army. Uncle Ro, furious with his own department for what he called "outrageous mismanagement" of the case, was desperate to be of help. But for obvious reasons, he had been shut out of his information network within the sheriff's office, and all Marshall would offer was sympathy. Rita wanted to come down to lend support, but that was the last thing I wanted. The fewer people I had to face and pretend to be brave for, the better off I was.

Finally, Miles decided that the best thing all our well-meaning relatives could do was to take charge of Melanie. Aunt Mart and Uncle Ro were assigned to take her on a tour of the Great Smokey Mountains National Park and from there to Myrtle Beach, where they would all spend a week with Rita. I don't know that I will ever be able to thank my aunt and uncle enough for the five days they spent sightseeing with a precocious eleven-year-old and her energetic golden retriever, nor my future mother-in-law for opening up her beach house to them all once they arrived. But that's what family does.

A week before the hearing I got a friends-and-family group text from Buck. *Sorry for the radio silence; wilderness camping. Just got back to an emergency in Mercy & they need me to start the new job right away. I'll be back next weekend for a few days & hope to see you all then with the details.*

Buck was gone.

I stood for a moment with my finger hovering above the "call" icon but put the phone away. There was nothing Buck could do. He didn't even work here anymore. And he would find out what had happened soon enough. I could only hope that by the time he did, it would all be over.

That night I lay in Miles's arms, staring at the dark, thinking about everything that was gone. Maude, whom I had known all my life, alive one moment and dead the next. Casey, the only brother I would ever have, who had flashed through my life like lightning and now was gone forever. Buck, who had never *not* been a part of my life, who had been my best friend since we were kids, who had taught me to fish and hunt and make a fire with flint, who had taught me to love him and who had broken my heart. I could see his little yellow house in the valley from my kitchen window and there had always been something reassuring about that, knowing he was there. Now when I looked out my kitchen window, what would I see?

So much loss. But I think the thing I most regretted losing was the girl who used to believe everything was going to be all right.

I said softly, "I'm sorry."

I knew Miles wasn't asleep. He rarely is. "About what, sugar?"

"Everything," I said. "I should have listened to you. I keep screwing up your life and you keep forgiving me even though there's no reason for you to, and I'm just sorry."

"You're not screwing up my life," he said, and kissed my hair. "And there's nothing to forgive."

"Casey said we're more alike than I'd admit. We came from the same father, both bad seeds."

"That's crazy." Now his voice was harsh, and his fingers tightened on my shoulder. "Nobody talks that way about the woman I love. Not even you."

I turned to look at him in the dark. "I love you, Miles," I said, and I felt it with all my being. "I want to marry you."

"I'm glad." He kissed me. "I want to marry you, too. Think I might have mentioned that once or twice."

"No," I insisted. There might have been the slightest note of desperation in my voice. "I mean now. Not in October with flowers and cake. Right now."

He was silent for a beat too long. My chest tightened with dread.

"Sweetheart," he said carefully, stroking my shoulder, "there's nothing I'd like more. And if that's what you want to do, we'll go to the courthouse in the morning. But you realize if we do that it's going to look like we got married so I couldn't be called to testify against you."

I sank back against the pillow, every muscle in my body heavy with defeat, every last bit of hope draining out of my pores. Even this. Even this had been taken from me.

Miles pushed my hair away from my face and kissed me again. "October," he assured me, "will be here before you know it. "

I managed a smile even though he couldn't see it. "I know."

The question was, Where would I be when October came?

CHAPTER FORTY-TWO

Mercy, Georgia

"**H**arrigan, you stupid son of a bitch!" Buck shouted into the phone. "What in the name of all holy hell are you thinking? You know there's not enough evidence for a conviction. There's not even enough evidence for an arrest! How in God's name did you even get a search warrant? Anything you found under that warrant is going to be thrown out if it's found to be invalid and that's basically your whole damn case! What were you thinking?"

Jolene came into the walnut-paneled study and closed the door behind her, an admonishing frown on her face as she lifted a finger to her lips. It was past 9:00 PM, Willis was asleep, and the big old antebellum house that was now their home carried sound like an echo chamber. She leaned against the door, her frown deepening as she listened.

On the other end of the phone, Brett Harrigan said wearily, "Buck, I follow orders, just like you do. York figured you'd react this way, which is why he waited until you were out of the picture to make the arrest. And we do have the evidence. You just didn't get a chance to see it."

"What evidence?" Buck demanded.

"The thumb drive. Raine Stockton had it in her possession and her fingerprints are all over it—along with Macintosh's blood."

"Of course her fingerprints are on it," Buck returned shortly. "She's the one who found it in the first place. And how do you know it's Casey's blood? The last I heard you couldn't get DNA."

Harrigan said, "You sound like you're arguing for the defense."

"Maybe I should," Buck shot back, "because what I'm hearing on your end is total bullshit."

"I'm sorry you feel that way."

Buck Lawson had been chief of police of Mercy, Georgia for a week now, and those had not been uneventful days. Hanover County might as well have been on another planet for all he knew of what had been going on there. The first he'd heard of Raine's arrest was when he received a request from the DA's office for an affidavit certifying the police report he had taken about the theft of the thumb drive, which was to be presented as evidence at her upcoming hearing. That had been this afternoon, and he had spent the hours since then on the phone demanding answers. So far, he had been less than successful.

He said, "This was an organized crime hit and you know it. All the evidence points to Petrova and his boss, whoever he turns out to be. We talked about it, for God's sake. We had it all laid out."

"We didn't consider other angles—"

"Because there *were* no other angles! And what about the thumb drive, anyway? Did you ever find out what was on it?"

"We've sent it to the FBI's cryptanalysis team for assistance. We hope to have some answers before the hearing, but I don't think the contents are going to make much of a difference in our case. We're talking about a crime of passion here, and there's plenty of evidence for that."

Buck said in a very low, very controlled tone, "Listen to me, Harrigan. I want a complete and unabridged copy of Raine Stockton's file in my inbox within the hour. I don't care how late it is. I don't care who you have to wake up to get it. I want it."

"Buck, you're not a part of this investigation anymore. You don't even work here. I can't just—"

"I'm the investigator in charge who opened this case," Buck returned brusquely. "You can do me a professional courtesy, or I can come up there and get it myself, in which case I can assure you there will be nothing either professional or courteous about our meeting. One. Hour."

He punched the disconnect button and stood there for a minute, eyes churning. Then he drew back his hand as though to throw the phone against the wall, and Jolene stepped forward with her palm raised. "You'll regret it," she warned.

Buck slammed the phone down on his desk instead.

"I love it when you go all badass chief-of-police on me," Jolene said, "but let's try not to destroy the electronics in the process. Or the furniture," she added when he jerked open a drawer then slammed it closed hard.

He scowled at her. "You should have known. How could you not know?"

Jolene sat down on the sofa adjacent to the desk and tucked one long leg beneath her. She was wearing a silky nightshirt trimmed in lace and an open flowery robe that fell to her calves. Her hair was loose in a thick braid that fell across one shoulder. Her freshly showered scent floated across the room to him. Just her nearness calmed him measurably.

She said, "I told you, I didn't leave my desk for three days after we got back from the woods. I was drowning in paperwork, and Stockton's arrest report was not among it. She'd been out a week by then and it was old news. Before I had a chance to get back in the loop on anything, I had to come down here and rescue your ass."

"You did not..." But at her mildly raised eyebrow, he let the sentence drop. He sank into his desk chair and leaned back his head. "Damn. I feel responsible for this."

"You're not," Jolene informed him matter-of-factly. "Did

you call her?"

Buck picked up the glass off bourbon his desk, looked at it, and put it down again. "I didn't know what to say," he admitted. "I talked to Ro—he's in Myrtle Beach with Miles Young's kid—and Marshall wouldn't tell me a damn thing. Can't blame him. It's still an open case. I thought about calling Young but..." This time when he picked up the glass, he drank from it. "I didn't think he'd want to hear from me."

The computer on his desk pinged, and Buck sat forward, looking at it. "That's it," he said. "Harrigan must have been in the office."

Jolene said, "Print me out a copy."

Two hours later Buck sat back, his eyes bleary and his shoulders stiff from leaning over the computer, and ran a hand through his hair. Jolene stacked her copy of the file, paper-clipped it, and dropped it on the coffee table. "Do you think she did it?" she asked.

It was not an offhand question, and Buck did not give the easy reply. He picked up the now almost-empty glass of bourbon and took a sip. He chose his answer carefully. "If somebody hurt one of her dogs," he said, "or, God forbid, that little girl, yeah. I can see Raine shooting a man in the face with a .44 without even thinking about it. Then she'd call 911 and turn herself in. That's just her. But something like this..." He shook his head. "No. Not a chance."

Jolene regarded him steadily. "Well then," she said, "you'd better do whatever it takes to get her off, because I can't be married to a man who'd let somebody he once loved go to prison for a crime he knows she didn't commit."

Buck glanced at her and then closed his eyes in brief surrender. "I don't know what to do. I'm a witness for the prosecution. I don't see anything I can do to help her."

Jolene got up and dropped the printed file on his desk. "Look harder," she advised. She kissed the top of his head, and he caressed her cheek. "I'm going to bed," she said. She tapped the printed report with her fingernail. "Start at the beginning.

Look harder."

When she was gone, that was exactly what Buck did. Around 2:00 in the morning, he found it, and a slow smile of relief spread across his face. Too tired to go upstairs to bed, he collapsed on the sofa and slept dreamlessly for five hours.

At 7:00 the next morning he called the Hanover County's prosecutor's office and left a message. "Please tell Mr. York that I won't be signing the affidavit he requested," he told the assistant who answered the phone. "I prefer to give testimony in person. I'll be there for the hearing at 10:00 AM on Thursday."

When he hung up, he saw Jolene leaning against the doorframe of his study, arms and ankles crossed, a vaguely self-satisfied expression on her face. "How'd you sleep?" she inquired.

Buck replied, "How would you like to spend the weekend in the mountains?"

She said, "I already packed."

CHAPTER FORTY-THREE

The day before the hearing, the letter from Maude arrived. It came in a sealed envelope addressed to me, accompanied by a handwritten note from Leon Whitmire.

Ms. Stockton,
I hope this finds you well. This letter to you turned up in my aunt's papers. I'm sure she meant to mail it before she went to the hospital for the last time. I'm sorry it was delayed.
All best wishes,
Leon Whitmire
P.S. Did you find a good home for the puppy?

I sat on Miles's deck in the gentle May sunshine and looked at the sealed envelope addressed to me for a long time without opening it. Somehow just looking at the familiar handwriting made it seem for a moment as though the person who had written the letter was still here, just out of town, that nothing had changed, that everything was normal. But if there was one thing Maude had taught me, it was to face the world as it was, head held high, even when it was scary. I opened the envelope and unfolded the paper inside.

Dearest Raine,

271

It disturbs me deeply to be the bearer of unsettling news, but I must tell you I have been diagnosed with a terminal illness and it is progressing rapidly. I selfishly hope this letter reaches you after I am gone, because I don't want my last memories of you to be the knowledge that I have caused you more pain.

I am so sorry for the trouble between us, which I hope has lessened a little over the past few years. I want you to know I never regretted loving your father, nor do I regret the product of that love, which is what I must write you about now. When I was a younger woman, very much in love and dreaming foolish dreams, I had a son, your half-brother. I never told your father about him. I couldn't do that to him, nor to you and your mother. I also want you to know that after I moved to Hansonville and came to work for Jonathon, our affair was over... until, of course, that last weekend, when, for reasons that will make no difference to you now, we found comfort in each other. I never stopped loving your father, but you and your mother were the loves of his life.

I placed my son for adoption with a fine family, and I think I turned my love for my child, my need to nurture and mother, on you. I want to thank you for that. The years I spent with you and your family will always be the best ones of my life. A few years ago, my son got in touch. His name is Casey Macintosh and he's a young man now, living his own life. I'm afraid our initial conversation didn't go very well, but last fall I was able to track him down again. I got the impression he has not been very successful in life, and I offered him the use of my house on Deer Run Trail, which was vacant at the time. I suggested we might meet there, and I must confess I was hoping to introduce him to you. I didn't mention that he had a sister, of course. I felt I should talk to you first. At any rate, he never gave me a definitive answer, and eventually the house was rented to someone else.

The reason I bring up these details is that I have left the property to you, Raine. Perhaps it wasn't the best thing to do, and will doubtless be more of a burden than a boon to you. But now that you know about Casey, you may choose to make a different decision. I have enclosed the latest contact information I had for him, should you choose to get in touch. I hope that you will meet him someday, and that the two of you will bring joy into each other's lives. Please know that both of you had parents who loved you boundlessly.

In my thoughts,
Maude

I read the letter several times, and with each reading, a deeper layer of peace settled over me. Maude had always had that effect on me. Whether it was coaching me toward a clean run in the agility ring or soothing my broken heart after my husband left me, she made me feel strong, she made me feel capable. And right now, she made me feel as though she was standing beside me, giving me a bracing squeeze on my shoulder and a firm, "You've got this, my girl."

And so I did.

CHAPTER FORTY-
FOUR

I never imagined, when I was a little girl playing with my father's gavel, or a kid dashing into his chambers to get him to sign an urgently needed permission slip for school, or a teenager listening with morbid fascination as cases were argued before him, that this courtroom would ever hold anything but welcome for me. I had always walked in here like I owned the place. Now I sat at a table surrounded by lawyers and guarded by deputies, and everything about the room seemed alien.

The judge, whom I didn't know, had declared a closed courtroom, which meant only lawyers, principles and witnesses were allowed to be present. Miles was there, sitting on the front row of the gallery, because he was being called to give testimony about the break-in. Detective Harrigan was there, naturally. Tony, who had found Casey's body, was there, as were the first two deputies who had arrived on the scene. And, to my astonishment, Buck was there, sitting on the opposite side of the room behind the prosecution's table. I did not know why.

Sonny sat beside me, more for moral support than anything else, and explained to me that a hearing was typically more informal than a trial. There was not a lot of protocol to be observed, no arguments were being made. The prosecution was simply laying out its case, and we were there to listen. Accordingly, Mr. Breyer and the two associates he had brought with him from Atlanta seemed very relaxed.

I felt good, until that handsome young prosecutor, Mr. York, started summarizing his case. "Your honor, the people intend to show that Raine Stockton, on February 20 of this year, shot to death Casey Kinsey Macintosh, her half-brother, then disposed of his body by driving it to the Cullowhee Gorge in the victim's own van and pushing the van over the ledge. We will present witnesses who'll testify as to motive—the theft of a thumb drive which, according to recent FBI analysis, contained access to offshore bank accounts worth in excess of twenty million dollars."

I whipped my head around to stare at Sonny, and then at Mr. Breyer, but of course both of them remained stone-faced. Sonny had a legal pad and pen in front of her and I scribbled on it, *What??* She just nodded and patted my hand.

York was continuing, "We will present evidence of Miss Stockton's presence in the van in the form of fingerprints, and doorbell camera footage that shows her driving the van toward the highway only moments after her own statement confirms a violent encounter with the victim. We will show her presence at Cullowhee Gap as confirmed by a text message on her phone. We will prove the defendant owned and was well trained in the use of the same type of weapon that killed Casey McIntosh. We will present police records and testimony indicating over an hour of time on the afternoon of the murder for which Miss Stockton cannot account. We have witnesses to testify to the fact that, on the day that Casey MacIntosh's body was found by a canine search-and-rescue team of which the defendant was a member, she actively tried to direct the search away from the site where the body was eventually located. Finally, your honor, we have as evidence Miss Stockton's own garments, stained with blood and hidden in her car, along with the thumb drive that Casey Macintosh purportedly stole."

The judge nodded. "All right, Mr. York, thank you. Let's get on with it."

And so, it began. Miles, verifying the security camera footage showing Casey breaking into the safe, telling them how he had texted me and how I hadn't answered the last four times, how he had called the police and how they had arrived thirty minutes before I did. They asked him if he had an app on his phone that tracked my phone's location, and where that app had shown me to be on the afternoon of February 20. He told them, with lips as tight as wire, that the app had shown me at Cullowhee Gap. What was he supposed to say? It was all true.

Hank testified that I'd argued against searching the north ridge, and then tried to explain how we argued all the time about things like that, but he was cut off. The neighbor who owned the doorbell camera testified he had heard shots coming from the direction of Casey's house that day, which was something we hadn't expected. Sonny kept patting my hand in a reassuring way, Mr. Breyer and his team kept taking notes, and everyone around me kept their composure with what appeared to be very little effort at all. Everyone except me, of course. It was taking a great deal of effort for me to stay still and stay calm in the face of so much mounting evidence against me. It was one thing to know what they were going to say; it was quite another to hear them say it. Until now I hadn't really been able to visualize a jury of my peers ever believing that I had murdered Casey. Now, watching the prosecution's case come together piece by piece, it not only seemed possible, but likely.

Buck was called to testify about the interview he had conducted with Miles and me on the day Miles had discovered the thumb drive was stolen. He took the stand and swore the oath and didn't meet my eyes. I didn't blame him. I knew what he was going to say, what he had to say. That had I come in an hour later than I was expected, muddy and disheveled and injured. That I had tried to get the thumb drive back from Casey and he refused. That I admitted to a violent confrontation with Casey and had ordered him off my property. That I had refused to press charges for theft which, I only now realized, might have been because I didn't want any further police involvement.

If only they would let me speak, I could have explained everything. *Everything.* But even then, I was starting to wonder whether anyone would believe me. I wondered if Buck did.

After asking Buck to identify himself and clarifying that, while he had been lead investigator at the time in question, he no longer worked for Hanover County, York handed Buck some papers with the sheriff's department logo. "Is this the police report you prepared regarding the theft from Miles Young's safe on February 20 of this year?"

Buck glanced over the papers. "This is the police report, yes," he replied, "but I didn't prepare it. I was transitioning out of the job at the time and my replacement, Brett Harrigan, was assisting with the paperwork."

York said, "But I see from the report Mr. Harrigan was present at the interview, as well as Chief Deputy Jolene Smith, is that correct?"

"That's correct."

York said to the judge, "We'll be hearing from Mr. Harrigan later, and I reserve the right to call Deputy Smith at trial if needed."

York turned back to Buck. "Other than the fact that the report was prepared by your colleague, Brett Harrigan, can you verify that the facts contained within it are, to the best of your knowledge, true and correct?"

Buck took a moment to glance again at the pages, and then he looked up. "No," he said. "I can't."

I felt Mr. Breyer go very alert beside me. Sonny gave me a sharp questioning look. The judge looked up from his notes.

York looked as startled as everyone else felt. "Excuse me?"

Buck offered the report back to Mr. York. "I had a chance to check the official report against my field notes from the day in question while I was preparing my testimony. I found a significant discrepancy."

York took the report and looked through it, his jaw tightening as he turned pages. "Could you explain what that was, please?"

"On page two of the report," Buck replied, "it says that Miss Stockton arrived at the interview at 4:45." He reached into his jacket pocket and took out a battered field notebook, thumbing through it until he found the right page. "According to the notes I made on the scene, Miss Stockton arrived in the room at 3:45."

The judge held out his hand for the notebook, and Buck passed it to him.

I could almost feel the ripple of excitement and confusion go around the room. My attorney said quickly, "We will be subpoenaing that notebook as evidence, your honor."

Mr. York said, sharply, "Chief Lawson, that's quite impossible. We have camera footage of Miss Stockton driving Casey Macintosh's van toward Cullowhee Gap at 3:45."

And I knew perfectly well I hadn't been in either of those places. At 3:30 I had been punching Casey in the nose, and at 3:45 I had been parked on the side of the road, sobbing my heart out. I stared at Buck. Had he just perjured himself for me?

The judge was looking over the police report and studying Buck's notebook. He looked up at Mr. York. "This is a problem," he said. "This discrepancy throws the entire police report into question."

"There were multiple people at the interview who can verify the time of Miss Stockton's arrival, Your Honor," York said quickly.

Mr. Breyer lifted his hand for attention. "Your Honor, if I may, the testimony of witnesses remembering an event months after the fact cannot be relied upon at trial to dispute or confirm an official police report."

The judge looked at Mr. York with a raised eyebrow. "He has a point, Mr. York."

My heart was beating hard. I could actually hear Sonny's breathing quicken beside me with excitement. I heard the main doors to the courtroom open behind us, but no one looked around to see who the latecomer was. We didn't dare take our eyes off the drama unfolding on the bench. Buck had lied for me under oath. Why had he done that? And had he just saved my life?

"If I have to disallow this police report on a technicality," he said to the prosecutor, "I'm afraid you won't have much chance of making a case for murder."

It was at that moment that I saw Buck's face. It had gone still and sharp, his eyes riveted on the back door. I half turned to follow his gaze when I heard a familiar voice from behind us.

"Besides that," said the voice, "I'm not dead."

I leapt up with such force that I knocked over the heavy chair. I stumbled out into the aisle, tripping over the legs of my lawyers, wrenching out of the grip of the deputy who tried to restrain me. "Casey!" I cried. "Oh, my God, *Casey!*"

CHAPTER FORTY-FIVE

I charged down the aisle and flung myself on Casey, careless of the crutch that supported him or the way he staggered backwards with my weight, and I hugged him hard, gasping, crying, clinging to him. And he hugged me back. He hugged me back.

Distantly, I heard the bang of the gavel, the judge saying something. Everyone was standing, staring, questioning. The deputy had my shoulders, trying to pull me away, saying something like, "Come on, Raine, don't make me cuff you. Back to your seat."

And when he finally managed to persuade me to loosen my grip on Casey and take a step back, all I could do was gasp, "It's you, oh, God, Casey, it *is* you."

He was pale, beardless and very, very skinny. His blond curls were longer now, pulled back in a ponytail at his nape. There were purplish circles under his eyes and there was something wrong with his nose—a slightly crooked bump, where I had broken it. His left leg was in a cast from foot to calf, and when someone handed him the crutch he had dropped, he leaned on it heavily. But when he smiled at me there was no doubt. Casey. He was alive. He was here.

I was vaguely aware that two men had come in with Casey. One of them stepped forward now, addressing the bench. "Your Honor," he said, "I'm Devin Childers from the US Attorney General's Office. I have with me Casey Macintosh, who I believe is germane to this case, and also relevant evidence which I think you'll find will be better explored in your chambers. May I approach?"

The judge beckoned him forward and banged the gavel hard one last time. "Miss Stockton," he ordered, "*sit down* before I have you removed from this courtroom." He glared at Casey. "Are you telling me that you're Casey Macintosh, also known as Kevin Christopher Kinsey, the supposed victim in this case?"

"Yes, sir, I am," Casey said. He added, somewhat awkwardly, "Sorry for the confusion."

I let the deputy pull me back to my table, but before I reached it, I heard the judge say briskly, "The witness is excused. Counsel, Mr. Childers, my chambers. Court is in recess for fifteen minutes."

Miles came from behind the gallery rail to embrace me, and Buck dragged over a chair from the prosecution table to sit across from me. Casey made his way slowly down the aisle with the crutch, the man who had come in with him walking watchfully beside him. That man looked oddly familiar to me, and as he drew closer, I knew why.

"You're that real estate person," I said. "George something."

He smiled, pulling out a chair for Casey and taking his crutch. "No, ma'am," he said. "I'm Special Agent George Detweiler, FBI."

Casey sat down heavily in the chair next to me at the table, stretching out his injured leg into the aisle. I looked at him in trepidation. "Are you... under arrest?"

Casey started to chuckle, and Special Agent Detweiler assured me, "No, ma'am. Casey's not my prisoner. He's more like my partner."

Casey frowned uncomfortably at that, and the other man grinned at him. "Well, damn, kid, no point in trying to keep it on the down-low now. You have definitely been made."

He glanced around the table at Buck, at me, at Miles, and even at Harrigan, who stood a few feet away, unwilling to insert himself but listening anxiously. Detweiler said, "I know it's a stretch to believe, but Casey's been working undercover as a special consultant for the task force charged with bringing down the Carolina Syndicate for a little over six years now. And I'm pleased to report that we have succeeded. That's what the lawyer is talking to the judge about now. I'm pretty sure all charges against you will be dropped, Miss Stockton. And I'm really sorry all this happened. It wasn't part of the plan."

"Plan," I repeated, staring at Casey. "*Plan*?"

He held up a defensive hand. "Please, no hitting. I don't have that many bones that haven't already been broken."

Miles sat down on the other side of me, his gently reassuring hand cupping the back of my neck. But his voice was chill as he said to Casey, "I hope you don't mind my asking, but where the *hell* have you been all this time?"

Casey cast him an apologetic look. "Um, in a coma?"

My heart was stabbed with alarm, and I reached out uncertainly to touch his sleeve. "God, Casey, what…?"

Detweiler pulled up a chair to the corner of the table, its legs scraping loudly on the hardwood floor. "Also," he added as he sat down, "in protective custody, until we finally got enough on Scarburg to put him away for good. That happened last week, when your guys turned over the thumb drive and our tech team deciphered what was on it."

"Jeez, Raine," Casey said, his tone annoyed, "I thought you would've turned it in to the cops the minute you found it, or Miles's investigators would have. That's why I put it in Cisco's vest. I couldn't afford for it to be found on me, and you'd already proved you didn't know anything about it so they wouldn't be after you. What took so long?"

Before I could answer, Buck interrupted, "Scarburg. Is that the guy who was running this Carolina Syndicate you're talking about?"

Detweiler nodded. "Nobody even knew who he was until he came after Casey. Ashton Scarburg. He's been running an underground network of petty criminals and thieves—money laundering, counterfeiting, identity theft, bank fraud, you name it—for over twenty-five years in these parts. But we've got him solid on two murders so far, and with the bank accounts painting a pretty picture of every crime he's committed in the past twenty-five years, I'm pretty damn confident he'll never see the light of day again."

I was thoroughly confused. "But... who was the body we found? He had a tattoo just like yours, Casey. That why I thought... why I was sure..."

Casey said, "That was a guy named Dimitri Petrova. We called him Deacon. He was a hit man for the old man—I mean, Scarburg. He did all his dirty work. He's the one who recruited me into The Chain Gang. We all had the tattoos, even Deacon."

Miles said carefully, "I can see you've been through something, Casey, and I don't mean to sound unsympathetic. But it's been no picnic around here, either. So maybe you could just start with why you stole the thumb drive in the first place and go from there."

Casey paused, seeming to gather his strength to retell the story. "I didn't exactly steal it. The fellow who lived in Maude's house before, Freddie Thomas, he left it for me. That's what I came here to find. It was a lot harder than I thought, and when I finally found the drive behind the outlet cover, I didn't have a chance to turn it over to Detweiler before Raine got there. Then Cisco found it and Raine wanted to see what was on it..."

He shrugged. "I hadn't intended to leave the drive with you," he told Miles, "but after I thought about it for a minute, I realized your safe was probably the best place for it. Only I didn't realize Deacon had followed me to your house. When I got home that night, he was waiting for me. He made it clear that if I didn't turn over the thumb drive by the next afternoon, he'd get it himself. They'd already killed Freddie for it." He looked at me. "I had to steal it back, Raine, otherwise they were coming for you, and Miles, and your family. But I couldn't turn it over to them either, not after all I'd been through—all everybody had been through—to get it."

Casey paused a moment, the lines on his face deepening as

he relived the memories. Then he went on, "When you showed up the next day, I saw my chance. I hid the real drive in Cisco's vest and turned over a blank one to Scarburg. I hoped it would buy me enough time to come up with a better plan, but no such luck. Deacon shot me three times in the gut the minute he got the drive."

I caught my breath, but Casey held up a reassuring hand. "I lived," he informed me dryly. "But I'm not sure either one of them knew that at the time. The old man went to check the contents of the drive, leaving me to bleed out on the ground, and as soon as he realized it was blank, he shot Deacon in the face. I passed out after that. The next thing I remember I was lying in my van, upside down at the bottom of a ravine. I don't know how long I'd been there. I had the phone Detweiler had given me with his number programmed in. I remember pushing the button. That's all."

Detective Harrigan spoke up then, taking a step forward. "Wait a minute. We have camera footage of somebody that looks like Miss Stockton driving the van away from Deer Run Trail. If it wasn't her, and it wasn't you, who was it?"

Detweiler answered. "We'll be needing that footage," he said. "It was Scarburg who drove the van to the ravine and pushed it over. He's got dark hair like Ms. Stockton's, and isn't much taller. No doubt you'd have been able to see it was a man driving if you'd had the equipment to enhance the video, like we do," he added.

Harrigan's lips compressed, and he didn't say anything else

"There were sixteen inches of snow on the ground when we got to the gorge." Detweiler picked up the story. "There was no way we could locate Deacon's body. We barely found the van and got Casey out of there. He was in pretty rough shape."

"My God," I said softly, looking at Casey. "Have you been in the hospital all this time? Are you… how badly were you… are you going to be okay?"

He gave a weak, dismissive smile. "Let's just say I hope you never need a kidney, because I don't have one to spare. Other than that, and the fact that I'm mostly held together by rods and pins, I'll be fine."

Buck looked him over thoughtfully. He had his investigator's face on and looked unimpressed. "So, all those arrests—your entire rap sheet—that was all fake?"

"Not all," admitted Casey. He glanced at me. "After I found my birth certificate I came east, thinking I'd look up my birth mother. I got sidetracked by an easy-money scheme and ended up in a South Carolina prison. That's where I met Deacon, and for a while we had a good thing going. But it didn't take me long to realize that that once you're in with these guys, they own you. I didn't like the idea of being owned, so I figured out a way to make a deal with the other side."

"So, consultant is just a pretty word for criminal informant," Buck observed.

"Yeah, at first," Detweiler said. "We didn't expect much, but the kid delivered what he promised, and kept on delivering. There's a lot of talent there, and we decided to put him on the payroll, so to speak. Of course..." He cast a sideways glance at Casey. "We had our ups and downs, but every time we'd plant him on the inside, we'd take out a few more bad guys, and get closer to bringing down the ring. But the real break came when he got hold of the passwords to Scarburg's offshore accounts."

Miles looked at Casey sharply. "You had the passwords?"

"That was by accident," Casey said with a shrug. "Rich paranoid people like him do the craziest things with their passwords. Turns out Scarburg had them etched on the back of a Piaget watch. I got close to Scarburg's girlfriend—former girlfriend, I should say—who got pissed at him and stole the watch. That wasn't even the hard part. The worst was convincing her to put it back before he noticed it was missing."

"Jesus," Miles murmured. "This is like something out of a John le Carre novel."

I glanced at him, then looked back at Casey.

Detweiler went on, "Of course, the passwords were no good without the account numbers, and that's where Freddie came in. He was a computer geek doing twenty years for fraud, and it turned out he'd actually done some work for the syndicate once upon a time. Casey convinced him he had the passwords and they'd both be rich if Freddie could only find the account numbers. Not sure if you know this, but those numbers are kept tighter than a vault. The only people with access to them are the account owner and one or two high-level managers at the bank."

"And Freddie, as it turns out," Casey said.

"So," I said, trying to put the pieces together, "this Freddie person—the one who skipped out on the rent and then was found dead in his car—you're the one who told him about Maude's house?"

Casey nodded. "Maude offered me the use of her house last year," he said. "I was actually going to take her up on it, thought it was a good time to make a fresh start and all, but then this thing came up with Freddie and I realized this would be the perfect place for him to hide out while he worked on finding the bank accounts. When he disappeared, I came looking for him."

"And the bank account numbers," Miles added.

"Right," Casey agreed with a tired smile. "And I guess that brings us up to date."

"Scarburg and most of his operatives are in custody now," Detweiler said, "and we're dismantling his operation as we speak. All in all, a good day's work."

"That only took five years," Casey pointed out.

There was a stirring up front, and the lawyers came through the side door. The deputy gestured everyone back to their seats. My lawyers came back to my table and started gathering up their papers. Sonny, who was walking without assistance today, winked at me. Before I could question, the deputy called, "All rise," and the judge resumed his place behind the bench.

He struck the gavel and, instead of instructing us to be seated, he looked directly at me and said, "In the case of

The People Versus Raine Stockton, all charges are dismissed. Miss Stockton, you are free to go with the court's profoundest apologies. Court is adjourned."

And that was it. Sonny hugged me. Miles embraced me, lifting me off my feet. The lawyers congratulated me, and I think I stammered thanks. I hugged Casey again, more carefully this time. Buck came over, and Miles shook his hand, thanking him for coming. Then Miles spotted Mr. York across the room, and his expression changed. "Excuse me," he told Buck. I watched as Miles walked over to the prosecution's table.

"Mr. Young." York glanced at Miles. "What can I do for you?"

"Not a damn thing," replied Miles pleasantly. "I just wanted to give you a chance to get a good look at the man who's about at destroy you."

York stopped packing his briefcase and straightened up.

"First," Miles went on easily, "I'll sue the county, and your office in particular. Malpractice, intentional infliction of emotional and physical harm, and false imprisonment should do for a start. Then I'm coming after you personally. I'll take your house, your car, your kids' college fund, and your law degree. I might even throw in a few criminal charges while I'm at it—malfeasance of office, misappropriation of funds, who knows? And when you're standing in your underwear selling bottles of water on the side of the road to make ends meet, maybe you'll have some time to think about the havoc you wreaked on innocent lives just to make a name for yourself, and whether it was all worth it. I don't care how long it takes. I don't care how much it costs. I really don't even care whether I win or lose. I just want to see you suffer."

York's nostrils flared and his shoulders went stiff. "It's a serious matter to threaten an officer of the court, Mr. Young."

"Oh, that's not a threat," Miles assured him. "It's a goddamn promise." He smiled. "Have a pleasant day, Mr. York. I can guarantee it will be the last one you ever have." He walked away to talk to Sonny.

Buck looked away from the conversation we'd both been

eavesdropping on, nodding his head toward Miles. "Remind me never to piss him off," he murmured.

But Miles's vendetta against the arrogant county prosecutor was hardly front and center in my mind at the moment. I looked at Buck in a mixture of confusion and profoundest gratitude, and I lowered my voice to avoid being overheard.

"Buck," I said uncertainly, not much above a whisper, "you lied under oath. You came all this way and… you lied for me."

He shook his head firmly. "I would never do that, Raine. You know better. I'm a trained observer, and I wrote down what I saw." He glanced at his watch. "I'd better get going, though. Jo and Willis are cleaning out the house and I told them I'd take them to lunch if I got done here in time."

It took me a moment to figure it out. "Is that your dad's watch?" I said, staring at the antique on his wrist. "Does it even keep time anymore?"

He smiled. "More or less. When I remember to set it, that is." He laid a hand lightly on my shoulder. "I'm sorry I left without saying goodbye. I didn't really have a choice. But we're going to be here all weekend, and we'll stop by before we leave, if that's okay."

"Yeah," I said. A big, silly grin spread across my face. "Yeah, that'd be great."

Miles returned and walked me to the door of the courtroom with an arm around my shoulders. Casey and Agent Detweiler were waiting there. We stopped, and Miles looked at Casey a moment before speaking, choosing his words. "Casey," he said finally, "I'm glad Raine punched you in the face, because if she hadn't, I sure as hell would. But I'm also glad you're alive." He offered his hand, and Casey shook it, smiling crookedly.

"Does this mean I won't be frisked by your security guards if I ever come visit again?" he asked.

"Oh, hell, no," Miles replied. Then he smiled. "I guess you're family now," he said, "whether I like it or not. If you need something, you don't have to steal it. Just ask, okay?"

Have I mentioned how much I love that man?

I turned to Casey. "So, what are you going to do now? Do you have a place to stay while you're recovering?"

Casey said, "Until the government replaces my van…" He shot a dark look at Detweiler. "It looks like I'm on my own."

Detweiler said irritably, "I told you, the US government is not buying you a new van." He frowned. "Pickup truck, maybe. Used."

"Extended cab," Casey argued, "heavy-duty tow package, XM radio, and don't forget my tools."

Miles kissed my hair. "I'm going to bring the car around. Meet you out front."

Detweiler said, "I'll walk out with you."

Casey told me, "I have to go back with Detweiler this afternoon. I haven't even officially been released from the hospital, and I guess the DOJ needs some testimony from me and stuff. But after that…" He looked hesitant. "I thought I might come back here and hang out awhile. If it's okay."

I pretended to be nonchalant. "I guess I could stand that," I said. "I might even know of a house that's coming up for rent, pretty reasonable."

He said, "I've recently terminated my contract with my former employer, so maybe I could work it out in trade. I'm pretty good with my hands."

I smiled at him. "I'll see what I can do," I said. I reached into the pocket of my blazer and brought out a folded envelope. I held it in my hand uncertainly for a moment. "I got this letter from Maude that she wrote before she died. I brought it with me today for good luck." I offered it to him. "I think she'd want you to read it. You can take it with you."

He took the envelope and looked at it for a minute, his expression opaque. "She had pretty handwriting," he said.

"Yes," I agreed. "She did."

Casey tucked the envelope into his pocket, and I looked at him thoughtfully. "Casey," I said, "that day that you found the thumb drive behind the outlet cover… you said you were going to turn it over to the FBI, but then I got there, and you didn't have time. But Detweiler was there before I was. You could have easily given it to him then, before I arrived."

Casey said nothing. He just looked at me with a politely interested expression on his face.

"So, here's my theory," I said. "I think you still have the passwords. I think the deal you made with Freddie was real, not just a sting to get him to hack the account numbers for the FBI. You have the passwords and when Freddie disappeared you came out here to steal the account numbers, not turn them over to Mr. Detweiler."

A slow, impish smile lit his face. "Because that's what you'd do?"

I shrugged. "If I were you, maybe. You put the thumb drive back when Agent Detweiler drove up because you planned to hightail it out of here that night. But Cisco ruined your plan."

"Not to mention Deacon," Casey pointed out.

"So, am I right?" I said. "Do you have the passwords?"

Casey held out his wrist, the one with the tattoo on it. The butterfly-shaped birthmark was still there. "Look closely," he said.

I took his arm in my hands and studied the tattoo. Very faintly, and with a great deal of effort, I could see a series of minuscule numbers, letters and symbols woven into the links of the chain.

"So yeah," he said, retrieving his arm. "I turned the passwords over to the FBI, but I kept a copy, so to speak. Nothing wrong with hedging your bets. That's how I convinced Freddie to go into partnership with me. And did I think about taking the money and running? Not going to lie. Every single day. But by the time Miles put the drive in his safe, I'd already seen the error of my ways."

"So, what changed your mind?"

He let his absent gaze wander somewhere over my shoulder. "Believe it or not," he said, "you did. You and Cisco and that broken down house. This place. A normal life. A good life. Besides..." he met my gaze with a wink. "What was I going to do with twenty million dollars in mob money? I'd never live to spend it."

"A million, maybe," I speculated thoughtfully, and he grinned.

"That's my sis," he said.

We walked out of the courtroom toward the front door of the courthouse, where Miles and Detweiler were waiting on the steps. I matched my pace to Casey's much slower one, and said, "The house is just like you left it. It'll be waiting for you whenever you're ready."

A corner of his mouth turned down wryly. "I'm afraid I lost my key."

"Don't worry." I smiled at him. "I'll leave the door unlocked for you."

We walked out into the sunshine together.

CHAPTER FORTY-SIX

Aunt Mart, Uncle Ro, Melanie and Rita all returned home Friday, and on Saturday I had everyone over to my farmhouse for an impromptu goodbye party for Buck. I knew Buck had already been by to see everyone at the Sheriff's Office, so I just invited family, close neighborhood friends and some people from church. Melanie and Aunt Mart baked a cake and we had homemade ice cream on the porch, along with an entire buffet table filled with snacks and drinks —most of them from the freezer, during the time that Aunt Mart couldn't stop bringing me food. The dogs were all turned loose in the play yard, and little Willis wore himself out playing with them. Everyone was in a buoyant mood despite the fact that we were saying goodbye to one of our own—even me. Of course, my ebullient mood might have had a lot to do with the fact that, for the past two months, I'd had nightmares that the only sunshine I'd ever see again would be from the exercise yard of a prison.

Miles circulated from group to group of neighbors, making everyone feel welcome, while Aunt Mart and Rita bustled around in the kitchen, refilling the buffet trays that were set up on a long table on the porch. I was in charge of keeping the red plastic cups filled with lemonade and sweet tea, and Melanie was in charge of Willis and the dogs.

Even Jolene, relaxed in crisp white shorts and a summer top, seemed like a different person as she sat on my steps and wiped sticky ice cream from her little boy's face. "I have to go, Mama," he insisted, wriggling under her ministrations. "Melanie's going to let me walk Rags on a leash."

Melanie was in her element bossing the younger child around, taking charge of the dogs, and reminding everyone that she had baked the cake. For the past hour or so she had also graciously allowed Willis to witness her skills as a dog trainer, but I was glad she had chosen Rags for the leash experiment. Rags had outgrown his puppy exuberance and would probably be the safest dog for the little boy to walk.

Jolene said to Willis, "Thank Miss Stockton for the ice cream and for your good time."

He looked up at me with beaming eyes. "Thank you for my good time, Miss Stockton," he said, "and the ice cream. You have the coolest dogs in the whole world!"

He skipped down the steps and I watched Jolene's face soften as, halfway across the lawn, Willis was intercepted by Buck, who caught him up in the air and swung him high overhead, demanding, "Where's the fire, big fellow?" I suspect my own expression softened in just the same way.

Willis squealed with delight, Buck set him on his feet again, and the little boy took off running back toward the play yard. Buck came to join us on the steps. "This has been great, Raine," he said. "I'm glad I got to see everybody like this one more time."

"I am too," I told him.

Buck sat on the step beside Jolene, caressing her shoulder absently. "We need to go before long, hon," he said. "Long drive tomorrow."

She rested her hand on his knee. "Look at that," she said in a voice thick with amusement. "That dog is almost as big as he is."

Rags had definitely sprung up over the last few months, and while I was fairly certain he'd reached his full height, he had a lot of filling out to do before he looked anything like a goldendoodle. He was still gangly and scraggly, his shoulders reaching to Willis's waist, but he walked with fairly good manners between Willis and Melanie, who kept up a constant stream of instructions about how fast to walk, how to hold the leash, where to hold the treat. Willis looked as proud as if he had just tamed a lion.

Buck chuckled. "That is one happy kid."

"And dog," I put in. "You know," I added casually, "he's still up for adoption."

Buck looked at Jolene. "Every boy should have a dog," he said.

She rolled her eyes. "Oh, please. Like I don't have enough problems."

At that moment Cisco wiggled through the gate that Melanie had apparently not entirely closed behind her. Corny rushed to secure the gate, but too late. Cisco raced across the lawn at full speed toward us, breezing past Willis and Rags. I lunged to protect the buffet table, but for once food was not on Cisco's top priority list. He leapt up the steps and into Buck's lap.

Buck, ever the fool for my golden retriever, laughed and wrapped his arms around Cisco while Jolene screwed up her face and leaned away, brushing at the muddy paw prints on her shorts. "Cisco, my man!" Buck declared. "You didn't really think I was going to leave without saying goodbye to you, did you?" He buried his face in Cisco's fur and that was the only time during the entire day that I felt the twist of pathos in my core, the sting of tears in my eyes. Buck and Cisco. It was the end of an era.

Fortunately, I was saved from humiliating myself by the arrival of Willis and Rags at the bottom of the steps. "Look, Mama!" he cried. "Isn't this the best dog ever? Did you see him walking with me?"

While I quickly wiped the corners of my eyes and Buck, still holding Cisco in his lap, looked up to smile at Willis, Melanie said with authority, "You have to make him sit. Every dog should learn to sit when you stop walking. Here, like this." She held the treat in front of Rags's nose, just like I had taught her, until he rocked back on his haunches to a sit.

I grinned at her. "Good job."

Willis knelt on the ground and threw his arms around Rags. "Best dog ever!" he declared, and Rags obligingly licked his face. "If I had a cool dog like this, I'd walk him every day and teach him to read and play basketball just like Cisco. And," he pronounced, "I'd name him Thor!"

Melanie said, "Hey. That's not bad."

I could see the corners of Jolene's mouth start to curve into an indulgent smile. "He's not much of a dog," she pointed out, although without conviction. "I doubt he could even be trained."

"He can count to six!" Willis insisted. "Want to see?"

Jolene's smile was full blown now. "Maybe later."

"He has a travel crate," I offered. "Corny can show you where it is."

Buck looked at Jolene. "What do you say, Mama?"

But I could see she had already made up her mind. "Well, go on," she said. "Pack up his things."

Buck gave Cisco a final hug and a kiss on the muzzle and got to his feet. "Come on, buddy," he said to Willis. "Let's go get this great dog ready to travel."

Willis's eyes grew huge with wonder. "Are you serious? Are you kidding me, Buck? You better not be kidding me. Is he really coming home with us? This dog? Really?"

I called Cisco back to me and caught his collar when he started to follow Buck, Willis and Rags back toward the kennel. Melanie skipped along beside them, eager to show the way. Cisco whined a little, and I knew how he felt. I would miss him too.

Jolene stood up. "I guess I should thank you," she said.

My chest swelled with affection as I watched boy, man and dog cross the lawn. "It's a good match," I said. "I think Maude would approve."

Jolene's gaze shifted toward her husband and child, and

then back to me. "I wasn't just talking about the dog," she said.

While I was trying to puzzle out what she meant, she said, "Look, Stockton. We're never going to be friends. I mean, you're a golden retriever and I'm a German shepherd. We've got nothing in common."

Rottweiler, I corrected to myself, but remained silent.

She went on, "We're not going to have Thanksgiving together or send each other Christmas cards. But I knew long before I married him that you would always be part of Buck's life, and that's okay. I just want you to know that if you ever need anything, you can call us."

I was touched. "Thanks, Jolene." And I smiled at her. "But I'm still going to send you a Christmas card."

She gave an eye-shrug and turned to follow her family. "See you, Stockton."

The party wound down around sunset, and the guest of honor was the last to leave, as it should be. Willis was spent, collapsed in the back of Jolene's SUV with his head on Rags's shoulder, sound asleep. Aunt Mart kept pressing plastic containers of food on them "for the trip," she insisted, and cried like a baby when she said her final goodbye to Buck. Jolene was in the car, and Buck leaned against the driver's side door while Miles and Cisco and I walked down to see them off. Buck made a big fuss over saying goodbye to Cisco, and when he straightened up, I said, trying to postpone the inevitable, "So, what are you going to do with your house?"

"We've decided to keep it," he said. I liked the easy way he said "we." "After all, it's not like we're never coming back here, and it'll be nice to have a place to stay when we visit."

I smiled. "Yeah. That's a good idea."

Miles extended his hand to Buck, "Good luck, Buck. I wish you well in your new life."

Buck hesitated for only a fraction of a second, then shook Miles's hand. "You know something?" he said. "The same to you."

Then he turned to embrace me and kissed my forehead. "Take care, Raine," he said, "and stay in touch."

I hugged him back. "Bye, Buck."

Miles put his arm around my waist as we watched them drive away. "They're going to be okay," he said.

I leaned my head against his shoulder. "So are we."

We smiled at each other and turned to walk back to the house.

BOOKS BY THIS AUTHOR

The Blood River Mystery Series

Don't miss this exciting first installment

UNFIXABLE: A Buck Lawson Mystery

Former sheriff Buck Lawson leaves the mountains of North Carolina to take a job as police chief of the small South Georgia town of Mercy, and soon finds himself in over his head. For one thing, his predecessor has been murdered…

DECK THE HALLS: A HOLIDAY MYSTERY ANTHOLOGY

Featuring Buck Lawson in **WELCOME TO BETHLEHEM**

Police chief Buck Lawson wants his first Christmas in his new hometown of Mercy, Georgia, to be a memorable one, both for his family and the police officers under his command. But while preparing to host the traditional police department Christmas party, Buck's home is burglarized by a Middle Eastern man who may be connected to far more violent crimes. As the investigation unfolds and unsettling connections to the past come to light, Buck fears this Christmas will be memorable for all the wrong reasons.

The Raine Stockton Dog Mystery Series
Books in Order

SMOKY MOUNTAIN TRACKS

A child has been kidnapped and abandoned in the mountain wilderness. Her only hope is Raine Stockton and her young, untried tracking dog Cisco…

RAPID FIRE

Raine and Cisco are brought in by the FBI to track a terrorist …a terrorist who just happens to be Raine's old boyfriend.

GUN SHY

Raine rescues a traumatized service dog, and soon begins to suspect he is the only witness to a murder.

BONE YARD

Cisco digs up human remains in Raine's back yard, and mayhem ensues. Could this be evidence of a serial killer, a long-unsolved mass murder, or something even more sinister... and closer to home?

SILENT NIGHT

It's Christmastime in Hansonville, N.C., and Raine and Cisco are on the trail of a missing teenager. But when a newborn is abandoned in the manger of the town's living nativity and Raine walks in on what appears to be the scene of a murder, the holidays take a very dark turn for everyone concerned.

THE DEAD SEASON

Raine and Cisco take a job leading a wilderness hike for troubled teenagers, and soon find themselves trapped on a mountainside in a blizzard... with a killer.

ALL THAT GLITTERS: A Holiday Short Story e book

Raine looks back on how she and Cisco met and solved their first crime in this Christmas Cozy short story. Sold separately as an e-book or bundled with the print edition of HIGH IN TRIAL.

HIGH IN TRIAL

A carefree weekend turns deadly when Raine and Cisco travel to the South Carolina low country for an agility competition

DOUBLE DOG DARE

A luxury Caribbean vacation sounds like just the ticket for over-worked, over-stressed Raine Stockton and her happy go lucky canine companion Cisco. But even in paradise trouble finds them, and when someone she loves is threatened Raine must use every resource at her command to track down a killer before it's too late.

HOME OF THE BRAVE

There's a new dog in town, and Raine and Cisco find themselves unexpectedly upstaged by a flashy K-9 addition to the sheriff's department. But when things go terribly wrong at a mountain camp for kids and dogs over the Fourth of July weekend, Raine and Cisco need all the help they can get to save themselves, and those they love.

DOG DAYS

Raine takes in a lost English Cream Golden Retriever, and the search for her owner leads Raine and Cisco into the hands of a killer. Readers will enjoy a treasure hunt for the titles of all ten of the Raine Stockton Dog Mysteries hidden in this special tenth anniversary release!

LAND OF THE FREE

On a routine search and rescue mission Raine Stockton and her golden retriever Cisco stumble onto something they were never meant to find, and are plunged into a nightmare of murder, corruption and intrigue as figures from her past re-emerge to threaten everything Raine holds dear.

DEADFALL

Hollywood comes to Hanover County, and Raine and Cisco get caught up in the drama when a series of mishaps on the set lead to murder.

THE DEVIL'S DEAL

Raine takes temporary custody of what may well be the most valuable dog in the world, but when lives are at stake she is forced to make an unthinkable choice.

MURDER CREEK

Raine and Cisco rescue a dog who is locked in a hot car in a remote Smoky Mountain park... and subsequently discover the owner of that car drowned in the creek only a few dozen yards away. Was it an accident, or was it murder?

DECK THE HALLS: A HOLIDAY MYSTERY ANTHOLOGY

*Featuring Raine and Cisco in **ANGELS IN THE SNOW**. While preparing for the annual Dog Daze Christmas party, Raine leaves on a secret Christmas errand and becomes trapped in a blizzard. Injured and alone, with a desperate criminal on the loose, a surprising canine hero comes to her rescue. But is it all a product of her imagination, or a genuine Christmas miracle?*

THE JUDGES DAUGHTER

The Dogleg Island Mystery Series

FLASH

Dogleg Island Mystery #1

Almost two years ago the sleepy little community of Dogleg Island was the scene of one of the most brutal crimes in Florida history. The only eye witnesses were Flash, a border collie puppy, and a police officer. Now the trial of the century is about to begin. The defendant, accused of slaughtering his parents in their beach home, maintains his innocence. The top witnesses for the prosecution are convinced he is lying. But only Flash knows the truth. And with another murder to solve and a monster storm on the way, the truth may come to late... for all of them.

THE SOUND OF RUNNING HORSES

Dogleg Island Mystery #2

A family outing takes a dark turn when Flash, Aggie and Grady discover a body on deserted Wild Horse Island, and the evidence appears to point to someone they know—and trust.

FLASH OF BRILLIANCE

Dogleg Island Mystery #3

Aggie, Flash and Grady look forward to their first Christmas as a family until a homicide hit-and-run exposes a crime syndicate, and dark shadows from the past return to haunt their future.

PIECES OF EIGHT

Dogleg Island Mystery #4

A deadly explosion at an archeological dig on Dogleg Island plunges police chief Aggie Malone and her canine partner Flash into a dark mystery from the past, while on the other side of the bridge, Deputy Sheriff Ryan Grady stumbles onto the site of a mass murder. As the investigation unfolds, Aggie and Grady see that the two cases are related, but only Flash knows how...and by whom.

FLASH IN THE DARK

Dogleg Island Mystery #5

Flash discovers an abandoned child on the beach, and the subsequent attempt to identify her leads to a secret organization with a plan for revenge that has been decades in the making. Unless Aggie, Grady and Flash can stop it they risk losing everything the love... even Dogleg Island itself.

DECK THE HALLS: A HOLIDAY MYSTERY ANTHOLOGY

*Featuring Aggie and Flash in **THE GOOD SHEPHERD***

A missing infant, a holiday pageant, and a priest determined to do the right thing no matter what the cost all come together to present Dogleg Island police chief Aggie Malone and her canine assistant Flash with one of their most unusual cases yet. When a routine call escalates into a kidnapping on the eve of the annual Dogleg Island Police Department holiday open house, Flash and Aggie are held hostage by a desperate man whose only chance for redemption may be the grace of the holiday season.

~*~

Spine-chilling suspense by Donna Ball

SHATTERED

A missing child, a desperate call for help in the middle of the night... is this a cruel hoax, or the work of a maniacal serial killer who is poised to strike again?

NIGHT FLIGHT

She's an innocent woman who knows too much. Now she's fleeing through the night without a weapon and without a phone, and her only hope for survival is a cop who's willing to risk his badge—and his life—to save her.

SANCTUARY

They came to the peaceful, untouched mountain wilderness of Eastern Tennessee seeking an escape from the madness of modern life. But when they built their luxury homes in the heart of virgin forest they did not realize that something was there before them... something ancient and horrible; something that will make them believe that monsters are real.

EXPOSURE

Everyone has secrets, but when talk show host Jessamine Cray's stalker begins to use her past to terrorize her, no one is safe ... not her family, her friends, her coworkers, and especially not Jess herself.

RENEGADE by Donna Boyd

Enter a world of dark mystery and intense passion, where human destiny is controlled by a species of powerful, exotic creatures. Once they ruled the Tundra, now they rule Wall Street. Once they fought with teeth and claws, now they fight with wealth and power. And only one man can stop them... if he dares.

Also by Donna Ball

The Ladybug Farm series by Donna Ball

For every woman who ever had a dream… or a friend

A Year on Ladybug Farm

At Home on Ladybug Farm

Love Letters from Ladybug Farm

Christmas on Ladybug Farm

Recipes from Ladybug Farm

Vintage Ladybug Farm

A Wedding on Ladybug Farm

The Hummingbird House

Christmas at the Hummingbird House

The Hummingbird House Presents

Romance Revisited by Donna Ball

MATCHMAKER, MATCHMAKER

He was a cowboy looking for a wife. She was a lady specializing in brides. They were made for each other… They just didn't know it yet.

A MAN AROUND THE HOUSE

He was the answer to a busy working woman's dreams. But was he too good to be true?

FOR KEEPS

He's an animal trainer who lives by one rule: never get attached. She's a social worker who knows all too well the price of getting involved. It may take an entire menagerie to bring them together, but eventually they both must learn that sometimes it's for keeps.

STEALING SAVANNAH

He was a reformed jewel thief now turned security expert and her job depended on his expertise. But could he be trusted not to steal the most valuable jewel of all-- her heart?

UNDER COVER

She's working on the biggest case of her life, and her cover has already been blown-- by the very man she's investigating. Now they must work together to solve an even bigger mystery-- their future together.

THE STORMRIDERS

They were thunder and lightning when they were married, and their divorce has been no less turbulent. But trapped together during a deadly blizzard with the lives of an entire community depending on them, they discover what's really important, and that some storms are worth riding out.

INTERLUDE

Sometimes a chance encounter is over in a moment, and sometimes it can last a lifetime.

CAST ADRIFT

She was a marine biologist on short deadline to find a very important dolphin, with no time to waste on romance. He was a sailor who knew there could only be one captain on his ship-- himself. But two weeks at sea together could change everything...

The Kincaids
Books in Order

Raging Rivers
Katherine Carlyle and Byrd Kincaid, fugitives and reluctant heroes, begin a journey west and launch a dynasty that will forge a nation.

Prairie Thunder
Legendary trailblazer Boothe Carlyle leads a wagon train west, where young Kitty Kincaid will rediscover her heritage and finally earn the proud warrior name she was given at her Shawnee mother's breast.

Westward Winds
Peril and promise await the children of Katherine and Byrd Kincaid in the high mountains and brutal plains of the American frontier they have worked so hard to tame.

Mountain Fury
The California Gold Rush brings turbulence and hope to the lives of the children of Byrd and Katherine Kincaid, and will forever alter the destiny of the wild land they love.

ABOUT THE AUTHOR

Donna Ball is the author of over 100 books under a variety of pseudonyms. Though she has been published in virtually every genre, she is best known for her work in women's fiction, mystery and suspense. Her novels have been translated into multiple languages, and published around the world.

She lives in the heart of the Blue Ridge Divide in a restored Victorian barn which was the inspiration for the bestselling *A Year On Ladybug Farm* as well as The Raine Stockton Dog Mystery series. She spends her spare time hiking, painting, and enjoying canine sports with her three dogs.

~